THE FUTURE'S
COMING
EVERYWHERE

THE FUTURE'S COMING EVERYWHERE

John Fraser

AESOP Modern Fiction
Oxford

AESOP Modern Fiction
An imprint of AESOP Publications
Martin Noble Editorial / AESOP
28 Abberbury Road, Oxford OX4 4ES, UK
www.aesopbooks.com

First paperback edition published by AESOP Publications
Copyright (c) 2020 John Fraser

www.johnfraserfiction.com

The right of John Fraser to be identified as the author of this work
has been asserted in accordance with sections 77 and 78
of the copyright designs and Patents Act 1988.

A catalogue record of this book is
available from the British Library.

First paperback edition 2020

ISBN: 978-1-910301-58-6

CONTENTS

CANDICE

I T'S HARD to find a library. They're not burnt – but if you find one, they are warm. Conrad spends his days there, sleeps, reads manuscripts and eats. Better than a hostel, better than the street.

What fun the old guys had – proud and sneaky, cynical and loyal. The name, the place – it bound you, gave you a side ... to be on, or to plot against. Plotting – that makes you, most everyone, a spy: the boss needs you, so you can scream at him, have huffs and loves, sleep on the heather, drink the hooch, take a musket ball full in the face.... The causes? Here, all are obscured, abstruse, odd: labyrinths. In other worlds, it still goes on, the monarchy, the faith, heads lopped and bodies hung.

That's our past, as we read the record – and someone's future.

*

The journal, the manuscript, says: 'I must acknowledge that I have not been brede a schollar; nor can I put this in a true stile...'

'That's the so-called Major, so-called "of Castle Leathers": really, neither rank nor house. Can't make much of that,'

Conrad thinks. 'No new edition there, no masterpiece ...
those wordy Scots! the Latin, the bad French, intrigues....'

'An amateur spy, like almost all of us, for little money,
just to live, to be near a secret, a confidence, false friends,
carrying something dangerous – a packet, our mortality,
juggling with it and what we might not discover, since it
probably won't exist.'

*

'Politics? Sex? Drugs? We're supposed to have had all that,
and now be connoisseurs of booze,' says Conrad. 'Where are
we headed? No one believes in anything their parents did. No
heaven and no hell. No nation and no friends. A false nation,
rather – invisible, voices bodiless. People with other origins –
they have someone to cling to, maybe.... But even they –
there's so many villages, so many clans to come from,
indelible sticky stuff, custom-designed bird-lime ... they
don't adhere to any of the rest.'

'The tolerance we claim – it's a veneer, a way of making
vapid gatherings,' says his pal, Paolo. 'When some threat
appears – they're all getting ready for a Hitler: a good death
in a structure, whether it's a regiment or a hospice.
Everybody dies, the song says: so long as your side has an
anthem, a parade.... Someone to hold your hand and tell you
you've done good. Everywhere – it's the same. The Russians
and the Yanks – it's "me first" everywhere.' He's gripping
Conrad's arm in case he moves away.

'Yes, I agree. It's the coming of the end. The candle flares
before the finish, brighter, quicker – dies. If it all can't go on,
can't go further – it's best call it a day. Enough. Start selling
off, and pulling down,' Conrad says, looking for the door.

*

It's a little false. Everyone says these things, everyone agrees. There's no impact. After, Conrad goes with Paolo to what they call the 'gym': for mental press-ups.

'We should wear our togs, our togas, tonight,' the organiser says. 'Let's try to get to that deeper level.'

They stand around, draped. Could be desert Arabs, or kids playing with some sheets. There's a coloured ball – you bounce it to someone you want to hear speak, or you throw it at someone who interrupts. That's copied from somewhere where that's done.

'Your husband – he was inarticulate. That's why he did those paintings. They say nothing,' Conrad tells his old friend Émilie.

'They're much admired, and beautiful. Significant people have written tributes,' she says.

'What's more to say? Tributes? He escaped, he isn't dead. He's gone on being beautiful, and staging all the past, as if it really matters, running it all through again. This time, with a knowing smirk,' Conrad says. 'All painting now's a requiem and an exhumation.'

'Well, what's new? Secret services and new age stuff. It's all the rage. Lovely bodies turning to spiritual perfection, swapping brains. What a bore,' she says. 'Everything's a dull party – like this one.'

*

Get someone in the bed, a body in all its seasons. You play the animal to show you aren't, that you are human. Another body, a different taste and smells, lies down beside, too tired to sleep...

*

'Dance! Dance with the person beside you, we'll all twist and twirl,' the organiser shouts. 'Spin! Spin like cotton bobbins! Things will go wavery, dissolve ... it's good! That's how it should be. Keep it up there, as long as you can.'

'You work for nothing,' Conrad says to Émilie. 'And then perhaps it turns into a job, and you get paid. But then you have to put out lies. I read old stuff, and broadcast the odd bits. There's this spy, centuries ago, a bendy trail ... then stories of a boozy trek – people love that... They were all naive then, like dogs.... Then, it all took off. It got to where we are: the massacres and the inventions, long lives, boredom … short lives and oblivion. Now we know: it speeded up, too quick, too desperate. It's like way back – you knew the play was ending because the horses snuffled outside – the carriages, drawn up for home....' Conrad knows he can say anything to Émilie – she doesn't listen, doesn't care: 'The play ends anyway,' he says, 'The horses aren't a part.'

*

'If you're a fugitive, the countryside looks vast, the people indifferent and uninformed. It isn't so,' Conrad tells Paolo. 'There's spies everywhere, ready to tell a tale, and fetch a party, a militia.... You should assume that everyone's a spy, outsiders, insiders too. Best turn everybody in, strangers, or just neighbours absent for a while.'

'Then came roads and telephones,' says Paolo, playing along. 'This century, running doesn't work.'

'Real voices, they existed already, and much better than a telephone,' Conrad says. 'They'd cut your head off, and no "ahh and ugh". It was the only way you wouldn't rise again. No mark set upon your grave, if grave you got.'

'There's always a regime. Those are the oldest things,' Paolo says.

'That country, that Scottish countryside – was a history of hamlets, of places with no one; but to sell land it has to have a name; mills and their streams, forced betrothals, early deaths ... the crows, who know the future. Then the rest, the other birds,' says Conrad. 'It's the northland – there's water everywhere. A tiny settlement is possible, is best. The south is different, they had cities, round a well, a river. Another kind of planet.'

'Going for centuries – all you needed to know at the start, and then at the finish, just the same. Unless you were invaded,' Paolo says, tagging along...

'It was terrible, of course,' says Conrad. 'A tyranny of little things, small lies, tiny people – a priest, a fear, a lord, a usurer, a husband, father, crazy crones and seers ... you fell down in the field and died, or a cow breathed in your face, gave you idiocy with boils... See the corpses in chains at the crossroads ... looks like you, Paolo. And me. Reactionary? you say. Returning somehow to what was? That has no appeal for me. We're moiling in the spate, Paolo, it's useless wishing you could die of thirst...'

The old villagers can't do poetry, they must put it in their lives. No old movies left, no sound, no sepia. You find the treatments, the sketches, in the court record, the land registry, no one knows who they were, poets, assassins, what they looked like, they'd be a few frames, no continuity, no character, no context, no lapse of time, no whiting of hair, the clothes change while you glance – families, expedients, a dash for somewhere like a vole, a stoat, a flash in the undergrowth – if you don't get eaten, you're disappeared for ever.

They did nothing for themselves – there was deportation. Clearances. Epidemics: joining a regiment to go and kill southerners, mostly. Where there are battles, not wars, things end quick. But, there's civil massacres ... after battles lost.

*

'You're not getting into depth,' the organiser tells Conrad.

'Maybe I'm getting whatever's the opposite,' says Conrad. 'Is it as precious? You know what you want of us, Lidia, but not what we want. I for one – have no idea. When I stop bothering, I'll say, "that's it". That's experience, the common state, known, done with, finished. We speak, communicate – we understand, and so – nothing we are or say is ours, special, unique. Then – you go "croak". Made in someone's grinning image, a toad's grimace, squashed by the years.'

How can you react to that? Lidia doesn't try.

'We have partners now,' says Conrad, 'as if we're panning for gold or founding Macy's. My partner's gone. She said, "You're a person, Conrad, who'll never get a medal for anything. Not for anything at all. Not even 'best dog in show'."'

'Oh, I see what she means,' says Lidia. 'It's her turn now, so off you go! You should be a big monster, Conrad. You'd know then why people treat you as they do – but you're a small monster. The treacherous kind.'

'I need a bed,' says Conrad. 'With electricity, where I can stay for months, then leave, not paying.'

'No, Conrad,' Lidia says, 'staying with me would not be ethical.'

She softens her voice, avoids the hand touch that should come with that. 'You're full of anomalies, my dear,' she says. 'Your search for justice: that follows great unpunished violence. Equality – comes after wars. Fraternity – found only in war, in the trenches, in flight, in marching in allegro time.... Your unchanging village – repressive – perpetuates the disasters you deplore – the famines, the rivalries, the sickness, the ignorance unto death, the bullying.... You must look elsewhere, Conrad – not in what you think you know, desire.... That only brings its opposite.'

'I didn't know that's what I want,' Conrad says. 'I'm thirty, Lidia – the good days are past, the brain, the heart – they are mature, ready to drop off the tree. I've a biography: already I've a past, I can look back, as if there's been an itinerary... That's what my parents thought – they wandered. Before that – no journey, just heads down for the struggle. Now – you can't do anything with us, Lidia...'

'That's your problem,' Lidia says. 'Not mine. I don't touch you. Think! Think about the future...'

'It's always being talked about,' says Conrad. 'The experts! But that's not the future – it's the present; that is all we know ... it always is. Anyway, Paolo will stay with you. He loves the music – "waiting for the golden light" – that's the line, that's what he wants.'

*

Jacobites and Jesuits.... Those Scots, their plots! Lives at risk – all for carrying a bundle of letters. No spying involved. Just escaping other spies. Playing both sides – who'd call it treachery?

'You're not Scottish,' Lidia says. 'No harm in that, of course. I'm sure you could be good at it, and learn. You're not a scholar, Conrad – why dive back in someone else's past? It's black as black – it's you that has to bring the light – and you're a person of the dusk, the waning day – not merry fearless drunks....'

'The past,' says Conrad, 'is always someone else's. Who's is the present? Not mine or yours, it's all laid out, and no one knows who by – and if it is a property to buy and sell...'

*

14   *John Fraser*

'There's no future in the past,' says Marcel 'Call Me *Colonel*': 'You'll never make a historian, Conrad – you're an anecdotist. A butterfly. Nothing more.'

'What's the new world, Marcel?' Conrad asks. 'What do you offer me – a *noir*? Do you want me as a spy, or a resister? Slightly dirty? Or a saint? The blue billiard tables, all in a row. "*Nous sommes Septembre*", Yves Montand and the rest of the gang.... All on the right side.'

'Humanitarian work,' says Marcel. 'You don't need be a humanist, just be a channel. That's the job – an intermediary, a facilitator. Guys we can't recognise – slippery in their friends, and their ideas – they need supplies. To keep them fighting, for the side we quite hope might win, or win a good position for the end, the endgame – they need assurances. They need materiel, recruits. Food to hand out, food to eat. Doctors. Magazines – to read in the bunkers, to fit to their guns. Arms, of course, prosthetic and ones that can go "bang" ... and systems.... Guidance. Locked on your target. There's no official supply, for all the good and useful stuff. You – you order it. You fetch it. You might even deliver it. Bring people in, take people out. That's how it's done – managing real things, real people....Not quite spying – illegal quartermastering.'

*

... 'Took horse; humm'd over some songs gently; at last attempted the *Dragon of Wantly*; slew him severall times, and was very weel pleased with myself.' That's the lord president – a famous boozer ... on the Major's other side, his similar, his opponent. If he catches the Major, he can have him hanged – or else recruit him. Unless they're on the same side after all.

*

'There's risks,' says Marcel, 'But not for you. Except your reputation, which you have not got. And for many unknown, anonymous friends, who'll never do you good.'

'Is there then a cause?' asks Conrad.

'Oh, you can be sure,' says Marcel. '"Many. And they shift. Liberals become nationalist, the nats turn to religion. In those places, you make your allies and you find if maybe they chime with what's in you, or maybe not. You'll fire on them, they'll jail you: you know how it is. It's serious, not logical.'

'I recruit?' asks Conrad.

'You guarantee,' Marcel says, 'that when the guys go, we look benevolently. After – is after. You transport. Enthusiasts and disinfectant. You do the publicity, write the letters home, even the last one.'

'The cities – I love them. The florid South! The nature too, once it was fine and ready,' Conrad says. 'There's Lidia. She gathers us, gives us philosophy – and yes! Of course! she organises us.'

'You see?' Marcel says. 'It's channels ... getting them to run down separately to the delta, and the sea.'

'The Major in the manuscript,' says Conrad. 'The rank. They weren't regulars – only an ephemeral militia regiment.... Do I get pips and crowns?' He laughs.

'That's the idea. Climb into his breeches, Conrad,' Marcel says. 'Though – beware: he said he had the itch....'

'I'm not sure:' says Conrad: 'I see I get an easy life, taking your offer. Travel – forced and not. Someone to help with parcels...'

'Trucks,' says Marcel. 'Huge trucks. It's all got bigger...'

'The battles,' Conrad says. 'Age of enlightenment. Reason, optimism. They were fierce. Drunk, hacking, with scythes and rakes, prisoners killed, the wounded left, mercenaries – soldiers arriving late, massacring the tired ones, a helter-skelter afterwards. Then dungeons. Lose your land, your language, your clothes – all proscribed.... Rebels for a new regime, restoration, the old religion, those highlanders wanted to win, make it all as it should have been – absolutely familiar, everybody doing the right thing.... "The eighteenth century for ever" – good title for a song....'

'Yes, yes,' says Marcel. 'What a laugh – the age of reason. How many times did we hear that? Now, your task. It's not just winning – you need to see enough good stuff gets through, so's they don't desert or change their side. You're there, whatever happens, whatever you may hear, or meet. Bring games and gas. All that – the aftermath – it's not your job.'

'Yes!' says Conrad. 'A job! With some purpose....'

'Being like other people,' says Marcel sternly. 'Doesn't make you less alone. Wanting to help – doesn't make you safe, nor liked. There's worse, of course. You're paid, you live well. Rent near a main road, no possessions to unpack, no protection – and you live so well, they think you're really spying. You know nothing – how could you spy? You live rich, but you're an outlaw, a fugitive. Someone's always after you, there's never time they give you to explain – and explanation makes it worse. Avoid the truth, but love it secretly. Remember too – your side may massacre, commit atrocities – it's still your side, it'll be so for ever: even if it wins, no one will plant a tree because you sent them stuff, forbidden, mislabelled....'

*

'It could even be quite noble,' Paolo says.

'I wouldn't say that,' says Conrad.

'It means supporting that hidden side, the side that might be noble,' Paolo insists.

'Don't keep on, Paolo,' Conrad says. 'You're annoying me. It's states, playing both sides, that's all. Betting on the outsider, keeping them going – in case. To make pressure, to have a voice if the wrong side wins....'

'It's lessening the pain,' says Paolo, 'of what continues to make pain.'

'No,' Conrad says, 'it's pushing people to fight on when there's no prospect for them, accepting the grimy side of the *guerilla*, the vendettas, the punishments, the paranoia, retributions....'

'Oh, that's the side that mirrors the other side....' says Paolo.

*

'Then – he was on me,' Paolo tells Émilie. 'Hitting out and screaming. A mad scene. *Lear, Lucia di Lammermoor*... If it hadn't hurt me so, could be as amusing as it frightened. Conrad's quite mad. It doesn't show, except ... when there's some hope of recognition, usefulness.... He knows it's all a lie: and of course, underneath, everyone soon sees, it's dirty compromise. Fame and reputation, naturally is also lies, but still....'

He shows Émilie his wounds – blood blisters, like he's just been cupped and leeched. Rips and bruises, as if from rusty swords.

'Poor Conrad,' Paolo says, resentful. 'He'll never make his name. One way or t'other, he'll end locked up....'

'He'll make a wave,' says Émilie. 'The crazy ones, enthusiasts – they make the ranting speech, everyone's fired up, and reassured. Then, the chief, the king of kings, the yagbo, goes back, back to his shabby room, and gnaws some wood, and razors at his thighs.... It's best to stick to art. My husband did – although, the devils came from tubes and ended on the wall. Of course, the sane ones – they do nothing, just sit beneath the tree, drink from a jug, and wait for mulberries to fall....'

'They won't catch Conrad,' Paolo says: 'He'll go to a lonely country. One where they don't talk to neighbours. Italy, France. They'll put him down to drink. That's how you get your anonymity – it's safer than madness. That way, in his fine room, he'll be the liberator, the *untore,* the greaser, the facilitator. Inside, he'll know he must take on the dark side, he will fester so that others can sing and say they're free.'

'You're wrong, Paolo,' says Émilie. 'That's how it was in books. People don't care. The chiefs; they organise, they prosper.'

*

Conrad tries to make out with Candice. His job – makes him do crazy things. She went once to Lidia's group, and found it silly.

'Don't touch me there,' Candice says. 'I feel I'm trapped in traffic, in a motor, and you're scrabbling at the glass. Do you want in? Or a buck?'

'Oh, I'm in a basket, rolling down the hill,' says Conrad. 'I don't care. You can't stop me. I'll go smash. You're all philistines: that used to be a good thing to be, a good place – Palestine. Filistin. Now they think your toothpaste can explode.'

'I don't think that, Conrad,' says Candice, 'I promise. There's been every kind of person – I don't follow anyone. I think I'm unique – that's where the trouble starts.'

'I'm not out for trouble,' Conrad says soothingly, touching her where he can.

'You're in business,' Candice says. 'In the traffic. What is it, Conrad? People? That could be creative. Don't tell me it's documents!' and she laughs.

'I'm the tortoise the world stands on,' says Conrad, quite embarrassed.

'You'll find it's bigger. Holds more people. It's a turtle, Conrad. Conrad the emperor, with the Weltenmantel. Printed by Liberty.' She laughs some more. It wasn't funny.

'This is a fine house you have,' she says: 'So many rooms! It's like America.'

'It's rented,' says Conrad. 'What it has is of no significance.'

'They've left so much,' says Candice. 'China dolls in a closet.'

'It's a metaphor,' says Conrad, winding down. 'They're all over this place.'

'You don't know anything about women, Conrad,' Candice says. 'It's fortunate – I don't either. Your people – I bet they know, but they don't tell.'

'They're women too,' says Conrad. 'And other sorts, like us, exactly like, except – they can't get out. I can, I can stop – whenever I want,' and he grins. 'They're at war, sealed in. I'm in trade – I can stop.'

'You won't,' says Candice, 'because you can. They can't – they're bound in, like leaves in a book. Can you imagine, Conrad – a book of leaves? A tree?'

'Mmmm,' says Conrad. 'Whimsy! I love it, it's like tiramisù, it's a sweet pudding, a sweet sweet.'

'You can fly,' Candice says. 'Where you sent the trucks. It's all aftermath, they say – the people will come back soon, they say that too.'

*

Aeroplanes – get up to all kinds of no good – some people even see them as erotic – it takes a stretch. They fly, Candice and Conrad, quite chaste.

*

A long dusty road, becoming, for a stretch, a short and dusty street. A café, all glass and showcases with ices, leathery sausage, a museum, a display: 'That pistaccio,' says Candice, 'it sums it up. Arsenic green.'

'The war?' the owner says, 'that's all behind us, we don't talk about it now.'

'I thought no one talked at all,' says Conrad. 'Or else only about the war.'

The man smiles a shifty smile, and charges lots for food which looks one way and tastes another – though it tastes not much at all. 'This bread,' says Candice. 'Wrapped in paper there was once some soap.'

'Yes,' Conrad says. 'That's it! Clever girl.'

The cafè's the only building that looks finished – the rest is like Bosnia before the war: guys who'd come back from building other people's houses up in Germany, came back to build their own.... No roofs, some brick, but mostly thick plaster sheeting, holes cut for the wires, like ghostie drapes, cement sticking out like grey ice-cream. Then came the war, no roofs, of course, what there had been was burnt or shelled like peas: the men – their throats cut, the women gone somewhere, or stayed out where they'd been.

'Here, you wouldn't call it victory,' says Conrad. 'There'd be trouble if you did. They lost – but there are promises.'

'I'd surrender,' Candice says. 'Except – it's worse. Better fight than be a destitute, in a tent.'

'Exactly so,' says Conrad. 'I stand for better tents and better arms – and on with the meetings. I work at it, Candice – it's like an expedition up the dark river. It's not enough to buy big hats, you need an entourage. I have porters, interpreters, my fellow travellers, my fawners, lickspittles – all trusties, all my confidants; sweet discourse, dirty deeds....
I'm the chief. If I wish, they carry me. I have the map. I drew it up myself. That's how things are done here, maybe everywhere. Only the barmen and the waiters work – the rest, they're courtiers. They journey with me, know they mostly won't come back. But – they don't care. For them, life is eking out; living out their time, and passing on the secret: 'nothing is resolved, not ever'. There's always poorer people, more determined, waiting for your job. The politicians – they act fast, they must rob, be popular, all that, and so they're slick. The bureaucrats – they are the lifers. They act slow, meticulous. They go nowhere, and make sure you won't. They guarantee – nothing will change.

'How many udders do I have, Candice? I have a train of mercenaries, my friends ... each waiting soft-mouthed for a teat.

'I act, Candice. The bosses – playing all sides, that is their goal, their guarantee. The terrorist on the lam today, tomorrow sits by you at the banquet.... Me, instead – I believe. I push my desperate guys, my dirty side, against the other lot. I help, Candice – no one else does. Others are optimist or pessimists – I've gone far far beyond all that.'

'Oh well,' she says. 'I guess you know how to be good and bad, and both together,' and she cartwheels down a gentle slope. 'See,' she shouts, 'how lovely is the grass! And how it breaks your fall!'

*

'You see, Candice,' says Conrad, 'those old Scots – all traitors: – to the crown, country – or their friends. No one blames them now. It's like the tires, for those old primal bangers – those first autos, shod with rubber from the Congo trees. Someone remembers Leopold – but all the guys who made things work, gang bosses, punishers – no one cares at all. They're shuffled into history, wearing their togas, and they disappear, hung up somewhere like albino bats, back of the cave – all that's left of interest is those tin lizzies running down the corniche ... laughter and cheers.'

'Yes, Conrad,' Candice says. 'I'm convinced. You're the best bad good person I have met. What does it mean? – you'll tell me that.... As if I care. All that I want – is hearing those tires squeak on the tarmac, guys in their goggles diving in the past.'

'We teeter, Candice,' Conrad says. 'We're linemen – and the line is in the air ... the dialogue's in morse ... tapped out through the telegraph....'

'I don't see you up aloft,' she says. 'Rather – there's a scent of burial about you – you keep your head well down, peering in the manifests, the chandlers' lists.... Anonymous, obscure. You're not exposed. I don't see that head, returning to us like the big chief's, foil-wrapped in a biscuit tin, shrunk to fit.... They don't do treason trials, no more. You're safe. Guilty in someone's eyes – no fear, you've won your anonymity. Those who care far more than me – still they're indifferent, or powerless. Leave it. Enjoy your life. Spend money, borrow and don't think of paying back. You're just a fixer, Conrad. You repent for what you wish you'd done, the boundaries you feared to cross.... But, you did none of it. You're in the middle, like the rest. If not you – then, someone else, they'd do exactly what you've done, not done. And so and so: a row of desks to the infinite, all you, all impersonating you.... If they, or you, are not the spy – the state's clerk does the same. The whistling.... Don't you hear, Conrad? If we're not here, not anyone – the whistling goes on; it's towers that's been built everywhere – the universal breeze, it catches on them when the world, the rock, spins by, and makes its tune for no one's ear....'

'Clearly, Candice – you're right. you've hit on it: it's poetry. Whistling in the dark,' says Conrad.

'How I love intellectuals,' Candice says, gambolling near a rhododendron – 'You appear, tall and grim, like Soter Megas – the great deliverer. Then – nothing is the same, nothing is as it appears, it all flows, a panto – I forget the phrase ... oh yes – *panta rhei*! It starts as water running – then you make a shore, a lake, a strand ... people it with mermaids, fish you swear are good to eat, eager to be caught – then ... it's gone. Sunk back into the earth, engulfed, drunk down. Maybe arising in another place, a dip, bushes of thyme becoming seawrack, waving slow and wise down in the green....'

'Yes,' Conrad says. 'Careful! The gold I found is real – I try to sell you pyrites. Watch out!'

'A threat? A rough patch?' Candice asks. 'I'm ready for all that. In life now, you pal up with someone, stay around a while, then you move on to someone else. It's not like being born with relatives, acquire a lover, stick with them, seep into them claggy, in the soil, coffins matching, the grave.... No!'

'I clung to you, Candice,' Conrad says, 'because your face is irreproachable. Our ancestors we share: simple and whitish, East African I'd say. Way back of course.... What we have in common – it is the smell, the smell of us, naked or clothed ... small rooms, reluctant food, needing to stew. No pretension, everything pawed over, bartered, left in a lockup to grow old ... those craggy vegetables. Smell of constriction, small lives waiting like Egyptian grain, a desert peony – an inclination of the sun, dew, scotch mist, then bursting out, after centuries – the strongest life ... flower for a day, *acheb.*'

'There!' Candice says. 'You've had your story. It's the end. We've visited the desolation that you made.. No doubt there's people ready to thank you for those bandages.... I don't judge – I move.... Those small rooms, though – you get the same smell from living in a squat, or with grim lovers, midst their installations, spread out in hangars. They've only cans to heat on single burners.... But, after all, I like your story. The nose points, bower of our memories. A kitchen shared – maybe in Deraa, Smolensk – bad times or ordinary ones....

'You're an artist, Conrad. Try making creation your next stage – get fresh horses, pal with them, tell them you'll ride them down to the abyss ... then dump them. The next inn – get more, tell them just the same until you're done, then lie down in the rut that everybody's made before you, try to sell your skin to make a purse, a sack. Maybe a rep will pass – Gucci, Fendi – make you the offer everyone is waiting for. Your body immortalised ... or a tote.'

'That's too dark for me,' says Conrad, holding her shoulder as she tries to spin around....

'You have to learn, Conrad,' says Candice, 'as it all spins, everything goes dark, then it comes light again. It doesn't mean a thing.'

Candice and Conrad – no one would say they suit. Conrad reads old histories, makes pop curiosities of them to make a buck. Then – the war zone, unofficial supplier to a shady front, makes lots of bucks, but there's complicity that gnaws. A far-away story, somewhere East, almost fairy-tales.

        Candice – is clean. She wants to know – what's life? Travel, taste everything. If you don't find out:

what attitude is it best to take, despite not knowing much, or anything?

There's no fit between them, so – they split.

*

'Some you lead, and some you follow,' Candice says. 'You can be choosy, but, well, you have your limitations. Travel the world, best not to carry cash or you'll be robbed. I love the art they left, the first ones. The people who live in it at present, they leave me tepid, everywhere. Still, there's nothing else – you plant your garden, sometimes with rutabagas, sometimes peonies. All has its use.'

'Perhaps,' Eva says. 'But you'll find nothing here. This is a corrupt society. It's rotten, rotting from the top – not just the usual bigots, reactionaries ... for centuries, it didn't move, it's stinking fruit that clings to branches – the wasps have made their tunnels and buzzed off; it's been pecked and penetrated. There's not one better part – the rot is hanging on the branch, or – on the ground.'

'I hadn't thought,' says Candice. 'Everybody talks that way – those that think. But it does nothing, it's no use.'

'When there was the *guerilla*,' Eva says, 'small as it was, they shot the generals. That was stupid – there's always more, every sergeant can become one – besides, here, the soldiers have no power. To be popular, you need to shoot the taxmen. If you read the books, you shoot the bankers. Who would be left? Poets and shepherds? Hmmmm. Not so many. Shoot the nonentities at their desks? What is the point? That's something we can all be, scribes.... No, Candice, there's no hope – they blew it all away, the gunmen, making it seem they were in some foreign bosses' pay. Who'd pay them to do that? Some country far away, far off in time and fashion....'

'Oh,' Candice says, 'I never thought of that, it's not my world. Shooting people to make things right? I'm amazed ... that someone thought....'

'People will fight, Candice, rebel,' says Eva. 'But only if there's hope.'

'It's all been long forgotten,' Candice says, 'No one at all remembers it – or if they do, it's a bad story.'

'Yes,' Eva says, 'stories don't happen again, and if they ever do, it was over so long ago, it never really was....'

'I wish I'd live long enough to find how my life turns out....' says Candice, wistfully –

'Forget that!' shouts Eva, pummelling her. 'Stop thinking butterflies and metamorphosis – when they get their wings, it's time up! – dead within the day! Lots lose things – wings, fins and tails – and as for loves and tastes ... those are the things that fly – away, away! There's no lesson there, no prospect. Change? It's a digestion. All those emotions just pass through.'

'Don't think it, Eva,' Candice says. 'Rebelling. They'd shoot you. No – they'd think of something worse – questions only they know the answers to. They'd give you another life, then draw it out of you – white flesh, like out of lobsters. People don't think of that, not here. When I was with Conrad – he'd read them out to me; the rebels and the law – they were all wags, piss artists, not frightened, or not all the time, forever wearing swords and daggers, taking snuff and trumpeting. Drinking those tappit hens, bad hooch....'

'Oh Candice,' Eva says, and laughs, 'The bottles were much smaller then, like the measures. Everything was, to fit the smaller people. Besides – the intimacy, the fighting – it's about places, clans, you and I have never seen, not on the maps, there's just sand and trees. I've never been there, but I can imagine it....'

'Well, not now,' says Candice. 'Don't fall into someone else's trap. You know it's not your theme, none of them are. You scare me!'

'You don't look scared,' says Eva. 'But of course, nothing that goes on now is mine, is up to me, is my concern. It's not that all's been settled, but it's not the time to speak. Another place perhaps awaits....'

'The mercenaries – they killed the wounded in the hospital,' says Candice.

'You have to be prepared for suchlike things,' says Eva. 'If they'd not been killed – for sure they'd not be here along with us today,' and they laugh.

'The locals – saw a soldier in a dead man's coat – yellow leather, unmistakable. Unhorsed him, then they drowned him in the burn. Of course, it was all feudal then....' Candice says.

'My! Your Conrad! What an impression he has left,' says Eva. 'You must be ready. But not seek, not trouble, anyway. Do what you must, but don't be an enthusiast.'

'Wait! – you've not done all this, none of everything, Eva; not even been, not found it on the map....' says Candice. 'Best leave it so, have someone else do it, in your name....'

'Oh, that old story,' Eva says. 'Complicity! I'm not guilty, not of anything, except what I do with my own hands,' and she spreads them out for Candice to admire. They're clean.

'Lots of the past is odd,' says Candice. 'Weird. Much of it looks like now. That's the past that interests me, Eva.'

'That's silly,' Eva says. 'What's different and what's now – that is ours. The rest is just a given. You want to know why, how, we are human, and why that shapes our destiny. Maybe what's past, what's constant, doesn't tell a thing. We have to harmonise with the unknown – or else it's all depressing. Pretend, Candice. Everything is new! No swords, daggers, no snuff mulls, no chiefs, no oatcakes, no blood pudding....'

'I'm sure you're right,' says Candice, telling a lie. 'People took arms....'

'Loyalty? Place, tradition? The name? The family name? The boss?' asks Eva –

'Foreigners. A little religion. Machismo. Desperation and fear. Resignation and indifference. Cash and food,' says Candice.

'Yes, my love,' says Eva, giggling. 'But in *kilts*!'

'Those went,' says Candice, 'The plaid, the toga, togs. The dishdasha: that's still around. When they lost to the professionals, they were all bevvied up, lots didn't feel anything at all. Language too, that went: and all those swords.'

'Yes,' says Eva. 'You remember Conrad, probably too much; and he remembers those old Scots – but, it's centuries ago.'

'I never said it was the same,' says Candice. 'But – first there's monkeys: then there's monkeys.'

They consider this: Candice says, 'They lost some heads, some land, a chief or two, a cause, a civilisation, you could say.... The deportations – they came much much after, and some turned out well....'

'All those come back,' says Eva. 'It's easy. Civilisation eternally returns: so do endings too. You don't need even try. It's a bad world, Candice, but – we have come through, we're here. We made it. I dare say they had hard lives, but it's a tiny interlude, forgotten, not severe. And we are on the brink – it could be paradise....'

'I'm sure you're right,' says Candice. 'It's just Conrad, his stories. He lives there, lives here... I couldn't even put my finger on his place, those places, not on a map.'

'Anyway,' says Eva, 'from what I hear, they weren't so separate, those sides. Just locals. On the fringe. They moved inward when they wanted, to make some cash, and, out –

when they had to think about their land. In those days, people weren't wicked, just feisty. Of course, there was exaggeration – you could say, as an example, Genghiz. What about Caligula?'

'My picture,' Candice says. 'It's firm, stable. That's what Conrad taught – he sailed on language, and he had so many – a sailor on the seven seas, bouncing on the waves, those ululating tongues. All the past was his, the landscapes, primal, and the stags that bellowed, the lairds sneezing brown snot into kerchiefs, all that stuff. And then the columns – walking fast, so fast, I couldn't make it, couldn't keep up. He was a genius, but it had all gone by. No one was interested – it was all in books. Put something in your head for keeps – that's a mistake.'

'That's right! You shouldn't store up your illusions about Conrad,' Eva says. 'From what you say, he was a waster, sleeping rough, or among the old books. Never accomplished anything. A loner, didn't have his ear to the grass. Talked big and acted small.'

'I fear you're right,' says Candice. 'Deportations though – he was an expert. Camps tented and in huts. All what you see on the TV. Quite ineffective, the knowing all about; whether you've the humanitarian bent, or just you feel you need to say it. Best just be a chronicler, avoid the powerful – if they fall on you, they squash... Conrad tripped on languages – you never knew which one. If people don't use them, they get clotted, turn into cheese. It's best to be like us. We understand enough, my dear ... each other, and ourselves...'

'Listen Candice,' Eva says, wriggling in the seat, its body-shape not quite up to hers. 'Maybe we should stop it here. Best not make friends, here in this visa queue. You never know who's who, and wanting to inform to score some points....'

'Oh Eva, I do so agree,' says Candice. 'We've been here for days. I want a permit to go in and out, you – one that lets you stay. They say it's better to be expelled, then try again – another name, another story. From outside.'

'They say the story doesn't count,' says Eva. 'No one cares. It's quotas, not your behaviour, your record. And the guy that keeps you out or in – they get a bonus, so they say.'

'It's like this everywhere,' says Candice. 'I need to move about. Go everywhere. It isn't one world any more, it's frontiers and entitlement...'

'You don't need to tell me that,' says Eva. 'Don't offend, don't be too clever, don't rock the boat. Don't say you'll smuggle something in or out, or that you have a mission, or don't agree with something that's been made a rule.'

No door opens, no one is called. They wait, suspicious of each other, fearful of themselves, their case.

They sit side by side and silent, waiting for visas, in or out.

*

Candice thinks – 'Maybe Eva was a spy, a provocateur. Or dangerous. What I said, whatever it was, I should not have.... I haven't yet needed to be a bad, a really bad, individual. Not like Eva says she is. Ditching eternity, that's grave. I'm sure if neeeded it would come quite naturally. The decency beneath – something you can conjure up, always go back to. Interests: those can't be bad, because they're in a system. Wars – you attack and you defend, there can be rules. The rest – good side, bad side – is incidental. But Eva? Evil is something you start off with, something makes you recognise it... it doesn't slip in by chance – you start with it, with doing it, and then maybe you look for an excuse. Your excuse – is the punishment you can get for being bad. Especially if you win clearly. You apologise. Or you lose, and that is that: no one listens to you anyway. Eva – she had the eye. She knows what it would mean – really bad, real evil. The cause – good or bad – irrelevant. It's the evil done, with no get-out.... Not that there's punishment. There's nothing. So – why bother, why worry? Maybe, if I had such a cause....

'Be as naive as you like, when you're in line, waiting for the visa. Never be sarcastic...'

*

Candice is smart – you can see. They give her everything she wants – she can go anywhere.... Could be quota, could be a mistake...

'Poor Eva,' Trudi says. 'They thought she was untrustworthy. She could be deported, but you, Candice, you have everything.'

'Yes,' Candice says. 'I don't know where to start.'

'Oh,' Trudi says. 'You have to start from here – even if you couldn't put your finger on it on a map.'

'An older woman, so they say,' says Candice. 'Makes a superb companion on a journey.'

'Well,' Trudi says. 'I'm older than some, but maybe not as old as you – so I accept, though you could be more gracious and ingratiating.... I heard you talking about those Scots. After they rebelled, they dispersed like spores. The opium, my dear! Those canny foxes! How they traded, squeezed in everywhere, careless of the decencies, of course. Empire and banking. Hongkong in thrall to them – they gave China a new life, now that too's dispersed like spores ... like opium. It's everywhere – we sleep on it, we brush our teeth with it....'

'Oh Trudi,' Candice says, quite flustered. 'I'm not a Scot, I don't know where they went. As for the drugs and banking – the opium... I put the blame on religion. Not what they insist is looking for the underside, the golden lining inside everything, even in the fustian and the duck.... It's the idea of stewardship, the offer to the emperors' sons, the Caesars: to open an account and see their money grow – slavery, my dear! That's where the money is! They say we have to grow, produce, or else we're poor for ever, even if it condemns us all to suffocate....'

'It will have been an example to the universe,' says Trudi, pushing Candice in a cab. 'No one has done all that before, not ever. Killing the planet, ours – like an exhausted horse, run out and desperate. Pushing the system to the limit means sometimes you go beyond, too far for comfortable lives. It gives you choice, dear Candice – you can be a banker, or a toxic, maybe a pusher – the thing not to be is grow and hoe the stuff, or cook it up – my! that is hard and dangerous....'

'You get me wrong,' says Candice, quite irritated. 'I might just be corruptible – most everybody is, but I am not corrupt. Not yet.'

'Of course,' says Trudi. 'You have not begun your trip. Forget about your origins – in a way, we've all been Scots, and milked the cows and shot the deer and eaten oatcakes ... now, that's done. Whatever you might want to do, remember, I can coach you in it.'

The cab goes swiftly down spacious avenues of limes – at the end there is an arch of Constantine, or probably a copy, and they've turned into a narrow street with tall buildings of brown brick, no windows, but, where they might be, grey wood loading-doors, each striped in red.

'The deals start here,' says Trudi, paying off the driver.

'It's too sudden,' Candice says. 'I don't know where I am.'

'It isn't necessary,' Trudi says. 'When you go somewhere else, you'll know where you have left – they have a stamp for when you leave.'

'All you people!' Candice says. 'They spring up everywhere, in caps and uniforms. You too, Trudi – as if you've been planted, and I'm adrift, on a shipping lane, or on a railroad track.... And none of you are people I could love....'

'If you can move around,' says Trudi, not put out. 'And it goes well, it shows you've saddlebags of cash. And if instead you smash – you're just a deportee. Either way, you'll be in company. Maybe you'll find a slot and win a prize – or maybe not. Love isn't part of this, though I, like Eva – I've an eye for it: seduction and betrayal, or the other way around – that's more usual, maybe....'

'Trudi,' says Candice, 'I'm sure you're good as toast. And, you Nordic six-footers, you're much desired. Finns, short Finns – they like their prostitutes tall, oh so tall ... like pines.'

'Be careful with that tongue, Candice,' says Trudi, irritated. 'I don't know Finns. I have a mission. If we travel as a pair, it's me that does the favour.'

'Tell me, Trudi,' Candice says. 'Travelling, one has one's secrets. But often – they are someone else's – are they still secrets? The woman in the film says "I seek. What do I seek?" It's like that with secrets. It's dangerous to have them, because you can't drop them off, leave them in a bin. They're with you for ever, longer by far than you're alive.'

'That's the nub,' says Trudi. 'The butcher has no insurance on his van – he sells his name – a mafia fleet of motors, all registered to him.... Things you know, that's just the start – it's the scut dropping down the hole, a beckoning finger. You will follow, like it or not....Some boys down our street – they were terrorists – I could be one, and so could you. Face years in jail – except we're on another side. This time, the finger didn't point, you weren't the chieftain, nor the patsy... And gangs – I was bullied, they wanted me to join. It's better to be bullied than to join, I promise you, Candice.'

'That's it, exactly,' Candice says. 'Secrets all round. What you know, and what you aren't. What they want you to be, what you resist: secrets all of it, that you carry with you, like in a trolley-bag.'

'That's a tiny bit naive, Candice,' says Trudi, as they go down the airplane steps into heat and dust. Kolkata, says the sign. 'If you have principles, you can tell everything you know. You must! Sometimes it's already known – someone else, the same principles – or else you precipitate the deed: or they give it up. Consequences. More secrets, different ones, but further down the path. Things you make happen, without having the intent.'

'Cairo was as hot as this,' says Candice. 'The sunset here – there is more green in it. How busy everybody is – some doing things I'd never do. They have Naxalites, a ways away, over in the trees.'

'Yes,' says Trudi, 'Cairo. We should have stayed awhile – it's famous, though it's not a happy place. I have the nose for suchlike things – my childhood was a mixed one, Candice dear.'

'We're safe,' says Candice. 'Look at all the cops we've seen. I fear I made an error – this is Kolkata, I thought I'd booked us into Calicut. In any case – I wanted time to see Golconda – but either way, we're kilometres away...'

'Oh,' says Trudi laughing, 'If it's gold you want to see, my love....' And she opens up her silk – there's kilograms of gold on her, she's caparisoned, a heavy belt, her biceps clasped, a necklace descending as a harness ... below the belt, a girdle, kneepads, is that a golden wig atop? – the shoes, how they must hurt and clunk, she's like the guy they weigh in gold, except he isn't wearing it ... sprinkled in the hair and eyelids, ear-, nose- and chin-plugs and earrings big as bells with plaited bellropes hanging down ... those you could see quite casually, but not the nipple cones, the shoulder-flames, the leaf-tights, and of course ... there's all those rings like cobras winding up the arms....

'What are you financing with all that?' asks Candice. 'Trudi – do tell. I'll keep a secret. How do you pass the checks....?'

'All that's for later,' Trudi says. 'Let's go down, my dear – I'm dressed: the estuary fish is excellent, full-bodied, so they say.'

'Next stop, Kucha,' Candice trills. 'If there's a flight direct. I hate those nomenslands, lounges where you lounge, like in the brothel, waiting for squaddies on leave to feel their twinge....'

'Quixi?' asks Trudi, laughing hard. 'Another city rich with past. We can't be tourists always, though, talking to cabbies, chambermaids and so – there must be something more ... though it was tourists bought those Scottish lands that gave young Conrad his poetic views... Ah, those hydros where they threw the porridge down at dawn, the finnan-haddies yanked from freezing seas like golden slippers off an ugly sister....'

'Oh, Trudi,' Candice says. 'We don't start with themes and motifs, some lesson to be learnt, passed on. We don't come out of travel with an action plan, still less with passive disillusionment.'

*

'And here's the sign,' says Trudi, fishing a glistening ring from out their *brochet*'s mouth. 'You see, Candice – we're never going home. If you think you had a home – forget it. And – I am your bank. No snide comments on the globe, its management, and "home is best". It isn't so. Most people leave the smoky hearth as soon as possible. At most, they take the roof-beam as a trophy: or the key. And "be content". If you can manage it. That's it! History, diplomacy – don't trust them, not at all.... Remember the Wee Free, Candice –

the scowl, the exaltation – thinking of heaven ... and of hell for all the rest – we're the Big Free, Candice – no heaven, and no hell. Find the best place on earth – what else is sensible? What else is free?'

'The metal, Trudi...?' Candice asks.

'Suppose I told you it was lead, and that I found the formula – would you believe?'

'Oh no, Trudi,' says Candice, and she laughs.

'Well, Candice – the secret is, it starts as little shiny bits of crap in streams,' says Trudi. 'Trust me, Candice – I'm your destiny. Let's embrace...' And so they do.

'Tell me Trudi,' Candice says. 'Your teeth – most people, going where we are – have sets of aluminium, or steel, some have gold, but you...'

'Oh Candice,' Trudi laughs, 'tomorrow, we are on the road. I love that Uighur food. My teeth – *au naturel*, of course. My heart – is metaphorically of gold, but I've faith in the flesh – the same for eyes. Don't touch those. I'm a treasure – but I don't exaggerate.'

'The problem is, where we have been, there's been a mound of people – too many, and by far, to make a judgement on,' says Candice. 'And, Trudi, it so saddens me to think that as we spend your treasury, you will emerge quite naked, unadorned, an innocent, they say. Then, there's the hunger, and the poverty – the patriarchs, the oligarchs, the fighting and precarious lives ... the Naxalites we haven't seen – and now to Kucha, the Han, the Uighurs, alas, poor silken path, now paved with iron... How do we sail ahead, our seas laid flat: our specie eliminating misery; the speciality our species majors in....?'

'Oh we're protected from all that,' says Trudi. 'Before they strip me, we'll need shave off our daily bread from ingots I have safely in my bags – and as for suffering, we, of course, in due time will face the furnace or the worms, our dust, our loam.... I've had a dreadful life, my dear.... The pain of womankind was piled upon the universal grind of being a defenceless sample of mankind. But – now, trust me. I have come through, our lives will be as everyone's should be. For us, the Revolution's been an unequivocal success. It hasn't been for all – but, that may come. And I shall let you share, Candice. Enjoy yourself! I shall....'

'Tell me Trudi,' Candice says. 'What power do we have? With all that wealth.... It must buy something, something beyond ourselves. The chambermaids, cabdrivers – that is ephemeral.'

Trudi doesn't answer.

'Do we have a stand,' asks Candice. 'On big things ... climate, say. Extinction. Comrades from space. Even – the continental drift....'

'Don't fuck with me,' says Trudi, at full height. 'It's those Italian chefs, indentured in the hydros, the lodges, getting up at three, hungover, "fuck the fucking porridge", they used to say, browning it intentionally. That's the shout, re-echoing. It's gruel, Candice, that stuff,' Trudi shouts. 'They'd eat it because they're poor, those few that stayed: "I want to drive like Marinetti," says the servant girl, breaking from the Gaelic, all lit up, eager to be off...doing the figure eight. That's what they wanted, that is what they say, all over, everywhere. Away, away! You want power? Over them? Scullions they became. Making them do what?... You want to have them run out in the sun, getting brown, if they're not brown already from their start?... brown, freckles especially, is a curse. Not fashionable at all.'

'Look, Trudi,' Candice says, pointing. 'There's fog over Xinjiang. We can't take off just now. We could ride, find an elephant, perhaps, and ride, ride to Golconda, Trudi dear.'

Every destination's open – when the air permits. They don't know where to go – but

'I *am* Golconda, Candice,' Trudi says.

*

'You see, Candice,' Trudi says. 'You lounge. You wait for what might come along and take your ticket, fly you away ... but there's another side. This is Arrivals, and Departures too. Two faces of the coin. It seems there's nothing more to see, and nowhere else to go. What you will never see is – who decides. We're passing through, and over, too – but who has tried to make the world their country, their yard, who decides to drop the bombs, and lie about who's who and what they want and how they live, and who recruits and writes the histories and puts it on TV – that, Candice, we shall never see. Not sitting here. And do we need to look more close? Those suburbs where the angels live ... they have an answer, to most everything. How they weren't there, or it was justified...'

'Americans....' Candice says.

'Quiet!' Trudi shouts. 'It's true they don't come here, they have their special airports ... but ... who knows? Those ears – they're bottomless. To everything, remember too, there's a before: – we know all that. An after, too – we have a good idea.... But who decides? – we transiters, we never see.... That's why we can't those judgments make, or analyse the crowds who need to go from here to there and back again. The world we see is one-dimensional – keep your voice down for the rest... We're vulnerable, we're statues off their base, triumphant or holy: even, we could end up bad, Candice.'

*

'My!' Candice says. 'Those places! How they were all different! Kucha especially, whatever it's called now. Siberia – if only I had learned to use a camera! All white! The snow, the foxes, and the white dogs racing on white ice, Trudi, the sleds a-trundling! Do you remember some of it?'

'Mmmm, the markets,' Trudi says. 'Those were nearly all identical, except – those hopping things. So hard to keep them down. I should have brought the recipe....'

*

'It's life, Trudi,' says Candice, sternly. 'Small though it was – yet vigorous. Expecting something challenging. Was it for that they leapt? Aspired? Worlds, autonomous and sentient – unlike the the stone we're sitting on, our rocky globe, its blinded circle – round and round it spins, wired in its socket like a robot's eye. And you – downing a monster poke of them, the crawlies....'

'I value life, Candice,' says Trudi, sternly too, 'but I have hierarchies. I am a humanist. Those hoppers fell below the line – they're food, not friends. What they are best at – is their taste. You must o'ermaster them, it's true, and thrust them down.... I explained – it's in the belch, expiring moments in the gut: in that you have their delicacy, a tang, a musty gust....'

'Some cultures,' Candice persists, 'see life as the sign that there is some thing – not no thing, and not just rocks and spume, spars from a broken necklace, gyring around in emptiness. Life, whatever is its form – even if your gut, dear Trudi, brings forth just worms – life! is the something.'

'Don't be a bore, my sweet,' says Tudi tartly. 'We didn't kill anybody, but you don't treat people all in the same way.'

'What do you remember, Trudi?' Candice asks. 'We went everywhere. Do you remember that? The too littles, the too excessives. The factories, the prisons, schools – all places set to rehabilitate and make us good.... And did it work for us, my dear? When you come home – of course, you must repent. Do penance for the strugglers. Apologies. "We saw, but it was dark." "We're sorry: history ... it made us do it'... "the choice was just political" ... "some rotten guys got on our ship and took your parents off for sale...."'

'Calm it, Candice,' Trudi says, coldly. 'Don't give me that "imperative to act on what you see..." It's all a theatre, they invite complicity and guilt – and yet they know: you want those bombs and tasering bad guys, and having parties, drinking vodka cocktails, all the rest... If you cared, you wouldn't drop a bomb on those unknowns, or ask those guys to shoot or lock them up, or steal their food...'

'Oh Trudi,' Candice shouts, bright red with zeal. 'Of course, when you get home, they'll run a test – and you're a clothes horse, Trudi, all that stuff you bought: and gold! No! – horse brasses, round your neck and in your navel pinned and leaching out corrosion green.....'

'Well,' Trudi shouts back, 'if it's green, it shows I'm nature's queen, survivor of the rites of spring; the Indian corn sprouts from my orifices....'

'Don't traduce the Indians,' Candice says, putting her thumbs on Trudi's throat. 'Remember Siva, Manitou, and all the rest ... how respectful we were to guides' delusions...' She pirouettes. 'And I love the veil – it's the cloak that gives invisibility, you walk not you, an unknown to yourself ... a film of armour, and it keeps out dust and smells...'

'Is that what travel taught, Candice?' sneers Trudi. 'Out comes the everything, a warm owl's pellet, you, a sentimentalist ... you pass everywhere, you're small change, a petty coin, a paisa, Candice ... good for the beggars, and you don't miss it if it drops....'

*

'I left my tall princess,' says Candice to herself. 'I shall regret....'

*

Those Hessians – they massacred the rebels. Those that survived joined the other side as soldiers, left the country, founded an empire, or went back to mind the cows. There's always a new loyalty, a project and enthusiasm. Once driven away, the title and the cause, they're made mock, clowns: part lodged in the archive, part in a memory-box.

'Conrad's off the Scots,' says Paolo, his friend. 'Reactionaries, then imperialists. Now, it's Scythians, in India – they came next in the alphabet.'

'Oh, we were there,' says Candice. 'It's a big place – we didn't see any. Maybe they were on the West.... The Hunas, Huns – they came in too. They had an abundance of war elephants, I hear.'

'You were true tourists.' Paolo says. 'Conrad is my site – I visit him and stay at home. He goes deeper – on the map, that is. I never travel to those parts. The lounges – how they do depress! You'd think the mountains kept them out, the peoples, straggling, warlike and ephemeral ... they are like water, they find a way you don't expect. Are they still with us? Clans, nations, tribes.... Your guide – maybe she said...'

'Oh, we travelled the rich way,' Candice says. 'No one was behind us, burning thatch and prodding us – everyone was way ahead, laid out for our inspection – an illuminated manuscript.'

'And you, the most illuminated....' says Paolo, quite fancying a fling with Candice.

'We covered all the space,' says Candice. 'Mule and camel, but not ships. Everybody knows – ships now are all the same, but slow, so slow. We didn't reach conclusions. We did no harm, no good. We studied....'

'Oh, but conclusions are the point!' says Paolo, tying a long grey muffler round his neck. He lets Lidia boss him – Émilie and he split up – nothing much occurred with either.

'Conclusions? Sure, you have to have a plot,' says Candice. 'With consequences. But what goes before, call it the development – usually it's inconclusive, random: the ending – usually, quite improvised. As for decisions – the ones you could pin down are mostly about cash, liquid and immediate. Empires occurred: but, the visionaries ... they were few, exalted, somewhat crazed.... For most, the picture was all blur and blot.'

'There's no conclusion there,' says Paolo. 'Look deeper, calculate. People – cogitating and resolved. People, Candice, they did it all, with brains alight. And – who are you, Candice? What did you become, with travelling around? Now, concentrate. No mental voyaging. Just – discover something absolutely new, that no one else was looking for....'

'I'm not sure,' says Candice. 'I've been everywhere, seen everything. To me, it was all new. Add something of my own? It's why we're here, maybe, but...'

*

'Cows and trees,' says Candice. 'They say those are important – we didn't see so much of them. Food and water – those, we found. Air – yes, we travelled on it – earthy colours, made the sun twinkle, like glass in a kaleidoscope....'

'That's the wrong track,' says Paolo. 'You need to stop over in a place before you know it all... And you'll need cash, dear Candice. You need to find someone who has lots – that means some kind of sex, that's normal, I guess you know by now....'

'We saw a host of people,' Candice says. 'But none were candidates. Trudi was a treasure, but I squandered her away.'

'You know,' says Paolo. 'This talk – it takes a nasty turn for me. Whether you melt away, Candice, or quest – a sadness comes, lies on me like a sky. Lidia says, "If you're sad, you cry." But you're not worth it, Candice. Maybe it'll come to that some time....'

'Well,' Candice says, pushing him outside. 'We'll have to wait and see.'

'Too bad,' she thinks. 'Everything is bizarre now – only the people aren't. We're living in the sci-fi scene – too many plots and all incredible. Paolo – that muffler ... hmm, he's bizarre, I guess, in subtle ways, but men come in sizes quite mathematical, none that you would want to wear.

'Implosion or explosion ... famine or obesity – how banal it's all become, nothing to think of but extremes, and how it all will look when we aren't here.'

*

'Tribal repression? Or repressive state?' asks Émilie. 'Paternalism and patriarchy – or welfare and marginality? You hear them laughing in the shadows, in the past – but then they must decide. Perhaps, it seems it's up to you. Modernity! You must jump in, full immersion, then follow the bubbles, up and up...'

'You're so caustic, Émilie,' says Candice, laughing. 'Of course, we still live in the gaps, or try to – sunlight sneaking through those tall leafy trees. Don't believe what's written down, Émilie – the words seem motionless and fixed, wedged in our clay. It isn't so. They're witness statements:

you don't need to tell the truth or take the oath. Someone
must go to jail – it won't be you, it could be a cop, the judge,
or a stenographer....'

'I can tell you who,' says Émilie. 'In confidence. I can't
change a thing. But – it's all decided.You know, I work on
the big brain. The one that knows just everything – what
you've done and do and probably... Who goes to jail, and if
they will come out.'

'Oh yes,' says Candice. 'We all know about that. They pay
you well – everyone is envious...'

'Oh yes,' says Émilie. 'But not enough, it never is. I can
offer you a secret ... how we get cash on the side – we sell off
info, tips and such, news from the stables and the banks, the
auction houses ... but, that brain's a monstrous giant. It
knows so much that we could never know, it has a memory,
but the kind that never fails.... It has its secrets, sure, but big,
enormous ones – you can't get into those.... They'd rock your
principles – the brain's set up to fetishise them, never to let
the values drift away. They're loaded in the mix...!'

She takes Candice, tiptoe and shush – to a shed, so vast the
shadows in the deeps – they go from green to blue, and that's
just the reception.... 'Where no one goes,' says Émilie.
'Because you're not supposed to know it's real. You ought to
think it's a hypothesis....'

And down they go, in silence, there are shelves, no sound,
no hum, no whisper, no Mahlerian pianissimos before the
clash, no storms, no Strauss, no heights unpeopled, and no
avalanche.... Doors so vast – you press a stop – so simple a
monkey could learn the trick and once they did...

'There's nothing here,' says Candice. 'So, it's all a hoax,
and what each person knows is separate, unique from all the
rest. Just empty shelves ... forever...'

'Oh no, Candice,' says Émilie. 'The storage *is* the shelves.
That is the trick. They are the machine – you can't put

anything on them. The emptiness is what you see – it's like
the universe, it's empty but for shards of stone and whiffs of
gas, but that is where we live, and hosts of tiny folks no
bigger than your spit have dug inside the shiny pebbles,
orange-sized, and made a warm and happy home, and learned
to breathe the methane, cling to chromium and the poison
stuff....'

'And are there people like yourself,' asks Candice, 'who
work here? Maybe in different coloured coats ... stripes, spots
– a homely something, makes you weep – and walk here up
and down, and dust....'

'Oh I've no doubt there are,' says Émilie. 'I've never seen
them, there is nothing they can do. I bring my sandwich
lunch, and eat it by myself....'

'It seems quite sad,' says Candice. 'Aren't there gardens,
with a bench?'

'Of course,' says Émilie. 'No one would survive if there
were no plants and birds – the plants that tell you what is
good and bad, and right and wrong, and which is the right
farmakon – the cure, the poison, both – and then there is the
folklore, and aesthetics too – the myth and saga, heroines and
heroes lacing up their corselets ... and the animals – they eat
each other, but so far we've eaten all the winners of the
fights; our competition. They sing, the birds, but no one
writes the music down, there are tone rows, and twigs and
branches too ... all playable, if you've the training and the
mind... There's universal strife, of course, and crunch of
bones and lapping up of blood. But we're the tops, dear
Candice – your journey will have shown you that. We are the
only kind that doesn't eat its own.... That is the basis of our
humanism,' and she winks at Candice; then winks another
time....

'You mean,' asks Candice, 'cannibalism? A tabu! Life's hidden pleasure... Like incest, eating snot and faeces, you can't mean ... despite....?'

'Of course,' says Émilie, 'in the book – they eat the apple. But, in fact – and I can tell the secret just to you – it wasn't fruit. It was the heart, the heart of everything. Up till then, they called their god "the everything". But after – there was desolation. Uncertainty, choice, a fork that led down to oblivion – what's now become the fate of everyone. There can't be punishment for breaking the tabu – just silence, guilt.... It must seem merely appetite: but – the heart! The bright and pulsing jewel! It's the first rule you mustn't break, and broken once, there's no return. A rule it was – though no one made it, set it down. It seems it is our nature, and our first desire – to open up the heart and then to raise it high – into the sun, an offering, the first transgression: and the end... Consumed, digested by our ancestors. Never again alive and pristine: it's finished, Candice dear.'

'It all sounds musty,' Candice says. 'The story's like the ones my grannie told.'

'It's a tale you should not tell,' says Émilie. 'Not about the brain here, nor the end at the beginning, the heart, the everything, a snack digested, then excreted....'

'I'm cognisant,' says Candice, 'of the everything – I never knew it ended on these empty shelves...'

'Don't keep calling them that,' says Émilie, quite irritated. 'They look like shelves. They could be shelves. They are not shelves.'

'Everybody knows, about the cannibalism,' Candice objects. 'How it pops up. And, that there's a big brain who sucks it in, all knowledge – and never tells you anything. True, Émilie, you seem to be the only one employed by it. You know a lot – but ultimately not much, besides – it may be wrong.'

'Think, Candice! Think of what you say!' says Émilie. 'The big brain knows more, and so it knows it differently from everybody else. It never says, it never tells: you'd never know how much you've spooned from it – oh brain! who knows even if she's he, or somewhere in between or off the end, unmoved by alll the sexual stuff and gender too – and if the humans have a special place in her, or if she's quite indifferent, hostile – or disgusted....'

'Oh,' Candice says, with a sneer. 'That's fantasy. A trick, a slant, a plot that's not a scheme, a scheme without a plot.... It's true, that something – someone – knows far more than we can ever know or fish: it isn't God, not even a One hidden, or resurgent.... A brain: nothing creates, nothing instructs, nothing reveals. It knows, that's all.'

'Suppose you had a synthesis ... an epic: a Ramayana of the world again, and all the monkeys and the monsters...' and Émilie touches, delicately, the shelf that's not a shelf: 'Another try?'

'What if you're right, dear Émilie?' asks Candice. 'You're stepping out from the sci-fi: what do you plan – a raid that brings conundrums to be solved? Banality? Come on, Émilie, be grown-up, do! Don't titillate!'

'Oh, it's useless trying to get in,' says Émilie. 'Not into me. You'll not learn secrets, not from me. I'm incorruptible, and you would need corrupt me – just to have me show you where is the entrance to the brain. No – maybe you should travel round, find someone else, a sweetie who's not clever, but cleverer, maybe more beautiful, than me.'

It's true. Émilie's not worthy, not the type. There is a drabness. And those grey slabs that are not shelves, lack eye-appeal. The eye craves an attraction. But, mostly, cleverer people try to do you down, or win their argument, make an ergone box or grow demented, marry someone quite incongruous.... She could be the best there is....

'It's an idea,' says Candice. 'Thank you, Émilie. I'll put it by the rest.'

'Oh Candice,' Émilie says, pinching her partner's cheek. 'Everything is sci-fi to you now. It's that Trudi's fault, the monster!'

'You're supposed to love monsters,' Candice says. 'I did. You get a credit for it.'

'Maybe what I've called a brain,' says Émilie, 'is not a brain. One of those metaphors we try to prove is not: and what a waste of time that is!'

'Oh,' Candice says, 'all brains are that. A metaphor. A box of wires that pets the llama – apparently impossible. A miracle that flies until the fuel runs out, a crash! – it joins the milliard of dumps, wrecks, black and silver in the sand, that licks them over, buries them. Forget! That's the lesson mostly that we've learnt.'

'Someone, some people – they must have decided the whole scene,' says Émilie, 'to set it up: the brain. Monsters, you'd say, begetting a big monster: and yet, you should see us, at the start: we're all monsters: then, a metamorphosis, we lose the gills and tails, and then we're born – as monsters. We must love us.'

'Knowledge,' says Candice. 'Trudi was innocent of that. She only wanted all the treasure in the world, to bathe in it, wear it – eat gold, perhaps. The men who made the brain – they wanted the biggest secret, to give the world its knowledge, but in a form quite indecipherable. All men think they give and take – from women too. But they can only give something that has no worth – and there is nothing they can take. Nothing there at all.'

'That doesn't fit,' says Émilie. 'Men and women don't come in. And it's a pity, but my suggestion limps. Rama isn't one of us. No epic's here.'

'You're right,' says Candice, 'though monsters are essential to the story, and some – they help you, they're your friends. Some may stay hostile, or else you hug them and suddenly they're beautiful. Much, much more beautiful than you. With others – it's the other way around. They turn against you....'

'That's a fine thought, Candice,' says Émilie – and they find a garden, with a bench, and sit together, close as possible.

*

'Émilie,' says Candice, 'I know you're a simple gatekeeper – though you see everything that goes in, comes out. Let's set aside the brain for now – do some gardening.'

'There's lots,' says Émilie, taking Candice's hand and pulling her through bushes. 'This is a little plot, needs a clean, a purging! – see, everything's just about dead or gone quite wild.'

'How sad,' says Candice. 'There's Socrates, in the middle – you can just see the bald head.'

Émilie laughs, 'Oh no,' she says. 'That's Lenin. Socrates is in another patch – that too needs a lot of work. There's these goddam crows perched everywhere. All the gardens help us breathe, but they all fall into disuse, they fail and you have to carry off the dead stuff.'

'I know,' says Candice, 'it's sad. A fungus spreads from one to another – the insects carry them, the wood creatures eat the bugs, and so they die – whole species, horrible deaths. Then there's the nets – underground, invisible, the mushroom roots – their filaments spread like underfelt, and run round everywhere.... Nature is so wasteful – inscrutable too, Émilie. I'm sure if we could find our way in, we'd see what the purpose is – the more you prune, the greater is the withering.

Plants that strangle one other, brothers climbing up their sisters' stems... Then there's the snow.... Who sends that, I wonder?'

'No, Candice,' Émilie laughs. 'Don't slant your wheedle at me! If there are secrets, I'm not telling you! And even if you got into the brain, or mine, you'd not know how to read the cues...'

'Look!' shouts Candice, 'I went after the Morning Glory – and the Bougainvillaea's pricked me to the bone....'

'You should see the Spinoza clearing,' laughs Émilie. 'It used to attract every kind of bird, even the cassowaries – but those red holly berries! Everyone got sick. And, if you think there's tendrils of an allegory here, well, you'd be right. These gardens *are* an allegory, nothing wrong with that. What other uses could they have?'

'I wonder, Émilie dear,' says Candice, reluctantly, 'is allegory the word we're really searching for? The halms, the bindweed – there's a phrase in there, but...'

'Yes it is,' says Émilie, starting to sulk. 'Allegory. That is the word. I know about these things. Give me that trug, silly! You don't know how to carry it.'

'These, I suppose,' Candice says, trying not to sob, 'are little things ... there's history round about, I'm sure....'

'You want to see the grave?' asks Émilie, heating up. 'A long mound, down the hill. There's been an earthquake here, it tumbled down the titans' walls.... Some tents? – if you stand on your tiptoe, you can see a camp – and hark! The rooks are coming home to five o'clock. My, they're regular, and how they love the mealtimes here...!'

'I'm sure you're right,' sighs Candice, 'although there is no trace of allegory: I love the rooks, their modest dress, community, matins and vespers to the same full-throated laud.... Time without sequence....'

'I appreciate them,' says Émilie, 'but they don't belong here. We're too far south. They've been driven out, and found these trees, so high. So high, my love,' and she kisses Candice firmly on the lips. 'There!' she says. 'Now you know it all.'

They root out more weeds, each busy with her doubts and probably her fears.

*

'Know all that you can and is good for you, Candice,' says Émilie, stamping on some small white eggs. 'We should cut down the rookery,' she says. 'Everywhere's infested.'

'Oh Émilie!' says Candice. 'Where would they go? They're so proud, so busy.'

'Oh, they'll go,' says Émilie. 'You won't see them around.'

'It's so drastic,' Candice says. 'Though of course – you're right. They're Scottish birds, like corbies. You don't want to get too close....'

'Oh,' says Émilie, 'I'm used to doing what has to be done. I've seen conflict, you know, Candice. Those guys, the hands, squaddies, boots and helmets, operators – they take lots of flak, but they don't enjoy doing what they must do. You have to show the locals – best not mess with us, don't feed our enemies, or you'll end up against the wall. Don't be a hero, an example – you won't like that at all....' and she runs through the phrases, smiling in between each one. 'It's in the book, Candice – you do it because it works. If you don't, they'll do it back to you.'

They strain at the weeds. 'Some might have preferred them left,' says Émilie. The hillside starts to look like Rwanda, little memorial plots, green and brown. 'We put the berries in,' says Émilie. 'Blackberries for Schmitt, blueberries for Burke, redcurrants for Hegel; Marx has the peperoncino. Then there's Wittgenstein – rosemary and forget-me-not ... memory was his weak spot...'

'Who gets strawberries?' asks Candice, feeling hungry. 'It all sounds random – besides, there's no one here.'

'Oh, the gardens wait,' says Émilie, opening her lunch packet. 'They're used to it. I think they like it. Besides – there's birds – they keep the faith. Strawberries? – I think it's Mill, but they're not the delicious forest ones – these are big and bland.... If you're hungry, you should bring something in – there's nothing here. You can have my apple....'

'I don't feel like that,' Candice says, finding a blue stone and sucking on it. 'You could pass away here, and just lie ... being eaten, twisting as the creepers and the branches come to life and lethargy, turning you slowly, like on a cold spit....'

Émilie doesn't answer.

'I've found the big brain,' says Candice. 'What's to do? Come upon its content shred by patch?'

'Yes,' says Émilie. 'While you wait. Lying here, through the year, everything said, quizzed, pondered. Over. You paint so well – that picture, like the Douanier's, the solitude in cultivation, the lion guarding the sleeper on the sand. Or is he curious? Hungry? Then, the lady dressed for a stroll – that branch laid on the path ... a rune? monkeys overhead? the seasons' cold in view....?'

'I love solitude,' Candice says, 'but I'm so lonely.'

'You should have brought your lunch,' says Émilie.

*

'Does the brain enjoy the gardens?' Candice asks. Émilie doesn't answer. It should be obvious.

'Are we lovers,' Candice wonders, 'and is that what I want?' – in silence.

'I don't believe in that,' says Émilie, as if she heard. 'Loving someone gets you nowhere. Solves no difficulty. Opens no door. You may get a ticket – but there's no destination, and no train.'

'Then there's the world,' says Candice. 'I thought I'd need to travel, but much of it is here, the world, in what you say aren't shelves, aren't perhaps anything at all to do with anything, just show, and custom-made. There's people outside too, down the hill, over the fence – what would they do, if they were in? What do *we* do? Besides, they're spoiled: – they're like those beasts you capture in the forest, take them to compounds, then you must decide – do you want them tame or wild? They're not the same as once you thought they were. Not friends, not enemies, but something in between. They are no threat – after all, I am their cop: but the tremors – in the foundations? In my legs? What would I see, travelling around? The same people, just a chapter back, waiting to start their travelling.... Suppose it comes to us, the earthquake, the shaking of the walls, the marshalling – I'm lucky, I don't have tattoos, no giveaways....'

'If it comes,' says Émilie, 'you'll struggle to survive: but you will. It's Paolo, Conrad, who will find it hard, surviving. Conrad's Scots – gentlemen, their trews in holes, the fishers smoking cutties on their stubby boats – a most precarious situation. Death natural and not: much coming at you unexpected, with whisky breath and arms lengths waving short sharp swords. Conrad wanted all to be evident. He took it on, a past not his: not anyone's. None of it is, it's a wandering orphan. Terrible and odd, even sometimes fun and rollicking. Not like here, and not like now. Lidia – she won't come through, she's been written down and everybody knows... Trudi – stripped, she'll make the other shore. She can change shape, knows when to snarl and when to purr.

'The big brain – she won't help, what could she do?

'These gardens ... let's sort out the weeds: some of those have flowers, and some have berries too. We'll save the best for now – they grow so strong, stronger than the rest. You have to shift your lines, your categories, genres – nature calls no thing "weed". She's indifferent to what we eat and see. But it's good, Candice, imagining catastrophe, and know that it will never come. Here – there's the antidote, the cure and the prevention.'

She winks again.

'Maybe catastrophe's too strong for what I had in mind,' says Candice. 'It's an easy word, it happens often – but look how we've cleaned things up.... In just a morning, so it seems.... Why, Émilie? Why did we, do we, do it? Do we have a tidiness thing?'

'Yes,' says Émilie. 'We do. Food too – we discriminate. We don't eat spurge. Nor harebells – but looking takes our mind off flesh. The brain – has no philosophy – and maybe it's like they say, things happen, there's no story, no narrative between them, chaining them together. I'm the humble servant of the brain, Candice. If it's demented – so am I....' She throws gasoline on a bonfire, lights it. It roars. 'Philosophy is of two kinds – do you accept, or do you rage.... Limitations, death and shaky circuits – or blue skies – black, of course, when you go real high, leave necessity behind – infinity....'

'I'm sure you're right,' says Candice, not following, relieved there's no request for sex. 'The first one's crap, the second's fantasy.'

'Too bad, Candice,' says Émilie. 'That's it – the choice. Lucky to have one, not that it makes a difference....'

*

'There!' says Émilie. 'A little of our time, or so it seems, and working in the times of nature, its spaces and perspectives... It's done us good. Not *very* good, but better than sex or a shower. Doing things together for the plants and birds, it establishes us, and is a rule set against our reason.'

'That's a fine thought too,' says Candice. 'I'm not sure we shouldn't worry about that smell, the reek, up from the camp....'

'Maybe another day,' says Émilie, hugging Candice. 'When there's more time at our disposal. Fortunately, the brain is not demanding. It lets things go – it waits for fruit to ripen when we'd rather stuff it down ourselves.... The smell – it's really not our business, but if you'd like, we can think about it, come back another day....'

'Meantime,' Candice asks, apprehensively. 'Where do we stay?'

'Not here!' says Émilie. 'I like the fast life! This place has no name ... and there's no inhabitants. We'd need keep chickens to survive, that's hard on them, besides, look! I've worn my heels down, dancing –' and she pulls off a shoe, shows Candice the stubby heel bones. 'Disco! Toes are worse! I can't do without... I love the noise, the booze, the flesh jouncing up and down. In any case, I don't want to live with you, Candice. This is close enough.'

It's a relief.

Candice wonders how Émilie manages to toss those old oak trunks on the fire, and laugh and shriek so fierce, while the gas flames jump about.

'Are you on something, Émilie?' she asks. 'You seem quite tireless.'

'Ah,' shouts Émilie, 'you noticed it! My strength. I'm strong, stronger than all the strong ones, with their weak brains and big armies, the militias and the cuirassiers.... I'm so strong – I don't need to stand people by a ditch and shoot them, find airmen that will blast them, seamen to carry them away and earthmen to bury them, firemen to burn their clothes and houses. I must be the strongest person in the century, Candice, and doesn't need to boast and fake....'

'I'm sure you are,' says Candice.

'So?' asks Émilie. 'What more do you want? I don't need pretend. I have no interest, I have a weekly wage, my passport's in the lake.... The brain is in the castle, as you saw, doing no harm, just knowing everything – everyone's on file, and join them all together, and you have human history; put in the foundries and the theses, the cauldrons and the circuit-boards, and you have history plus. Is it a surprise that I can make the flames go high, the flames so high, higher than the trees?'

'No Émilie, it's not – except – they say there is no story in it, that it's disconnected pieces that collide, like clicking bearings on a desk....' says Candice, trying to remember her philosophy.

'Well, Candice, maybe they're wrong at that,' says Émilie. 'I'm not out for punishments, responsibilities – but some things are unplanned, some are deliberate – and taken all together, it is clear – they're planned. It's that the plans are multiple, not each one comes to term or is set out: but the consequence is only what it is, the one....'

'And with your insight, and your strength – what do you do with those, Émilie?' asks Candice.

'I wait,' says Émilie. 'I wait, to ride the horse. When it comes bucking – I hold it, tame it – then hop on! And ride!'

'You're picturesque, dear Émilie!' says Candice. 'This horse – where does it come from? Its rider?'

'They always come,' says Émilie, chuckling. 'It's always you, dear Candice, who isn't ready.'

*

'Remember Conrad?' Émilie asks. 'He read those old guys' tales.... They lived in turf huts, heated them with turf, and stabbed and axed each other on the heath.... Conrad thought that should have brought the end of all the roistering and eating oats ... the snuff, the powder flasks, the bones left lie... He thought by now it would all have changed...'

'Well, evidently it has,' says Candice, irritated.

'He thought the difference would go his way,' says Émilie. 'The gentler way.'

'Oh well,' says Candice. 'If you're a humanist and anti-tech, it's turned out bad, a disappointment ... but that's not me. I see what is, and live in it.'

'Yes, you'd like to think that, Candice,' Émilie says. 'I have my place, we all do, but I hook on to all the forerunners – front runners, you'd say, and runners too: you have to run and sweat.'

'You're only ever what you wish you were,' says Candice. 'You're a success in that, dear Émilie.'

'It's about ancestors too,' says Émilie, to finish off discussion. 'Everyone has some: you never know them. They could be anyone. In fact, they're everyone. That's Conrad's take. They should instruct you, but instead....' And she throws more stout timbers on the fire.

'There's so much to be done here,' Candice says. 'Plants. But it's grey – like the castle. That should be ochre, but it's grey like its inside....'

'The work can never be completed,' says Émilie. 'Painting – never finished. That is its point. The castle walls – delapidated, rebuilding is our task, eternal, while the brain – it feels no pain, splendid and silent, junket white – but never, never seen. It needs no service, and no touch. For sure it knows who's in the castle, if it is inhabited... True, the prospect's grim. Yes, it's dreich here. We are never warm. Conrad hated it, the cold, and then the fug inside. He came from Egypt, half of him at least – that's why he couldn't get some cash, a room...Or maybe it was Ukraine...'

'Well,' Candice says, 'I'll not go to Egypt then.'

'It's all turned out more complicated,' thinks Candice. 'Even our bonfire: ill-advised.... So bright, so hot.... They burned the shaman by the sea – in a tar barrel ... must have left a fog...'

*

'Enough banality, Candice,' says Émilie. 'I love you. Don't insist. Goodbye!' She strides up towards the brain. All's said and done. Service before everything, says the sign above the door, and in she goes. She doesn't run, that's maybe something that she doesn't do, but she knows what's necessary and often tells the opposite. She leaves no option free for Candice. That's the way!

*

'Is this another brain?' asks Candice, knowing that there should be only one, and yet – the doorway looks alike, the motto is the same...

'Oh no,' the guy says laughing. 'We are the body. And we train. The brain – is just a set of tentacles. We improve ourselves,' and he shows Candice a row of tubs where muscled people lie in brine, their skin like turtles', tendons like wistaria roots. There's others, white cameos in blocks of ice, their fishy eyes a-stare – then there's the 'hot' room, in barrows full of tar, in retorts of methane bubbling up like acne, there sits a row of muscled lads... There's cloisters, ex votos in kitchen Greek tacked to the wall, old graduates, old amputees. Around the walls there's rows of muzzle-loaders, screw-guns too, the mules all ready tethered – and you can hear the range: a ploff, a platt – and then a fugue of pots and shots..... The women on the ropes climb thick as ants and at the top run along the girders, float down as destroying angels or as chanterelles, their parasols landing them with quite a shock.....

'And all these bodies, firm as angle-irons,' says Candice. 'Sturdier than robo-cops – is there a super-picture they are figures in?'

'There musn't be,' the guy, Damian, says. 'We're soldier-nurses. For emergencies. By definition, there is no defining corps. It happens, we react – no one foretells. We do what comes first to mind – we shoot the casualties, exchange the warriors, cure our allies, starve our foes.... We must be tough, prepared.... Success is needed every time.'

He waves across the scene, a vast stockage, a house of wares – there's bundles here of everything – 'There has to be,' he says. 'There's more here than at rest, even in use, on all the earth. Emergency requires we give out everything, and half as much again....'

'I'm sure brain helps,' says Candice, much impressed.

'You're wrong,' says Damian. 'We have all it needs, and when the window lights –' and he points up – a rose window in the wall, crimson and pink in waiting, 'we're off, we pack up everything and half as much again, the dogs of war and peace are on their leash, we leap into our boat or plane, or on our camel and our horse. Away! Away!'

'And so,' says Candice, 'you are our humanists?'

'That you might say,' says Damian, slowing his discourse down. 'Not always so. Where people may end up – maybe they had rather died. For us, emergency runs, floods, subsides, comes to its end – to them, it is eternal.'

'I don't see it,' says Candice. 'It must be eternal for you too.'

Damian squints at her: doesn't she understand? – he's body. Not brain. He says, 'We shall have children. All ranks shall reproduce. and we shall be better far than you.'

'Someone stronger pays you, though....' Candice ventures.

'Oh, we make, we buy and sell,' says Damian. 'And someone must pay up, it's not a choice. All can be destitute, but all cannot expire. We're like the fibres underground, of mushrooms, like an underfelt. We keep the forest standing. In the fall, the people come, seek us out, and pickle, preserve, rely on us, for harder times.'

They stroll on, to an area labelled 'Heavy'. Guys are lifting cement slabs, raising chimneys, standing upright horizontal walls and floors. 'You can run the same clip,' says Damian. 'Earthquake or bomb – the same techniques apply, even without us using gloves. White phosphorus – that's the worst.'

'Putting mannikins together?' Candice asks.

They're sticking scattered arms and legs on torsoes, trying to get a fit. 'We used chimps once,' says Damian. 'They're best at recognition, but in the end....'

'The results all looked like chimps,' says Candice.

'In the field,' says Damian, 'it's true, the monkeys love the little ones – with them, you can haphazard be ... and the relatives are pleased to have a something they can hug.'

'Well, it's true of all of us,' says Candice, laughing to lighten up.

'Partners in uniform,' says Damian, quite stern. 'As mates. That's how we get the thrill. Sex. We multiply. Civilians break.'

'I know I'm omega,' says Candice apologetically. 'You, Damian, are a fine strong alpha type. And yet – body, face, the rest – there's no feature I could get out on a pin and hold it up, and say "that's you", "that's Damian, you'd recognise him in the dark..."'

'I know,' says Damian. 'I'm really insignificant, not like the people who are fictional and don't exist, or else look lots like somebody – or everybody – else. When we execute, or rescue – no one remembers what we're like. Would *you*? Do you remember characters anyway, and how they look? In plays, the decription's summary; in movies, they're distinctive but you know it isn't really them, they're quite different from the person laid out, non-existent, in the script. We are self-created, there is no prime creator for the human being – as you know, we start as slime, then tadpoles, there's no template, no original, all's chance, there's no grand imagination behind us.... We, the doctor-generals, we invent our bodies, without a hitch, a blob, a facial tumour, or big teeth – whereby you might distinguish and remember us....'

'Oh, I understand,' says Candice, much relieved. 'It's all like movies, where you know everyone went to one acting school, with one selector who hires people who look indistinguishably beautiful....'

'Here is a guide: Karine,' says Damian. 'See how beautiful she is? If you lose sight of her, you won't identify her, small-talking with the other lookalikes....'

'It's rather facho,' Candice says, 'but makes life easier...'

'Yes,' says Damian. 'And you, Candice, are a special case – your beetle-brows, your crows-feet, elk's nose and dormouse eyes ... we'll know exactly where you are...'

'Candice,' says Karine. 'Forget the insults. Damian's a stone – he doesn't recognise the beautiful – as for the true, he said it: he's not brain.'

'Beauty and truth should be self-evident,' says Candice. 'But I guess it's like the gardening, it's laid out when you get to it, and all the plants are named... Some ancient seedsman has sorted it all out, there's nothing left to do, except to weed...'

'Oh, gardens,' says Karine, 'that's a mystery to me. When we arrive somewhere, the trees are flat, they're boiling up the grass for lunch, there's loosestrife in the ruins – that is all....'

'And you go in everywhere?' Candice asks. 'Quite recently, you used to wait and see and see....'

'Oh, naturally,' says Karine. 'We only go where we can win.'

'I don't grasp it,' says Candice. 'How do you judge?'

'We could be everywhere, always, and be everything,' says Karine. 'But it seems there's always a proximate cause, and so – we can defer to astonishment and wonder, seeing a catastrophe, ponder and delay, calculate our risk. There's a fear of being overwhelmed ... disasters spread and grow....'

'One day, you could be overcome as well? And yet, that's what you live for – like warriors, you're outpacing death....' says Candice.

'We *are* warriors, Candice, and it's your death as well as ours,' says Karine.

'I know,' says Candice. 'Tell me something new. Causes shouldn't matter...'

'But they do,' says Karine.

'So,' says Candice, 'you have a plan? It's not just that you react? You must have started off as liberals – mending tears and helping helpless people – but that's no philosophy. Where have you got to now?'

'Try and work it out, Candice,' Karine says. 'There's nature. And there's states. Who's more responsible for making things fall down?'

'You're like the Bolsheviks would have liked to be,' says Candice. 'But without Russia round your neck....'

'Oh yes, without all the countries too, and fusty dress-ups, – the moustache wax, men's corsets and pile creams, opium and codeine....!' says Karine.

'And you still try? Despite everything? To make the change, break the chain, strike new coin...' asks Candice, pretending to be incredulous. 'I'm a modest sort – I don't flock round men, still less jump over the pommel horse with them – suppose I got infected, the virus, had a man child? What would I do!'

'Oh, I'm not so scaredy!' Karine says and laughs. 'If I had men children, I'd say "How clever! I can do anything!" Those babies are as helpless as the rest!'

'The physical stuff you do here,' says Candice, 'it attracts. Not much, but, making those arcs, like callipers.... A robot can tone you up, without you lying in the snow and making angel wings....'

'Just think, Candice,' says Karine, pointing. 'In that box, there's enough socks for all Peru....'

Of everything, there is abundance.

Karine – she's symmetrical. You'd love to love her, wherever you come from, and who you are, the experience is perfect, though you might forget the rest, the detail, what was said or not.

'And in emergency, if you survive, it's primitive,' says Candice. 'Primitive communism....'

'Of course,' says Karine....

'But that's where lots stay,' says Candice. 'Stay all their lives, their childrens' too. Just like in reality.'

'It's not all macho,' Karine says, dragging Candice along, who's panting hard. 'Look! We dance!'

There's a wooden oval, couples of every kind dance – in all-sorts couples, singly, in lines and rounds – some stand and twitch – some pulse in time, and others – out of time....

There's a bandstand ... trombone, marimba, citole and erhu – you hear them all, but that blue light! it blots: you glimpse the fingers, elbows, working hard, but not a face....

'Every tabu's respected,' Karine says. 'If you disapprove of music, we can plug your ears.'

'When you dance,' says Candice, touching Karine's cheek, 'There is no future, whatever you believe, you believe it lasts for ever and goes on exactly so.... And is it good? Some of us live wholly in the dance – my old friend's people, his obsession; before they were recruited in the empire – they lived like that, those ancient highland Scots, walking, riding, fighting, drinking: it would never stop. And then, of course, it did. But what came wasn't Bolshevism, nor gymnastics. It was the imprisonment of peoples. Under arms, on desks, for ever, in service for pale faces...'

'I'd have liked to dance with you, Candice,' says Karine, pulling her along by the forearm, as you do a pig. 'But – you've grown, developed, Candice, swelled: and so, you've gone quite tarnished. You envy other people who don't have your darkness in their eyes, your acceptance, your resignation,' and she draws Candice past the rows of crates, big as cottages, guys in flock suits at ease, waiting for the rose and crimson light to bloom.... 'I know,' she says. 'We have no turn of phrase – we don't believe in all that windy stuff.... "Envy? Darkness? Excuse me!"' and Candice finds she is outside, through the back door, no Karine, no Damian, no sound of bodies straining....

'They think they look alike,' thinks Candice. 'Like the Pharoahs – who don't look alike, but you know immediately what they are. Training for eternal life. They don't believe here, not in that eternity, but you do the exercises, and the belief must come – it's what you want, what we all want, and the thin time when we don't want and don't believe – that will pass, and the illusion will come again, and we shall find in death our goal and purpose....

'Too bad,' she thinks. 'I'd not be wanted here, in body. And how banal their thoughts! Noble their actions, mixed their accomplishments, usually inadequate....'

*

Conrad drops by.

'I left them all,' says Candice. 'My partners, my supports. They may spin it different. They got on my nerve. They were ignorant; they disagreed; they were mean with cash. People are like ideas: – you open up to them, they squirm, then, you see there's bits have fallen off, or they repeat themselves, get sick – so you must move on.

'Parents and siblings – even worse. You never get the chance to have a *coup de foudre.*'

It's obvious – how you say it, that must be why it can still sound fresh, and even true.

'Do you have a cause you'd risk for?' Candice asks.

'Look at me!' says Conrad. He's torn, air-broken like a paper sail. With a white face, gothicked out like his – the eyes should seem a tiger's ... his, though, look small. 'Busy, short, deprived – my life...' He keens.

'Reading? Eating bad? Spying? It doesn't seem like much to me,' says Candice. 'I'd never be you, Conrad, a wreck. Heroic ethic compromised. Not even a comma in someone else's story.'

'Oh Candice,' Conrad says. 'It's enough to look into the box, the peep-show. It's terrible, unspeakable – first, life hard and ignorant, then came the omnivores, they looked like us, they weren't us, surely, they were us, they were me.'

'I've seen all that,' says Candice....

'And you, Candice – you're some kind of designer, surgeon? You can handle it? The misery, the awfulness?' asks Conrad. 'Heroic ethics were a part for me. The greater part, now – is poverty. My contract was not renewed. I trucked them, Candice, the pain and the relief... As for the evil, the horror....'

'Sure!' says Candice. 'I have the riposte. I survive, and put a mental frame around the everything. You look at what doesn't suit and do the opposite. Come on, Conrad – you can do better than surrender! Remember Lidia? Said go deep? Don't look up at the rockface, say it's too high: you only need climb it, not cart it off in baskets.... Or – you can just gaze, like you've done ... take a tumble, even.'

It's the end.

'Look, Conrad,' Candice says. 'This is the end. You're right for someone, maybe it's for you alone. That's sterile. Your only exit can be to goodness. Inner peace, with sarcasm.'

'So be it then,' says Conrad. 'Farewell, farewell. Adieu, Candice, and your curiosity....'

*

'Right!' says Candice: 'Enough seen, enough experience, enough time spent living. Now come the accomplishments, the doing. I've visited the past: the present – forceful, insignificant people, my lovers, teachers, comrades, I've explored them all. Now I must climb the rock, ignore the bat-holes on the way, and reach ... the top. The top! Above the rock, there is the mountain, and above that – the clouds ... when you clamber up the clouds, you see the distances, the heights above – the emptiness that stretches on and leads – to more clouds, more distances, and there won't be time to cross them, but you see how far you'd need to go to find ... more distances, and then – the end, the nothing more. The higher is the emptier, greater the view, without the detail. The birds have laid the tracks up there, but they don't speak, they sing what's printed on.... Not many humans fly those routes....'

'The murderers' paradise that everybody talks about,' says the boss. 'Where no one's been. Heaven, for the holy fools.'

'I know,' says Candice. 'When you say it, it sounds trite. It's a metaphor, is all.'

'You're not suitable,' says the boss, Roman. 'But if you were, I'd need to watch you. The ad says you are to assist. No! You're here to do my job, while I am free to do my next. I'm elected, so your faults are just the voters'. Such a fuss!'

'But when you're prince, Roman,' says Candice. 'I'll be your counsellor. Much power to me without the risk....'

'Don't be too sure of that, Candice,' says Roman. 'It depends how many wolves there are behind the sledge. We are all weights, not dead but on the edge. The shadow line is that – we're always on it, though we may pretend.... To lighten loads – anyone can be tossed out. The line, Candice, is everywhere – our sex, our ethics, life itself – always we walk the line, cross, re-cross, end up crucified, or in a book.... That line's a safety code for "edge" – one you can fall off. You don't end up always thrown to wolves, but you are always on the cliff, above the drop.... Nothing is granted, Candice, nothing can be taken so, as if there were a judge who weighs your faults....'

'Thanks, Sire Roman,' joshes Candice. 'My first lesson.... "Don't expect your help...."'

'Exactly so,' says Roman. 'We all know the sound wolves make.... They're there to clean a dirty world.'

'So,' Candice says. 'I can do anything I want.'

'Exactly so,' says Roman. 'Anything you can.'

*

'An assistant,' Candice thinks. 'That's what I need. The killing – and the pardoning – I'll keep those for myself.'

*

'I'm here to help?' Pandora asks. 'I guess your projects must be mine....'

'No, no,' says Candice. 'You leave me free, is all. My plans – they give me lustre – you get none. You plot. You climb the tree to which we cling, the lot of us... The sweetest fruit is at the top, but will the twigs support our weight....?'

'Best stick to gardening,' Pandora says... 'The flat...'

'I thought of that,' says Candice, thinking of her Émilie, fertilising plants and pruning old philosophy. 'My benevolence! A vast reserve, some grateful beasts, almost extinct: a place to roam in, disport myself. Space, Pandora! Not in the air – here, on the ground: animals – not constellations, ones you can stroke and cuddle....'

'A mobilisation, Candice? A new aesthetic? A scumbling of the past, a burial, and a fantasy?' Pandora asks: 'Electro-shock? The world stood on its head? A win, for once, instead of protests? Away with billies and the mace!'

'Think of the animals, Pandora,' Candice says, laughing. 'You can work with those. People want cash, to show where they, this place, stand in the universe.... Remember the fruit, Pandora – people see wealth and want to climb, to turn it into pineapples....'

'But Candice,' says Pandora. 'Pineapples....'

'Don't be a bore, Pandora,' Candice shouts. 'I know how the damn things grow – right down to earth. But – you have to think in metaphor to work with me....'

'Instruct me, then,' Pandora says. 'What must I know?'

'People don't share. They covet; and they think they're best,' says Candice. 'So – welfare, defence, finance – they'll never quite succeed. Always a step behind the passions. That is the truth – accept it, or you'll try to change what is immutable. That's it. That's all you need to know. If you want a satisfaction – choose an animal, a plant, a ruin ... with those, you can enjoy yourself ... feed, manure, cement. Those are the materials, Pandora dear, those bring results. Remember, though – we're in a forest, there's a host of trees, like ours, but some are short, and some have thorns, some are for squirrels, some for owls. We all go climbing up the trunks, each wants to reach the top, and then....'

'It's so depressing, Candice,' Pandora says. 'It seems we're monkeys – up we climb, and eat the nuts and stuff, and then ... descend ... or fall....'

Come, Pandora,' Candice says, and laughs. 'Of course we're monkeys! But – I lied. You have to climb! The air is foul below. You have the view! Beneath – there's slip and slide, fungus and rot. The musty dark. We love the height, Pandora! It's our destiny, our designated goal! Ever upward, till we're in the clouds, along with gods ... eagles ... the winds that shape the continents, that bring the rain, the snow....'

'I see it all,' Pandora says. 'There's no alternative. That is our way...'

'Our destiny!' says Candice. 'So – it's yours, you love it, there's no other way.'

'Order,' says Pandora. 'Science, management. It all fits in – the massacres too....All to climb the trunks...'

'My reservation,' says Candice. 'A park, the animals put first, they run it, and there's room, so's if it's us who run, we'll make a getaway; they know the saying, they'll do no harm. It must start primitive, disorderly, and purposeless – it all fits in. A chaos, jungle, an eating fest, of gristly stuff that mostly gets spat out. Does it end orderly? In equilibrium? I'm not so sure....'

'I'd love to think so,' Pandora laughs, 'but it's just animals, and flowers, and you.'

'It's not easy,' Candice says. 'There's the expulsions. Then, to stop the people coming back – the guards, the shotguns. And – is this the end, or the beginning? Maybe it doesn't matter.'

'Well,' Pandora says. 'My idea is, bet on what develops...'

'Oh, I imagine!' Candice says. 'Order. Sophisticated communism. We all pass through that. But to grow the white cedars – takes a century, and we never live that long. It usually goes for firewood long before you put the roof on, make the city, then call it forbidden...'

It's fascinating – the two sit, the master – Candice, the mistress: and the pupil, perhaps a genius. They talk and jot, the grand scheme and the details of the joinery, the roof-ties.... 'Lay religions,' Candice says. 'Nothing transcendent-al,' and Pandora says –

'Yes! How perspicacious!' and she calls Candice her dear, and blushes, as she's stepped across the line, and Candice hugs her in forgiveness: it's *lèse majesté*, but after all, it's play, and inspiration, and the majesté is recognised, so there is no harm.

'Maybe, Candice, I should start a dig,' Pandora says. 'What you seek, and what you find – it must prefigure order of a kind.'

*

'Remember, Pandora,' Candice says. 'Once in the forest – there are no tragic figures. Don't try to be one. Deal with what comes at you – there is no other way.'

Of course, the animals love Candice. If only they could express themselves. The people expelled – they hate Candice, have no difficulty with it – but in general, she's a heroine.

Besides – there's larger difficulties.... Pandora's excavations – they go well, why not? If you want, you can fill in the hole again, down there's where our intolerant forebears went long ago – they won't see the difference, nor shall we. But – there's problems...not quite peace, land, bread, but updated, yes, for sure ... you can hear the shouts from here.

'There's people in the streets, Candice,' Pandora says, excited but alarmed.

'It's good,' says Candice. 'Once they said they'd stay indoors, be lonely, not know what was wrong. Roman's miscalculated: big prices and small rain: trouble's all predictable.'

Pandora's comforted. 'Here is a secret, Candice,' she says. 'My father – wished for a child white, working class. Instead – I'm curious and clumsy....'

'We might be twins then,' Candice says, laughing. 'I'm curious – but I'm dextrous. Look!'

She takes off her top – there's rivers of freshwater pearls, flowing like white water down... 'See! I pierced and threaded them – they say that gold discolours you – but these are limpid, and you take a tumour from the shell – do good, and profit by it... Don't eat the oyster....'

'Magnificent!' Pandora says, her fingers rafting up and down. 'And are we doomed?' she asks. 'Our tree....?'

'No, no,' says Candice. 'See – the growths around the trunk are green – the underfelt of mushrooms, spreading through – it guarantees stability. You need the parasites to keep you vertical. We shall come through, Pandora – without the storms, sickly timbers need be propped – we'd have to shoulder them, no, no – let them fall, they must! They must!'

At the window, they look down, arm in arm – there's the street, guys in black, with capes, all orderly. 'See,' says Candice. 'Those guys in black, they clean the streets. And if

they don't, bacteria will celebrate, life sprouts, it multiplies....
See, the bad stuff – it does good....'

'Oh,' says Pandora. 'The people, yes! What if I went and
talked to them....'

'Stay here,' says Candice. 'That's someone else's job.'

'Make your mark, Candice,' Pandora says. 'Promise them
the choice – either be rich, or else be free. It's up to them....'

'They'll choose the hard one, Pandora,' Candice says. 'Oh
– I'm reminded, have you ever seen an eland? I'm unsure
how they look – I have a pair that's been despatched, what
might they eat?... all that. It's new worlds and decisions. Find
me some experts, Pandora dear....'

'The people. Quite free, quite rich, then, Candice,'
Pandora suggests. 'Or fre*er*: rich*er*?'

'It amounts to the same, my dear,' says Candice, irritated.
'They want the world they live in changed – and I am all for
that.'

'This is the moment, Candice,' says Pandora.

'Yes it is,' says Candice. 'Let it pass. It will pass. Don't go
down, Pandora.'

'It could be my moment, Candice – even better, could be
yours,' she says.

'History is crammed with them, Pandora – moments,'
Candice says. 'It's like love stories – moments full of sex,
then moments of not having it. Politics is similar....'

'It isn't politics, Candice,' Pandora says. 'It's history.'

'Politics – make you live. History's what kills you,'
Candice says. 'Of course – if this moment were truly
revolutionary – I'd be out there, on the balcony. But – there
isn't strategy, it's crowd scene. The system hasn't stopped
and jammed – it's in the stockroom handing out the night-
sticks.... It's not our moment, I am sure, Pandora. We'll
wait.... Who doesn't long for shake-ups ... upheaval ...

turmoil, followed by justice. But – I don't know how to do it, Pandora. I don't have the plan, the fantasy....'

'You think it's like being in a rock band, Candice?' Pandora asks, irritated. 'Not knowing how to play an instrument, but there you are, you're up....?'

'That's my nightmare fear,' Candice admits. 'Plugged in. The lights, the fires, up go the flames – it's judgment time. The outstretched arms – nothing to put into them....'

*

'There!' says Candice. 'All over. Just a show – not the great change. Take nothing for granted, Pandora. Like the old Scots – a change of monarch, that's the most they get. That's the best, and of course, they didn't manage it – and, oh! I made an error. I didn't want those elands – it was kudus, with the corkscrew horns. True magic, useful too!'

'The idea seeks reality, as reality seeks the idea,' says Pandora, still looking out the window.

'Exactly what I thought of,' says Candice. 'But you'll learn – you need to see how the merchants jump: in the market, bazaar, the souk, the City. They're the sensitives.'

'Other people – they're difficult to talk about. Other *peoples* – I think anyone should avoid ... it's so presumptuous,' Pandora says. 'Once, the writers took it on themselves to put on every different kind of skin: you couldn't do it now. The same if you have power, even if you're given it.... Whatever you say about the mass – you're bound to condescend.'

'We know all that, Pandora,' Candice says. 'And no one gave you anything – you're here thanks to an ad, some family pull and push. I know about those ancient Scots because of Conrad ... and of course, neither of us knows a thing. It doesn't matter: they're all dead – most people are, Pandora, it takes them out of sensibility, out of range.'

'I never claimed a thing,' says Pandora, seeming offended. 'Where Scotland is, or was, what they all wanted. It's getting through this.... I need to know what breaks, what flutters, what dies at a touch...'

'Don't think of it, Pandora,' Candice says. 'It'll all come to you – what is to be done. Remember – don't be provocative, stick to your own sex, especially if you don't fancy them. Don't get involved – you'll slip, be expelled, and have guilt put upon you, like a cache-sexe. Don't be too curious... Poking about on my desk! – those friendly fellows in the tank.... Don't prod them! They don't bite, they sting. They needn't even look at you, they do it with their tails, quite irreverent. We'll have to cut your hand off. There's a ceremony! Bring on cuirassiers, the memorial wall, yours tacked up with all the other hands, exemplary, the kids brought in to see! All hands to the wall! Cemented on the sidewalk! On deck! Hands off!

'And as for backhanders – *pourboires, mazzette* – don't think of it! Those gangsters don't give bribes, they take; they buy you. You don't need be in a gang, Pandora – you can run one, if you will. Taking cash – means you're afraid of being chased, kicked out. It's your insurance, but the company won't pay.... Don't be afraid. If you show fear – they'll sting you just the same, but you'll have wept with angst, just waiting for it ... I guess – it's for the best. That's why we have two hands. Take care of which is left.

'You think because my reservation's flat, there's nothing been knocked down and nothing built, land cleared and cages smithed ... security, the keepers armed. Building stuff – is vulgar, shameless – all nature's for the animals, and yet you have to do it – denature them with architects. Contracts, all that. Stalls, like in the opera-house. They'd be happy –

running unclothed and sleeping rough. Those antelopes –
they do it in the open, don't even seek a bush. Fear, Pandora
– you mustn't show it. Most people don't get eaten. Don't
take cash – plan your next move. You'll get more pay there
isn't time to spend. What you want – someone will give it
you, quite openly, without an envelope ... without a fondle or
a kiss.'

'Roman steals?' asks Pandora.

'It's his already,' Candice says.'He can't steal. He owns.
Roman's a throwback – doesn't need a kickback!' and they
laugh. 'It's like he doesn't know we're a developed country
now. You start rich if you want to run it. Everything is yours,
the people love you, your success, and hope you'll fall....'

*

'"Where the Wolves Drink..." how I love that poem. I'm sure
Tristan wrote for me, if only he had known....' Candice says
to Chavez, as she turns over some curiosities in his shop. 'If I
were to collect – apart from the big musky things I put into
my park,' she says, 'What would you recommend?'

'Round things,' says Chavez. 'Tiny ones.'

'A button, a coin,' he says, sifting out a handful. 'A
bottletop, glass off a dial, a lens. That's off a femur. This was
a fraud – the glass eye off a racing camel. People suffered for
that one...'

'Yes, that one I like,' says Candice reluctantly. 'But –
what...?'

'You collect,' says Chavez. 'That's all. It's passion, not a
sense. These roundels, they're nearly infinite, and each
original. Some may have belonged to famous guys – look ...
here's fifty kopeks. Lenin, pointing out to somewhere.
There's the Aurora on the twenty, pointing too.'

'Are they costly?' Candice asks.

'It depends on the association,' Chavez says, 'and the design.'

'They're intimate,' Candice admits. 'I've lots of cash, and animals and sandy space ... so, I'm not so sure the micro satisfies. But....'

'People are beginning to like *things*,' says Chavez. 'At last. And these might be the last. Although – people say collecting people is their goal. That's your business, Candice, I know, but it's unsatisfactory. A risk.'

'Well,' says Candice, 'I want a person I can trust, who'll not betray. Here, there's eyes, all eyes,' she fingers them, false eyes, turns them over like a turnstone turning stones.

'And fingers,' Chavez says. 'Here it comes! A prevision, Candice! Your trek: a button off a boot: – the drinking, racing, spying on the moon, or on the random but insistent shapes the stars appear to make – wolf, bear, giraffe. On to the fall: buying your way out, you hope....'

'Big troubles,' Candice says. 'What I brought in to you to trade, Chavez – the wolves – is planetary. A constellation I have here: purity, and music. Mother love – and persecution. It's heroic....'

'I can't give you anything for that,' says Chavez. 'I have no room. It's the little stuff that brings you down, but I can trade it. The Great Wolf – in the sky. How'd you get him down, confine him here? Make a sale?'

'It's all Pandora's fault,' thinks Candice. 'She pokes, she pries.' She says aloud: 'I can deal with eyes. Fingers, though.... The poem, it was full of immensities, and things as small as me.'

'Poems are like that,' Chavez says. 'Big and little, all together, doesn't make them easier to read. As for eyes, here, I can help...' and here's a drawer of evil eyes – singly and in rosaries...

'Ah,' says Candice, joking, pointing, 'the eye of God. Is that an evil eye?'

'Oh Candice,' Chavez says, 'you joke. But every evil eye squints for the distant hazy good, and vice versa, naturally.'

'Nonsense, Chavez,' Candice says. 'Slack and flabby nonsense! That's the song sung while people disappear and hiding-holes are dug... I'm not going down to someone's banal plot. I'll not be shuffled, from *piano nobile* to the basement, martyr to a fine project that's been washed and clinked – like a chipped cup in the coffee-room.... Done down by rhetoric? No – I won't accept. Wars and famines: here, exported, cheered on, fuelled, deplored with winkings – no! It is my vanity, but I'll not be party to all that. I am the centre. I say it as it comes to me. Something you've never heard before.'

*

'Oh, I love Chavez, and his stock,' Pandora says. 'And did you find a little thing for me, Candice? And are you always in retreat?! Railing against what shouldn't be and always is? Never a construction, always a talisman, an incantation, your good faith that isn't faith in anything? Things that are, and shouldn't be – your vain anathema still heaping on?'

'More respect, Pandora,' Candice says. 'I'm still sorting out positions. Chavez asks too much for quite a little. Anyway, I am the Brahmaputra – polluted, deviated, much reduced – the smaller and more contorted is my course, the more you know without me it all dies, all disappears.'

'It's not my fault, Candice,' Pandora says and laughs. 'You don't know where to make a stand... Maybe with the beasts?'

'Yes, Pandora, maybe the beasts,' says Candice.

'Driven out,' thinks Candice. 'Just like Chavez said – running, then carousing – there's the blind camel somewhere, capture, then the ransom, and I'm on my way again. No title, obviously, and no house.'

*

'Candice – I'm sorry,' says Pandora. 'I wanted to get rid of Roman – instead, he passed the punishment to you... It's you the culprit, Candice – my condolences, obsequies too....'

'And my work, Pandora,' Candice says, emptying the scorpions on the floor, and gathering up her cash. 'The reforms?'

'Well, there's an irony, my dear,' Pandora says. 'I have your job. Be sure I'll plot to reach the top and make the change the greatest.... Now, make your escape, Candice – they're on your trail....'

'It's just a moment,' Candice thinks. 'Other moments will come, and go in strictly measured time. Survive, and it will pass....'

*

Here's the reserve, the park: this is the climax – unintended flight, disgrace – probably expected. 'Bless me,' Candice says. 'For I may yet sin.'

'Where's your flag?' asks the metropolitan. 'I bless flags, not people: people flap, a flag you stencil on a wall.'

'It's my ritual,' Candice says. 'It was all described, flight and tumbling, captivity, then the ransom dressed up as my salvation... New life! If I've survived....'

'A person in flight flees with a lover,' says the prelate: 'Where is yours?'

'If you've had many,' Candice says. 'None shows up.'

'Of course,' says the metropolitan, 'I could draw you a flag, then bless it. You're a nativist, that's clear, but I don't know who'd be your similars. On the curve of belief, you're at both ends – foolish convictions and scepticism complete... Hmmmm. Yet, you cling on. You still love yourself, and you alone.

'The rest – they steal and jostle, imprison and dictate the faith – and yet, you are the center, and now – you the goal, the target: it's you the fox, the prey, the beast with bad repute.'

'I'm used to misunderstanding,' Candice says. 'Pandora said, "I wanted to get Roman – I'm sorry – I got you, Candice..." They'll regret going in my office – but it will all go on, despite the stings... Pandora needs an assistant, who'll understand the scene, and scheme, knock it all down. The bosses – they'll mostly end up "in-between" – who knows what colour, what shade, that may be, in between their guilt and innocence? Guilt's banal. Justice would bring the palace down, and in the end – who cares? Justice is not a word we use upon our friends, nor on our boss. Guilt – still less....'

'Well then,' says the metropolitan, 'why ask my blessing? See – the veldt, savannah – the sand you've made – it stretches over: here comes the pampero, the libeccio, the foehn, strong warm winds at whisky strength – you'll run, you'll reel, you'll have a wooden head, wake being licked, not out of passion, but in comradeship. A cuddly lion, fends off hyenas – how fortunate some long-tongues feast on carrion alone....'

'I need some coins,' says Candice. 'Shrive me, give me cash to place upon my eyes: a fanam, sequin – a pagoda! underneath my tongue.... I'll not be ferried otherwise....'

'Ah!' says the metropolitan. 'A fifty piece? A twenty? But – I'm out of gold.... I've just the obsolete scrapings I've found in the collecting bag...'

'Tiny round things?' Candice says. 'All that, Chavez thought, foretold. The stages of my flight. Ineluctable. No flag. A camel, though....'

'Yes,' says the metropolitan. 'My friends, the imams in the bothy over there, they may have a racing camel that would do: you'll need outrun hussars. It's blind, of course. But, you've no cash, no flag to trade. We'll need to take your soul....'

'Cheap!' Candice shouts. 'A bargain. Take – I'm not using it....'

It's brown, no bigger than a button from an ostler's boot – not for re-use, you see the metal loop is broke, it won't fit on a leather coat.

'Once, people died from hunger. Then – people died for being the wrong kind. Now, no one looks for the great change, that makes us be right kinds. Dying of hunger once again,' says Candice. 'Even from eating, mounds of it, all of the wrong kind.

'I'm different. For me – it's neither of those ends, but quite another: my escape; or else their tally-ho. If I'm the person they are looking for, the object of the chase – it's a mistake. They should be after someone else.'

'Maybe it's a mistake, but only partly,' says the metropolitan. 'You'd better run as if they'd got it right. And – as you go, remember – it's just about the politics, not your beliefs....'

But Candice doesn't hear, and if she did, she wouldn't care.

*

Off they go, her, the camel – the expanse is vast... Candice expects to see the beasts, her friends... No hopes! They're in the bushes, or the bush, indifferent to where blind camels run,

veering here, then there – no pattern and no destination...
'Unjust!' shouts Candice. 'I stood, and stand, only for the
right. You can't accuse me!' But they do. There's a good
chance they're partly right.

A horse gallops, in desperation: its course is limited, it
tires quite soon. A camel is a Maserati, though: it can go for
days, it doesn't think, or look, its blindness leaves it quite
indifferent, unless there's competition. It must go straight, no
turns – though "straight"'s not geometrical...

Candice is free to think – 'The themes are justice, reason,
and where I might fit in. I don't, of course, and no one has...'

She stops. The camel stops. Here comes the fall! The
camel has the power to scent a risk, but often she won't say.
Off Candice tumbles, and lands bad.

'Oh no!' says Candice. 'My leg! I'm not sure to mount
again – although the camel, quite unlike the horse, does make
it easier by crouching down....'

Here's a mound, of sand, like the Douanier imagined.
What's this rough beast, big teeth, all-over fur?

'They're all my friends,' thinks Candice. 'I saved them all.
Here, they're free. Their nature runs untrammelled, wild....'

Then it occurs: 'Suppose I've saved the one who eats them
all – all the rest, those that graze, that slither, fruit-gatherers,
those that relish grubs, and those that grub for roots ... eaters
of the dead and – oh no! Eaters of the living! What terrible
arithmetic – this ochre moloch, one wild card takes all the
rest – it will devour the whole reserve, and then into its mind
will come the Armageddon – the battle of the beasts, the
predators, man and his *semblable*, his brother omnivore....'

Aloud, she tells the lion, 'I bought you special food that
tastes of all the things you mustn't catch...' Then, 'Oh no!
Not my transport! Not the camel...' as the beast sniffs round
the camel's sightless head.

'I have no ransom, beastie,' Candice says. 'I've sold my soul. Seventy kopeks for my burial – those, and my body, I must keep....'

There's no way out. The human's lost, has brought on her own fate. The frolics and the talk, the rhetoric, the gardening, the judgements made upon the universe – in vain. Sheer vanity. And will you hear the crunch of your own bones? Think of atoning to your lovers for the silent criticisms you made, betrayals of all shape and size.... What gods may there be, or not, to make an estimate on your – what? Remember? You sold it, sold the soul you didn't think there was. A soulless shell...

'At least,' thinks Candice. 'I've ensured oblivion, the void. My soul was sold, pouched by that venal metropolitan. I'm anonymous, unclassified, although – if we're recycled, sent back like gerbils on their wheel, to live it through again, what should I be? A ghost? A robot? A machine that does what humans do with more enthusiasm, and more accuracy?'

*

Even a big beast, though ... its appetite is finite. Reducing a camel, a philosopher, to meal-size, it would be a feat. This one decides it isn't time to eat a monstrous joint – the guts, the shit, the soft and gooey parts.... Not to be considered with abandon, *joie de vivre*.

No ransom asked or paid. The beast trots off. Candice remounts, no lesson learned, nor taught.

*

'All my hardships,' Candice thinks, as the camel jogs along, releasing its rasping joy at her release: 'My life, addictions, drunken years, booze, de-tox, skiving and skivvying... The slurs, the fosterings, the molestations: fears and cures of Venus's ailments, hopes raised and dashed – all this conforms to nothing reasonable, nor just. Reason and justice, those are themes that ought to drive the species, me as well ... and yet... Two days of jail, deserved or not, that would be far worse than all the periodic hurts. The boredom, expense of fragile spirit, the diet and the mates – the ones you longed for and the ones you hate when they're tossed in ... the smell of guilt and innocence, the guys in wigs that send you there.... No, it's too awful to foresee. Better the chase, the pursuit and – freedom! you see it, a wall of thorns to climb, and then ... the other side! Maybe, the other shore is like my park, full of rare beasts you never see, that fear each other – cannibals and omnivores, all on manoeuvres, each born with a strategy of claws and paws....'

They lope along, the camel and Candice, comforted by their woolly thoughts...

'Where are the others,' Candice wonders, 'all the animals I bought to populate the park?' At least the camel heads to nowhere in particular, and everywhere in any case appears the same... Blindness means there's no direction, Candice has her leg, together with the pain.... 'How shall I fix this? Find a shaman, medicine man?' Candice wonders. 'Traditional medicine – a wonder cure? – or something mechanical, a wonderful replacement, that lets me leap and climb like – a gibbon, a macaque, plus their healthy diet, comradeship. A limp is dignified – but then, the *manga* theme, of drilling out the lower part to make a pipe, is naff. No, I don't feel in a fluty mood. Maybe a radical response: a leg full length – the knee, a hinge: a flail! That would be epic; a vengeful horseman, a weapon that can stun, but sheds no blood.... Then there's the camel – a good runner, nay, the best. But – she has no compass, no vision and no helm...'

'Doctor,' says Candice, and the sage, the philosophical doctor, uncrosses legs, puts on his magnifying glasses, looks at her with curiosity – 'I want,' she says, 'a leg like one of yours, and eyes too, potent and matching, for my mount.'

'I'll take your gammy leg our of its sheath,' the doctor says, 'and set it straight, then put it back: a limp is noble. You can't run, but also can't be made to carry loads.'

And, talking wisely on, he repairs poor Candice. 'Who knows, ' he says. 'If there is body resurrection, you'd need leave an artificial leg behind, and walking through the heavens, scaling holy mountains – that would be a pain.... Here's the old one, straightened, your old friend.'

'I'm quite convinced. And now the camel,' Candice says.

'My dear,' the doctor says. 'Therapy – it costs. Your camel's blind. There's nothing to be done. Remember, Candice, the other animals are the opposite of us – they're happier when they are not seen. Your camel sees no others. Does it think it's all alone? Invisible? It has only fear and safety. Leave it with me: the creature pays for what I've done for you.'

'I can't agree,' says Candice. 'But, this way the prediction's true – the ransom, the escape.... We ran randomly, and so, the pursuit's been shaken off. If they were led by reason, and also sought out what is just, their principles must seem quite hollow now. That way, they'd have learnt the limit to their trust.'

*

'It never saw me,' Candice says, 'so it didn't know I'd gone. It didn't hurt.' The camel hasn't turned her head.

'Well, it's an accomplice – innocent as nature, naturally. No knowledge means no guilt,' says Elsa. 'But you'd run away. It let you go much faster, though it didn't know to where. They never know. The crimes – did you bring them with you, or leave them behind? Don't tell me there were none, there always are.'

'The modern thing,' says Candice, 'is you're born somewhere, live in a country all your life, you serve the boss – help in its crimes, you'd say, but you're not one of them, not deep down, not ever. You don't come from there, but from a place unnamed, unknown to them. For you, the scenery is different, you think things differently.'

'Yes,' Elsa says. 'That's exactly how things are.'

'The crimes – they're different too. Sometimes you can start to think they are not even crimes,' says Candice.

'Putting those animals where we can't see them – that was kind,' says Elsa. 'Now, it's getting heavy. Enough of this talk...'

'I'm not escaping,' Candice says. 'Reason and justice – back in the saddle now.'

'I saw you talking to the medicine guy,' Elsa says. 'We all use traditionalists now – we mustn't live so long in apprehension and decay. The first sign of rot – we're off, dead, and then the shamans link us to our living friends.... I love your camel – unbeaten on the straight. See no evil – that could be her name, and you, Candice – you're sighted still, I see... If I were you, I'd give it up, your search....'

'Oh no,' says Candice. 'Since they could speak and write, the humans talked of reason, justice too. Maybe more the first – justice seems to have no rules....'

'Exactly so!' says Elsa, releasing some kittens in the wild. 'We've tried for centuries – maybe the time is here to think of something else, if it attracts, and is as distant and as bright as sunrise... Or as sunset too....'

'The animals,' says Candice, as the little cats run off and hide. 'They say it's good we cannot see them. But – how'd we know they're there?'

'Ah,' Elsa says. 'Epistemology. Never my strong suit.'

'Quite delightful, those kittens,' Candice says.

'Delicious,' Elsa says. 'They're food. Doesn't it occur, my dear, your quest was one that used to interest the Greeks – among the other things.... A simple ask and never a response. You may feel the time is up. Too many rowing in the other sense. Neither justice nor reason's possible, not if you're free, and compromise and shift your ground... What you need is immortality – endless time. Alas, that too's a boat that's sailed and won't come back. Laden with deities, Greeks, Hindus. I deviated, went for the big invisible one, the good life. I never raised a sail...

'Love and resignation, that's the more attainable goal...'

'And gardening,' Candice says. 'I feel that should come in too.'

'You can't use chemicals, of course – so if it's radishes you want, the voles will eat them all,' Elsa says.

'I'm not too sure where I have ended up,' says Candice. 'I came straight here, but don't know where. What do I need to know?'

'Power is safely in the hands of guys like your boss and you,' says Elsa. 'You can accept, or sigh. Ignore. It's sorted, anyway, and you can be sure, they're no smarter than you are, you were. Whatever language it speaks in, power's plain and straight. It's not a fan of tolerance, but, Candice, you don't want that. You wanted order, justice, and those you will not get. Be content! You need belief. That brightens up, puts shading, hatching, in. Otherwise, you're blocked, a single line, a kid's sketch: – a mum or dad. Neither role fits you, naturally,' and Elsa gazes into Candice's face: 'I see love there,' she says. 'No gardening.'

'No,' says Candice. 'You're mistaken. There's nothing there. There's just a face.'

'For sure, I can be wrong,' says Elsa. 'Nothing hangs on it, my right or wrong. But – look into my face – you'll be drawn into my eyes.' There's black, that's true. Ah yes – and depth. Unending voids.

'Here, it all looks like what I left behind,' says Candice, ignoring the invitation. 'I wonder who is chasing me.'

Elsa shrugs.

'What are you, Elsa?' Candice asks.

'Can't you see?' she asks, surprised. 'I'm a failure.'

'That's new to me,' says Candice. 'I've only known success. But you're right. Failing at difficult things – maybe there the future lies. Maybe it was so too in the past. Perhaps we should get used....'

'That's comforting,' says Elsa, dropping her basket and hugging Candice. 'Though I've also failed at easy things. It may be that damp hand in mine's the Zeitgeist's.'

'I should tell you, Elsa,' Candice says. 'That I am lonely. A lonely person. You may think it's an emotion, to be avoided – it's not. It's a statement, a state. It excludes failure, of course, by definition. And it doesn't mean that I want friends. If anything, quite the reverse.'

'That's enviable, Candice,' Elsa says, guiding the new friend, companion, happenstance, through a long vestibule, adorned with plumes of Amazons and Lorikeets. 'I prefer viewing envy as emotion, rather than as state – that would be humiliating, Candice. Stay here, explore – look in your loneliness, but don't expect I'll lend a hand. I'm out of almost everything, except my paints. And – no, I only occupy the house, don't own. It's rather big. I'd need to fix the roof, and there's subsidence too....'

'Better not to own it then,' says Candice. 'You do well to not.'

'The doorhandles are special,' Elsa says, whisking through. 'All Wiener Werkstatte, ended bad, and cheap. No doors, you see. The worms got those – the handles are up there – people steal the oddest things –' and she points to the ceiling. 'The carpets too. Cats – untrustworthy: and one wing I painted on in trompe l'oeil. The eye – so easy to deceive ... mind you don't hurt yourself....'

'Oh, I know about the eye,' says Candice, recoiling from some walls.

'My own work is hard to sell,' says Elsa. 'As you see – some is immovable, some isn't what you think ... the paint, the brick, it's easy to confuse... I end collecting myself.'

'Who knows the price of work original,' says Candice wistfully. 'Some cultures exclude it totally, most pay hugely for a tiny part, and cannot see the mass of it.'

'That argument leads nowhere, Candice,' Elsa says, quite sharp. 'If you want something here, make me an offer.'

'Cash? I haven't any ready, Elsa,' Candice says. 'I could take a loan from you, and then... But if you sell off bits of house, where will you go? You can't paint another one and live in it....'

'Don't patronise me, Candice,' Elsa says. 'Your project is a total loss, where mine is pretty, and well-crafted too.'

'You're right,' says Candice. 'Our projects aren't compatible. You arrange other people's stuff to make a crazy space, decayed and aimless –'

'I bodge,' Elsa says. 'Do nothing new. You want to make an order where there's not. How can we agree?'

'No one will look for me here, in this house,' Candice thinks. She says, 'Are you an aesthete, then, Elsa? I never met one, not till now...'

'No, Candice,' Elsa says. 'Not exactly, no. I think, in brief – I love chaos. Disorder. Not troubles – no, those I dislike. But general disorderliness. Situations and responses to them: chaos. Unreason.'

'Injustice too?' asks Candice.

'If called for, yes,' says Elsa. 'Your reason and justice caused those crimes....'

'So did unreason and disorder,' Candice says. 'Besides, I avoided absolutes...'

'There!' Elsa says. 'You're bitten both ways, my dear.'

*

Candice wanders sleepless round the dark, the black, house. There's snoring – is it Elsa, or more food, relaxed and fattening? – a pig, maybe, about to farrow; joy! Yumyum!

'And if it starts in chaos, there it will end,' she thinks, 'and so my order is a moment, probably pure chance, a lemma, a sport, in a disorder that prevails. And Elsa's fooled me – for I thought I stood not for order, but for reason, a higher kind of order, or a lower.... Or – was it justice she denied me, put me on order's trail? None of these is here. But...' And she stumbles, nearly falls – there's black holes in the paving, and she looks, and hey! mind! down, down it goes. 'In the universe,' she ponders, 'there's more nothing than there's something, and even something isn't stuff you walk upon and see the daffodils a-blowing... Is there a nowhere, where these endless holes don't end, or maybe a somewhere where they turn to something – a random thing, disorderly, that could rise up, a kraken, pour dense nothing, exude a dust embalming us and freezing everything – the Wiener tables and the Basquiats, the imitation Twomblies and the Kleins – all fakes and remembrances, things that don't belong to Elsa and to no one else, unsaleable, unwanted, like the cannons on a sunken ship, corroded, silted up with hermit crabs and carpet sharks....?'

She nearly falls – it's the attraction of the deep. Dry oceans: tumbling through emptiness with asphalt sides that's written on – 'dear duke of Kang, thanks for your killing of

those Shang', in everlasting gratitude, and shards of blanc de
Chine and moulded glass, bronze cash by bucketfuls,
'propitious years', and then the masks lined with men's skin,
and wiry hairs from elephants, and fetters for the feet and
wooden presses that crack hands, and empty trilbies like snail
shells, stuffed thrushes, old gas bills and paper targets
peppered through and salt from mines that's built from ice....
So you go down, and reason dwindles, and your order starts
to fray until it's bones and shells and reptile plates and
plaques from armoured flying things, then black and black
until you reach the end – the tiny button at the start of every
sequence, brown... that randomly explodes, producing order
and disorder, reason and its brother: guess; understanding of
the false, mistaking of the maybe true, making gold from
chowder, boiling souls in mayonnaise...

'I should go down,' thinks Candice. 'It could be my
mission, even if I don't come back – to have been
everywhere until I found my nowhere – except,' and she
pulls back from a hole, 'I'm always going into nowhere, and
I've never, ever, journeyed back, it's always different and
unexplained, the people gawk and carry on, and you are not
the same but don't know how you're different ... the future,
re-invented every second, all's different and the same.'

The snoring stops. 'Elsa!' shouts Candice. 'Sort me out!'
But Elsa doesn't come, maybe it's good because you're not
quite certain where it is that she belongs, and if that place is
saleable and how it's anchored on the nothing that those
holes are fastened to.

'Haven't you left?' Elsa asks, at last appearing, straw in
her hair. 'I supposed you'd fallen. Those holes – I must cover
them. Or widen them. Make a pool.'

'What would you put in the pool, Elsa?' Candice asks.
'Water?'

'Nothing.' Elsa says. 'Myself.'

'It's all so dark...' says Candice.

'You have to pay for light,' says Elsa. 'Who'd have thought?'

'Where shall I go, Elsa? Is there eats or something here?' Candice asks, at a loss.

'You don't want to be food, I expect,' says Elsa. 'So eating's wasted on you.'

'That's very smart,' says Candice, quite impressed.

'Maybe it seems so because you're not, Candice,' says Elsa. 'As for where, you could just go straight. That's how you got here. We're all middling sorts, no special place, no special destination. Try living with that, Candice.'

'Oh, I shall, I do,' says Candice. 'It's – I thought we'd be lovers, me reluctant. Spats and splits.'

'What you want won't happen in this world, Candice,' Elsa says. 'Maybe in the next. Think of that, think of the next world. Think very, very hard.'

'Will it be like down those holes?' Candice asks, heading to the wind that blows in through the doorways.

'I'll get those fixed,' says Elsa. 'The next world. Like this? Or the opposite? Think of it, Candice, don't bet on anything.' Candice feels disoriented. She cries.

'You're not a lovable person, Candice,' Elsa says. 'But not exactly horrible. I'm a realist, and live with what there is. You're shallow. It's not kindness, Candice, to wish things better – it is vanity.'

'What....' Candice starts, but finds she's out, on her park's perimeter. 'The next world,' she thinks. 'I wonder if someone's taking bets on it?

'Into the park? Where the animals are lurking. Or into the world – where for the crimes of someone else and my complicity, a someone lies in wait for me,' she thinks:

'I could have made those Jacobites succeed, and opened up a European world. Enough of slaves and empire, better to do without the rum, tobacco, those expensive woods.... think of the tall grey streets of Lazio, the plaques, 'Henry the Ninth slept here...' A straight world, pre-scientific always, worldly, paternalist.... Wider, at least, than what they have, without the deportations maybe... Conrad saw, repeated it, gave up. He found this story, ran it through, became a nobody, down in the reading room.

('Maybe you wanted "Jacobins"....' pops up.)

'The Soviet exploits –' she thinks on. 'I could have changed how those concluded, stirring in more justice and more reason...Kronstadt? The re-shoot? These are the other, the next worlds, now quite untouchable, not to be modified, even if you change the laws. Americans? What could you do with them? And all the rest...

'It's Elsa's fault. These fantasies – I'd not want all of them, or any of it. Nonsense. Histories, stories unlivable and irreversible. No! Absolutely not. Not me. Leave them all be, those past next worlds.

'And Conrad, Émilie too...'

*

'You're right, Candice,' the doctor says, holding up her clicking wand. 'I've looked everywhere. There is no nowhere, everything is somewhere. It's the question of the change, and making it: that's quite another thing....'

'Oh, I know about gender,' Candice says. 'And how they say it makes us one. Or many. But, doctor – you had no right nor reason to scan inside my head.'

'You were sat there, Candice, on a log,' says the doctor, Rose. 'That way, you put in doubt your place, your situation, the little space you occupy.... You were physical only – your identity was obscure. You railed and ranted, too. If there had been animals ... hearing the call of civilisation ... they hunger, always.'

'It doesn't excuse you, Rose. And – there's no cure for hunger,' says Candice, quite confused.

'If there's no nowhere, then there's no excuse: nothing is changed, nor changeable: everything is where it is, eternal, fixed, and everything you do is there like writing on a wall of infinite extension, neither keeping in nor out, but permanent,' says Rose.

'There's me, and there is my identity, and are we two, or one?' asks Candice once again.

'Your head,' says Rose. 'I found the conceptual areas quite pronounced. I'd like to follow you about.... Not for a purpose, just for scientific curiosity...The two of you...'

'Rose, with your machine – you are a child,' says Candice. 'Children – they're nothing special. Will you grow out of being one? I have a doubt.'

'Tell me what you want, Candice,' Rose says. 'I'll try to find it – the brain's become a park, we're rooting out the animals, testing the plants – there's hallucigens and cures for them...'

'No, Rose,' Candice says. 'I want a starting place. Not a silly utopia – I want a real no-place. Not something imagined, with all the decor, birds in cages, singing in ragtime. I don't want an invention, running all our history. A place called nowhere, that *is* nowhere ... that would do.'

'You want a rebirth of the universe, Candice,' Rose laughs. 'The moon sleeps with Endymion, for sure. There'll be offspring. Pandora's smooching Roman – they'll have immortal twins – justice and chaos. You left when it was interesting....'

'That's all wrong,' says Candice. 'And – it's not to do with brains.'

'Don't be so sure,' says Rose, slipping off her white coat, passing into a kaftan. 'Justice – must be universal, from all to all. That's a behaviour. Reason – that's a procedure. It must all be in there – potentially,' and she raps Candice's head in play: 'It's brain, Candice.'

'I wish I'd not been involved in this,' says Candice. 'It started with wanting a straight path I could follow for myself. Treasure: that was Trudi. Eva, keeping me company, for my document... Money and a visa – that's all you usually need to reach a top. Please – no check points at my synapses, Rose!'

'It's not you can't have what you want,' says Rose, despairing, slumping in a chair like its loose cover. 'It's that I can't find it; you're not predisposed.'

'Well,' says Candice, tearfully, 'if science is based on reason, and all I have's a brain ... what's to become of me? My brain's like all the rest. Don't tell me I am monstrous: body, brain – and wants quite unattainable.'

'Yes,' says Rose. 'Maybe you should just be normal. You've no curriculum, no job, no friends, no capital – so, you've no position to defend. You're open to be liberal, but until you have a job, you don't know how useful that might be.... To me, you're normal, all the signs are that there's nothing different in you – you could be Hitler, Mary Wollstonecraft: – the waves I register are the same.'

'You mean we can all be anything?' asks Candice, cheering up.

'No,' says Rose. 'I don't think I mean that at all.'

'What, then?' Candice asks, turning aggressive.

'Don't try. Seek love. Bless the world, and don't insist,' says Rose, as if all her subjects get the same.

'Oh Rose,' says Candice. 'You are soft! We all have the sickness in us, terminal. Best set off – a Kriegszug, with servants and treasure chests.'

'I don't see those, Candice,' says Rose, alarmed.

'I shall gather them;' says Candice. 'You can be beside me, taking my pulse, seeing if I'm still alive, or dead.'

*

'Your park,' says Rose, 'not at all a girly thing. So flat, lunar – a heath, like Pomerania.'

'You can't order hills from catalogues,' says Candice. 'I want the scrub to look like bronze corroding. It does. Don't drag on, Rose – if only speaking could be like painting, everything would be over quick. A colour and a scrawl...'

'Is that the point?' asks Rose, struggling to ease her thinking out from her career.

Medics – they're not allowed to ask where you're from, what class, who'd you identify with – only your age, and if your origin carries some disease: 'The look of things?' asks Rose. 'Or is it that the park lies on a frontier, so's you could get away? Beware, Candice. a document – and you're hooked back in, in to a tiny crowded room, perpetual light, nothing to see in it...'

'Relax, Rose,' Candice says. 'You've peered further into me than any lover. Before I met you, I knew I was one, indivisible. Besides, we are all Africans. I'm an innocent, one of the educated poor, brought up to know it's useless working to be poor some more. Can I be thrown back? – the golden age of plenty, hunter-gathering, before the torment of the weather and the crops, grinding little bits on stones. Nomads, Rose; or temple-priests, stretching up and prostrating, yoga – keeps them supple. That's the best. The sedentary life – it leaves you vulnerable, it gives you boils ... avoid it if you can.'

'But Candice, there's no justice, no reason in the wandering....' says Rose, throwing away her medicines, tucking her kaftan in to make some baggy trapsalteerie pants ... a Sinbad running rockily after her nemesis.

'Then let them be,' says Candice. 'Let them look for their future by themselves, those abstracts. They're in a hiding place, deep in my skull. Let's be off. Away, away!'

'I'm not sure, Candice,' says Rose. 'I'm ready, but unsure. Friends, a garden, a soft chair ... they summon me. You're a threat, Candice – I foresee you throttling me, my modest aspirations...'

'Nonsense!' shouts Candice. 'States, neighbours, porous sex, diluted nationality ... do you cling to all or some of that...? Look at me! The future – can't be stopped. The past is unattainable. The present – impossible to justify. Just contemplate. You can't be elsewhere than you are – but, imagine and select. The past – where it all began, before the first philosopher passed his begging-bowl, when we loped through the bush, apologised for our pork chop to mother pig... And later, where it began, more and more times, and ended too – tradition, rebellion, where did they lead? It ends in Roman and Pandora, Rose.'

Candice starts to trot. 'I'll not put my seal on anyone – no tsar, no hero, no elected freak, and no community of these and those, no campaign that binds me, puts me into uniform with boots too small, képi too large....

'Oh Rose, what is to do? The past is in our bones, lived and sedimented, it bodes no good. The future – how long? A year? A million? – and all the same, in fear and gadgetry, eyes blinded by the midday sun. Flocking and wheeling, starlings we shall be, every mathematic shape experimented to foil the predators. Join me, if you will, we'll wander through what was and is, and maybe steal a future.... Do you really care, Rose? Or did you choose a palliative, limp humanism, patching up the moribund? Your medicine – puts off what will come, and soon.... Stay here. I'm quite indifferent. Your padded chair, the couch where subjects lie and fear the worst, the garden that you tend when you have told them that – it's yours, and yours alone!

'*I* shall be free, Rose. Relatively. But free.'

Rose runs after, but she's slow, further and further off, a dot.... The flesh, the will, perspire and flag. 'Your conclusion, Candice – is that your true last word?' she gasps, but Candice doesn't hear, maybe already she forgot. Her message terrifies: 'I live. I'm glad. I don't agree to living anywhere.'

'Dear Rose,' she thinks. 'Oh Rose – you'll be my secret, my lost love. I'm ready! Our first kiss – for ever in the bottle, sealed like the virgin pack. Cold love – no booze, no blackjack, and no liar dice. No embrace. No poker.

'I can do no more. I have nothing, no place to be expelled from. I'm running, I've crossed one border, I'm ready for a number more. I've no capital, my body's worth the minimum; even if you savage it – it's not worth extra. Why, then, bother?

'New life! So, this is failure, this stale escape? What have I misunderstood? It's all gone down – reaction, revolution. Will it be capitalism next that falls? All comes to its end over and over, and rises grey and dusty from its ash.

'I'm galloping – those buildings coming down – you don't want being trapped beneath.'

*

'Poor Candice,' Rose thinks, relieved she's not going anywhere. 'Being a nomad means you're watched and trapped. Forced to go where you'd not wish, and beaten too....'

*

Candice dreams – quite inconclusively. They're ghosts, the figures, who don't age, don't work or earn, perhaps they play their luck, wavering between the up and down, the nearly visible, the nameless – no! Not fantasmic – they must be sporty chancers. Of course ... it's poker ... no, it's blackjack! She plays, the hand is polydactlylous, a split thumb, awkward – but even with six cards or more – it's rubbish, and the other guys are forceful, shouting, lying....

Clémence pokes her with a stick – the rose it propped up flops on Candice's face.

'They'll beat you if you sleep down there,' says Clémence. 'There's no Douanier's lion here to keep you safe. I have a badge – wear it, it will keep the vandals off.'

Candice takes the badge: it says 'Cop'. 'I'm not so sure it works, Clémence,' she says.

'You've none,' says Clémence. 'So how'd you know?'

'Being free is good, Clémence,' says Candice. 'But – it's all the rules! The ground – is hard, or wet. And people. It gets tough,' and the tears come, as she thinks of highs and lows, invisible animals, the goods done unrequited, and the bads seized on, the pasts shared, futures planned – 'Oh no,' she says, 'not another night down here, the roses, roses everywhere, and brothers snooping round....'

'Oh yes, Candice,' Clémence laughs. 'If there weren't people, we'd be truly free, our path would straighten up, and we could do the good, and only that.... My son – at first he couldn't talk, do good, or purify himself. You have to be severe, Candice. You make them learn a book, they mustn't look at girls, nor boys if they are so inclined. Hate – is a great organiser. It drives. You've not been in an organisation, where you do what you are told, Candice?'

'I guess I have,' says Candice, 'but I'll have disobeyed.'

'You didn't take resentment far enough...' says Clémence, sternly, raising her loud voice louder still.

'It seems simplistic,' Candice says. 'You'll find some follow rules, impose them – others think their destiny's a keyless lock....'

'I'm simple,' Clémence says. 'Simplistic if needs be. It isn't about punishment, it's doing what is right, and what I said.'

'Food, Clémence,' Candice begs, 'and quiet, perhaps?'

'No house, Candice,' says Clémence. 'And no park. But you can come with me....'

'What do I have to do?' asks Candice, quite resigned.

'Oh, the job's not doing, Candice. All you have to do is be,' says Clémence, pushing her inside the trailer, locking the door.

'Oh, Clémence – don't we move? I see us parked here....' Candice asks. 'Where is the traction, Clémence?'

'On the road? Oh no! You've been, Candice, you've seen it all. Conclusions: now's the time,' and Clémence blacks the windows out, and waits.

'I thought I'd be a servant here,' says Candice, 'then move on, taking valuables... Instead, it seems it's slavery. No work, no destiny...'

'Oh dear,' says Clémence. 'My! You're so conventional. House slaves have it good – like office slaves, and army slaves, and factory slaves. The thing is – don't forget the book.'

There's shelves of them on cookery. A thousand recipes. 'I guess we eat good here,' says Candice, in hope.

'Yes,' Clémence says. 'But I send out. These are the books the kids must learn. It sharpens appetite, tells you what's right, and if you get it wrong – it makes you vomit.'

'My conclusion,' Candice says. 'However pithy – does no good. No good, no bad. All that transpires, my lessons learned – is aphorism. Now, let me eat, Clémence....'

A lad bangs on the door. His box says, 'Pandora Eats' –
'So, she did well,' thinks Candice. 'Me, it doesn't help. She's
found priority, but only modestly...'

'What's this?' asks Candice, opening up her food. 'There's
panforte, ostler's biscuits, ship's tack and prison porridge.... I
thought at least – delightful Roma food, the hunter-gatherers'
delight....'

'Remember, Candice,' Clémence shouts. 'The saying:
"you eat exactly what you are'. Ponder that, with every
chew.'

'There's K-rations in that bin,' says Candice.

'My son's,' says Clémence, snatching them away. 'He's
too young for his fatigues – he changed his name. They gave
him food. How'd they get here? Which side are they from?
He's hard, I'm hard – we don't get on. I'm older, so I can't
say I hate, but I had training so's I'd turn out as I am. He has
only faith. That's worse than a cold shower. Everything he
does, must be done down to the last nail and knot.'

'No luxury, and no machines?' Candice asks: she knows
there's not. 'And yet – machines and luxury – that's what we
are. Still – you let me in. It's an anomaly, I guess. You're all
poor here, so soldiering's the only course. This is rich
country, so you can discipline the rest. Obey and fight? I am
more liquid, Clémence,' she wheedles, hoping for a softer
ride.

'Don't you want posterity, Candice?' Clémence asks. 'All
you have has ended, or will soon – the past imagined, your
life misremembered, sepia and already foxed. Something
different – you might spring to soldiering, a trek all planned
and mapped, nothing you'd need to show except
enthusiasm...'

'I might,' says Candice, 'but I'm locked in. Besides, it's
time to add it up – the bill, subtract what you can, the

credit.... A life's account. Don't add the rubbish food, Clémence ... just all the rest.'

'You have no house, no rank, Candice,' says Clémence. 'But I spot class. Rough sleepers often have it. Anyway, you're locked in, so it's easier to let you out, if you don't suit. It's quite a paradox – a tenant you can't evict: but a prisoner let out, runs, flees as though she's wanted still for the same crime whose time she has already served. Do you have unfinished business, Candice? It doesn't seem so. You're free; now you know freedom's price – your wishes, unattainable. As for your sanctuary, your park – it's a mystery. Were your animals in hiding? Maybe they became extinct. Or someone took the cash for them, and they were never there. Which side were you on? Which cause? Something you did? A threat? I'm sure you'd want to be a spy – most people do, it's more decorous than mere betrayal, treason, cowardice. The penalties are all the same....'

'You end your sermon, Clémence, saying "here you're safe",' says Candice, laughing. 'Except I'm not. My safety isn't on your minds. I'm sure you've rulings, rules – all unimaginable... Demands, requirements...'

'Companion, servant, slave – there's always something of them all,' says Clémence. 'I'm Jungian, deep down. The Jocasta complex, possibly. You're not a bit like me. That's why I seek you...'

'No,' Candice says. 'This isn't me. I am not I. Let me out. Don't save me, love me, nor keep me safe, obedient.'

'Suspicion, Candice,' Clémence says. 'It prowls through the trailer park, where we're all parked, through everywhere. We're all locked up and tolerant, but we won't mix. Nothing's to be trusted. I thought we'd be companions – you'd be a slave because in this trailer, there's nothing to be done... All's brought to the door, except some love for me.'

'The door must be kept open,' Candice says. 'For your son. They'll bring him back, deliver him like biscuits, in a box. Parts, at least: a head. Fighting in Africa – it's the start all over, that is why we left. Once there was space, then we became territorial, domesticated beasts. That was the turning point, the buying, selling animals: then it was us as well, and so we left....'

'It's not at all like that,' says Clémence. 'I'm sure it was more complicated. Stay with me, Candice, we all need power, power over someone.... Something we can do that machines can't....'

'I've had all that,' says Candice. 'I'm running out of people.... I've no beginning to return to, nowhere to set off from. Maybe I'm a refugee, and perhaps – if you take one in, you're paid ... paid to keep me so's I don't run out and steal....'

'Oh Candice,' Clémence says. 'I wouldn't trust you, not if they cased me in gold leaf. There is no peace – there's stasis, boredom, and you wait. There's no reward – your sons and daughters change their names, flight and fight, causes unnameable, causes with a thousand names, last words inaudible, forgotten.... All us here – we lost our homes, the animals, relatives whose everyone's laid underground; a mesh – don't pity me, Candice, I'm harsh, lived on the wrong side, beneath my love is deep indifference, you could call it hate....'

'No, Clémence,' says Candice. 'I know how it is, the everything, I don't call it, or anything, any name, not good or bad, just let me go, go outside under the sun, cover my head before it does me harm.'

*

Instinct spurs, Candice runs. Clémence was the weakest and the worst.

It's an electric brae – the eyes say it's downhill, the legs know it's up. The legs surrender. Ah – here's a tall lady....

'You don't engage, Candice,' says Flora. 'Think. People don't do what they're told. They make a scene and sometimes they conjure leaders who take them partly where they think of going.... You expect a peaceful garden, but you forgot the eggs and seeds – the flowers, the serpents: perfumes, and hazards...'

Candice, exhausted, is sat upon a stone.

'The city fell,' says Flora. 'This milestone doesn't tell a distance, it's just a memorial. Remember that. Scatter, not pattern. Climate, not class. Letting go. Unknown and disappeared: not sad and disappointed. Lions and foxes, Candice – each comes around, neither is admirable, but there it is. Patience!'

'You're right, of course,' says Candice. 'I left lots out – the worst, the best. I saw, I was the middling sort, but my conclusion can't be based on ignorance, on what I haven't seen, people I've not met. To me, my biggest mystery is where those animals went. Inventions and campaigns – I can't do anything. They're unstoppable, like dew. Pandora had the gift of making results she didn't want. She engaged. She hoped to spread the gift of intervention out to everyone. But who knows what each wants, Flora? And how to get to it?'

'That's boldly said, dear Candice,' Flora says, waving onward a bus that slowed to pick them up. 'But – I know exactly what, and how.' She grips Candice's arm above the elbow, pulls her to the vertical.

'What you say,' says Candice, 'is so like ... what reason has always predicated. Sit back, sit tight, pretend the worst won't come, and bet both ways, just to be sure. But, Flora –

the worst *has* come, it always does, it always will, and now we have a date for it. Forget the justice aspect, forget the flowers, the bowers – they'd be for painstaking guys. The sun, Flora! It's everywhere. Our centre: all we have. And the soot, the dark, the floods ... leafcutting creatures great and small ... those are here, a destination beckons – the primal garden gasping under the cement.'

'That's not the point,' says Flora. 'Who knows you, Candice? What weight would your conclusions have? The point you miss – is that you're pointless. Jedermann? We all are, it's banal. Sin and repent, Candice, fear death and pray – except, you're passive, don't pray, don't have the cash to do good deeds. You watch, that's all. To be a powerful Everyman, you have to *do*. Sin, fear, despair. And then be damned, forgotten, tossing on invisible waves....'

'People remember me,' says Candice, much irritated. 'By my aphorisms. My life's an aphorism. There's substance beneath – there's nothing I haven't lived, put in its nutshell.'

'You're tired, Candice,' says Flora. 'I can get you out of here, this dangerous stretch. True, you're just a failure, you're used to dodging dangers you can't see. You'll never have an answer – you can't look down ... you aren't up high enough.'

'My bestiary?' asks Candice. 'Oh, you can't seek what isn't there. It's Heidegger – it sounds, it *is,* the deepest sound, so grave it can't be heard. Only the animals, perhaps, the few big ones, but they aren't here, extinguished, scattered among rocks.'

'Don't be so sure. The tiny raptors lurk beneath those stones. There's danger everywhere,' Flora says. 'It's open road. All round, the sea: a porridge laced with mince. Trust me – I'll save you. Go! Don't come back. This argument is closed.'

'Rose...' Candice says, with extreme difficulty, holding on to Flora so's to stand....

'Forget all that,' says Flora. 'You had a name, Candice, but neither rank nor house. I have friends and followers – they'll get it all from me, all you found out about the world, its destiny. They trust me.... You're unknown.'

'It's a hollow secret, Flora,' Candice says. 'The world: it's been scooped out, it's just a shell. A Pulcinella's secret, what transpires. Enough: it's all known, all investigated, all set down, even shelved and locked up in the library.'

'Love. Perseverance,' Flora says. 'The old-fashioned stuff. People, especially sceptics – they adore it.'

'I hadn't thought of that,' says Candice. 'It seems improbable. I never found them dynamic, not the moving parts you need. They're for the losers, surely.'

*

They're on a bus route. That means there's a here, a there, a to-and-fro, two places you can go to.

'Just suppose,' says Flora, 'someone hit you with a stone ... no one would see, and on and on it goes...'

'We should have stopped the friendly bus,' Candice says. 'This road – exposed and perilous. Suppose they put me in the jail, hang me by the heels, and you can feel you drown yourself.... I'd leave all that to body and to brain – they're made to deal with drastic scenes. I as I – I can't imagine it, going on and living afterwards. I have no answer and no strategy. It's all systems – body and brain have theirs, often they cope, the universe runs like an exploding clock, and then there's everyone, each with a system...'

'You need responses,' Flora says. 'Distance yourself. Ask yourself – do all the animals think about them, the bad ends?'

'Of course we do,' says Candice. 'If you chant and hold your amulet real hard, until it hurts – you're cured – people do that, I hear. No trauma. No memory, no fear. There's systems all around, and you must fit in talismanic things invisible – the gods, of course, they pack up small, and sunsets, all that stuff – owls love those, it means dinnertime is near. The sun, the sun! You have to cherish it,' she says.

'I work this stretch, dear Candice,' Flora says. 'There isn't room for two. Your talk is fun, but now, enough.... Go!'

*

'Flora usually gets you out,' says Candice to herself. 'But there's threat here – answers without a question. She takes the credit for walking with you down the road.... She has the name, passed from long lines of prostitutes, the first, the best courtesan in Rome, but only one left now, Flora, ushering the lost ones off the road. It's good. You could be knocked down, or out.'

'Countries bemuse me,' she thinks. 'I know nothing of each one, except all stand on some odd principle, a mixing what shouldn't be, practices that I don't do: families, and cults. Each different, they say, each sedimented, fossils in a sand. The dynasties – those are all the same: they're boxes – some with scorpions, some with mice. A puzzle. What I see is – everywhere there's offices, gardens, a stretch of road that's being worked, people in headcloths learning verbs. Lines drawn in deserts. It's meanders. Do you risk your head to straighten out a river bend? Someone must. Not me. I believe in just wars, don't make me fight in them.

'Flora paints her face – you can't see it. No one else will paint her. I could go to the forest – there, there's people with painted faces you can see, being snapped, filmed, hunting, gathering: and animals you never saw before or since. Once there, you don't stay long. But where there's real war, you never get away. Stay overnight? Or in perpetuity? You can't just travel round, looking for pieces that fit into your puzzle. No jungle, then. No deadly wars....

'No. Not the case. Where, then?'

*

'You're right,' says Tania. 'To settle where there is delight and luxury. I see you quite exhausted – usually it means you have accomplished nothing. No matter – all lives are cinders, even if you've taken photographs of how it was – those childhoods solemn, rather out of focus.... The cakes here are excellent: they'll cheer you up, and make the world look appetising.'

It's true.

'I'll treat you,' Tania says. 'I come here despite the babble and the boasting. It's the gin that makes for pessimistic bars – here, they sell vodka. It's tearful, but you get to sing in tune. It's our little happy kingdom. I'm in the regal line,' she says, and laughs. 'But it would take a massacre before I'm at the top.'

'What would you do?' asks Candice, not much interested – massacres don't happen every day, or if they do, it's probably not here.

'Would do?' asks Tania... 'I *do* do. This is a poor dull town. But here, we live our best lives. We spend our cash, each pays their round, and what you say stays here, you don't complain of what goes on outside, at home – or past and future, we don't read papers here, though we discuss philosophy, or how you build a bridge or change a tire.'

'It sounds a long process, Tania,' Candice says. 'I've never been in one of those *novelas*, discussing everything and whether you are happy.'

'Maybe you are in a process, and didn't recognise,' says Tania.

'I like to drink,' says Candice. 'Lots. Not being drunk.'

'We come together here,' says Tania. 'To gather strength – guys from the air base, the fire station, waterworks, the landfill – the offices, and after mosque and mass: it isn't hard to understand. It's peace, Candice, even if the drink can fire you up – soon, it all calms down, nothing here lasts, harsh words forgotten...'

'I know, Tania,' Candice says. 'I've been in bars before – I've never heard of one that's like a universe....'

'I told you, Candice,' Tania says. 'The town is flat and dull, goes on for ever – you can eat here too –'

And so they do.

'Peace,' Tania repeats. 'Information, if you want. Sometimes you get work, sell stuff, buy a dog.'

'It's *huis clos*, Tania,' Candice says.

'No, that's purgatory, Candice. Two days in jail – I'm dead,' says Tania. 'This here is always. But it's peace. Eternal, if you want.'

'That's why you talk to me, Tania?' Candice asks.

'To anyone,' says Tania.

'Well,' Candice says. 'You're all used to it. I bet the masters never come down here, and this is where you're free, free to assess, if you want.'

'That's exactly right,' says Tania.

'There's not so many here,' Candice goes on. 'And those – they look quite drunk to me.'

'Oh, you understand enough,' says Tania. 'Once, everything you knew came from the media, you knew the places, where you were in them. On the screen. Walking up and down in Diyarbakir, drumming crazy in Los Angeles. Now, we're in them, in the media. It's swallowed us – turns out we're all normal. Even the hunters – they help you run. We all help each other, Candice.'

'I'm not stressed at all,' says Candice. 'I don't need help. I don't think in my life I've needed to help anyone.'

'You must look for patterns, Candice,' Tania says. 'There's always one. Rose the reticent: selfless and reluctant, then Flora the prostitute, helpful, abrasive. Clémence – a bad dose of death...'

'I don't see it,' Candice says. 'First, there was intrigue – with no rank, no house. Then butchery; more butchery – the invention of the metre, then the camps and people running, like the book we read at school – the *Völkerwanderung* – how the continent became all hugger-muggered off the steppes, and then the butchery, spread all over, the roots in Africa torn up, boiled and scraped, lithe guys fettered and whipped, the drugs to China, denims to India ... then it was animals, made into rugs, waste-paper baskets... No, Tania, I'm the ball in a machine – I rack up a score of thousands, a record, then I'm guttered and game over, tilt....'

'Oh,' shouts Tania – both are far gone, the vodka's made behind the bar, potatoes give it a kick grain can't. 'You didn't play our games! You flip a coin – it's arc goes spinning from the dynasty – the head – to capital, the value, or the price: tails.... It's hegemony setting up, and the chances are, if you do it long enough, between the rulers you owe deference to, and the wage you get, there's mathematical equality. Parity. Chance is certain – fifty-fifty. Kopeks or cents. That's history – and no conclusion, nothing settled, ever. It must go on, the world is one, then hundreds once again – it cannot stop until it stops. Our games here, though – they aren't arithmetic – they're quoits and skittles, threading a wisp into tiny holes and fitting boxes into boxes....'

'The age of reason, Tania,' Candice says. 'From optimism into pessimism, back again; enlightened guys who rode white horses, sabred the priests; where did that end?'

'Enough, you sceptic!' Tania laughs. 'No rank, no house! No side – that's you. No beliefs improbable and juvenile. You've mastered every cliché, every topic – and don't forget the women, and the Choctaws! Remember! Remember everything!

'Now, I'll take you to the cave. You'll see the monster bones – now, there's a thing that's disappeared: big animals!...'

And she pulls Candice down the slope.

'I love the monsters,' Candice says. 'I have affinity. They must be, they are, my kin...'

'Oh nonsense,' Tania shouts, dragging her friend along: 'You're fun, you're buttered toast, you ran in time when things were looking bad.... Outpacing monsters, that's your sport...'

Bones: ladies, gents, and kiddies too – with wings like sun umbrellas, torsoes like skiffs beached, bleached.... Some look like us, inside, and others don't.

'What does this mean?' asks Candice. 'Were they dumped here, a past? Or as a puzzle you must join up, breathe life in, put them on camera, see them chase the raptors on the veld, charge for a trophy shoot? Then boil them up, the skulls, theirs, ours, and test to see what, who, they have ate, and maybe one's Napoleon, another's – who? The nameless one, the resurrected. They all seem the same, but you must choose a name familiar, a tsar, a commissar, a star, a starman, astronaut....'

'Oh, Candice,' Tania kisses her and laughs. 'So solemn. You must enter in – the spirit!'

'The last battle, possibly,' says Candice, trying to fit a femur to a pelvis – *Dragon of Wanton*, was it? something like. Those were the days! abundant sex, and berries big as rubies hung on every neck. Life was profligate, the species came and went, and someone fleet and wily survived the witches and the hungry pigs and ... here we are! No magic. All pigs cooped tidy in their huts.'

'Well,' says Tania, 'and all the better! Yes, there was a battle here – our side had axes, like the Niebelungs, the rest just paws and claws, fangs as long as claymores, sharp as katars. Armageddon, Candice – and our species won, it rules, it can do anything it wants – it has done everything because there is no challenger left, your animals – they didn't last a week ... if they were there at all, and either they were cannibals, or else bushmeat....'

'Is this true?' asks Candice, much dismayed.

'Everybody saw,' says Tania, quite maliciously. 'I told you, we're all in the media now. It isn't just nature, meaning plants-and-animals, it's ours; our nature, that's consolidated.... Ours is the tops. Yours, mine, Candice – we'll see it battle out, the dialectic: ... creation and destruction: life and death... Which wins? I know, Candice, you'll say death always wins, though you don't seek it ... but rather, the goal is life, except, here in the cave, you see the losers and the losers, tangled up and indistinguishable –' and she clinks long bones together, a marimba sound, the bone's long gone, they're chalk like for the blackboard – that shows irregular verbs, the fricative and palatals in rows.

'The animals have gone,' Tania goes on. 'No problem there. The sun's a difficulty – but out of reach. The air's invisible – what can we do? The plants – you pop spuds in the ground, and so! they work it out....Into the vat with them! Ferment! Up here, above ground – big wars or big machines? Wages or sins,' and she laughs. 'Of course – the dialectic's not an either-or, you get a bit of everything; it's soup. Your army goes to selling door-to-door, from GI Joe's to Barbie with décolletée.... It is our last, our decisive battle, Candice. My! it's a long tough one. Kindness and medication? Or pack-drill. Nativism or inclusion? It's both, it's neither – in the end we'll have redrawn the boundaries, unmade, remade the countries and the histories, the what is true, the what is beautiful, the who lives where, who doesn't live at all. This is our epic, Candice.'

'It's a danse macabre,' says Candice, quite appalled. 'How'd you know all this, Tania?'

'It may well be a *Totentanz*,' says Tania. 'That's what being grown-up means. You play with all your chips, so you can lose them all. There's no big beasts to challenge us, so it's clean, the fight. Us against us.'

'Well,' says Candice, 'that has solved a lot, all my doubts and shuffling – quite unnecessary.... I thought I'd found the secret, that I had it with me all the time, and now – you've got it Tania – you, who else, and how many more of them, those secrets, can there be?'

'This cave,' says Tania. 'See how well-lit? In olden times, they looked for dark, obscure niches, cracks in the crags, hidey-holes, shades – but this charnel house, where the bones of everything are tossed, it's frontal lit. No hiding here. All must come, learn: and go, do likewise.'

'I see why you need the bar,' says Candice. 'Yes!' Tania jumps in. 'It's where you go for a respite. The Truce – its name. Time out.'

'It's civil war,' says Tania. 'Not each against all – that's crass, that's what the animals do – just gobble up the first that comes along. No, it's organised. There's sides. We love, respect, our fellow individuals: it's a war between some sides that change from month to month. It's destiny, not malice, Candice ... and of course, as the flow goes, the allies change, we must relax. The Truce.'

'Who will survive?' asks Candice. 'What's the principles?'

'Oh someone, no one,' Tania says. 'Who knows? Survival's for the moment, not a project. The principles – are often good. Or bad. Usually, banal and basic. Bring values in – as someone said, "everything has its argument". Chaos, naturally.'

'I've heard all this before,' says Candice. 'It seems each species has its destiny – and ours is battle to the end, an end uncertain till the last and after. The final scene? – maybe an unkempt garden, full of asps, two naked women, a sad victory....'

'Yes, Candice,' Tania says, pulling her out of the cave. 'It might be us.'

'Which side are you on, Tania?' Candice asks, slyly.

*

They go back to the Truce – Tania's name for it, it's not written somewhere.

Tania's dancing. 'She loves to twirl,' says Rupert, sitting down beside Candice. 'She's quite exhausting, tries it with everyone.'

'Is that the civil war?' Candice asks. 'Her part in it?' – she's quite drunk, or she wouldn't need to ask.

'She's one for sci-fi,' Rupert says and laughs. 'No science, lots of fiction. It's not that it mightn't be the truth – it's just irrelevant. It changes nothing. It's a thing you say. Sides are tides, rivers, glaciers. I know – I did the training for an astronaut. I was too tall. We had all sorts – some too short, some too tall. Some took up too much space, but – the shorties – what a sight, if you meet aliens three metres tall!' He laughs some more. 'Then I went to be a guardsman. Too short!'

'The Pomeranians?' Candice asks. 'They're on parade for every boss – I guess they must be uniform.'

'Be uniform and in it,' says Rupert. 'I have no more goals. I petitioned every side. I failed at everything....'

He weeps, strokes Candice's knee, under the table.

Candice is much preoccupied. 'Rupert,' she says. 'Stop. I've no idea which side you're on.'

'Hahaha,' Rupert cackles, in a falsetto that turns heads.

Tania returns. 'Rude soldiery,' she says, tweaking Rupert's ear until he drops his glass. 'If Candice is anyone's, she's mine,' and when Rupert stumbles off, she says, 'Just to be alone, us two, and nothing more.'

'There's nothing more than being alone,' says Candice, misunderstanding what Tania means.

'See – I said there was a pattern,' Tania says.

'That idiot, Rupert,' Candice says. 'At least, his rocket, his regiment – always part of your army – our army.'

'You can bet on that,' says Tania, firmly.

*

'I see the history,' says Candice, 'the past! Those squads of elephants, still in military file, trudging to the cemetery. Big warriors, deserting possibly, slipping in the sea – a safety quite illusory. The rest, turned *maquisards*, skulking and scavenging in the bush, or else too tiny to be seen, still stinging, bearing fevers, buboes – almost invisible. But, Tania, why is this not widely known? Is it the evidence in the cave that only we have seen?'

'Lack of interpretation,' Tania says. 'Confusion too. Some want to kill the stragglers, stuff them, decapitated on the wall, others to imprison them and stare. There is no policy. Everyone who's seen the cave's a drunk. Then, there's new concerns: guys like Rupert. Obsolete. Those wriggly arms and legs that helped us win – now, they don't fit the new machines...'

'Oh, Rupert could be something...' Candice starts –

'Oh really?' Tania says. 'Then, what?'

'My animals?' says Candice, tears starting, fear rising –

'It's over, Candice,' Tania says. 'Hypotheses race comprehensive in the messages I'd plan to write – not widely known, but brilliant. Guys only all read the manuals now. Those tales around the fire, they're *vieux chapeau.*'

'You're genius, and it's a miracle I came across you in this bar,' says Candice. 'But I'm not sure it helps myself...'

'Oh yes!' says Tania. 'It does. It's your last chapter, the last scene – the curtain falls and everybody disappears. It's always so. What keeps you going, though – is belief, like me...'

'Religion?' Candice asks. 'Invisible things, ghosts, forces, all that stuff.'

'No, no,' says Tania, and she laughs. 'Not belief in ghasties and divinities! Belief *in* religion. Nothing spiritual. Only that. That is the coming thing.'

'My dear!' Candice says, touching Tania's hand, its multicoloured nails. 'Write it all down, though no one else will ever see it. It's the record – like clay tablets, diaries, writing on the wall. In the cave – someone will come, piece the relics into: – a Winged Victory! In this case – a Winged Defeat. Remember Vienna, the art museum: only defeats! A country smaller, ever smaller – petrified: the rock-hard brownshirt prophet on his shrinking stone.... Defeats, victories – sides of the same coin. No matter that it's tragedy, dear Tania – you are the chronicler, the Homer and his kin in one....'

'What's it all worth?' asks Tania, snatching away her hand, passing it through her multi-coloured mèches. 'The bad of yesteryear? A city, country, century? Nothing is changed.

What it is, it is, and always will be so. Written on paper, birch-bark, electricity ... it's fossil, Candice. If only ... something might persist, a Sapphic line, arch of eyebrow, a turn of elbow.... Candice: it's all in vain!'

She weeps.

'My poor beasts,' Candice says. 'What fate.... Nothing to say, dear Tania.... What is to be done? Bind some wounds? Whittle a crutch? It seems so little in the spate of years.'

'You never saw my room,' says Tania. 'My Harley up on bricks. Vinyl and plastic – outlawed memories.... Gerry Mulligan. Fluffy dice. Oh Candice – into the memory bin for all of that, and all of us. Drop us your aphorism; and depart.'

'Vodka!' says Candice. She squirms through her clothes. 'Somewhere, so long ago, I kept my fare, gold under the tongue in case there's thieves, two paisas for the eyes. I won't spend those, but all the rest.... Another round....!'

'You do well, Candice,' Tania says. 'We should all be so prepared. Let's play a game, and dance. They have the best, the latest music here. See, the tables are all full, the guys here talk philosophy – some will dance with you, they're light as spirits, and they lift you up – high, higher, higher than you've ever been ... ever so high....!'

FRIENDS

'We are the glue, Susannah,' says Danièle. 'We women. The boys – one's a general, one's in the party, one's a commie in jail, and I got the exile poet. He doesn't do that, of course, but that's his space – creativity, fantasy, the writing down. Naked reality.'

'Did you convert?' asks Susannah, unconvinced.

'Oh,' says Danièle, laughing. 'The pillars? If you don't have a belief, it's easy to convert. It's routines, you fit them in, Walid doesn't mind, doesn't ask. It's me that does them, he doesn't. You can imagine him – a pilgrimage! People, hotels! So many people milling round, not enough rooms! All smiling or quarrelling, all the same, all doing the same thing... "Home?" he says, "I've no destination and no home. My brothers? Pitiful. No general lasts in the war against his officers, the strategists – he'll never sight who is supposed to be the enemy. And who'd that be? The Americans betray their allies, insult them, make war against their friends, and bomb the few who're innocent. Communism? There's been no proletarian revolution in the world, nowhere, there'll never be.

'"Brother Mohammed must like jail. He feels safe there – he's much mistaken. The regime? Its overcoat, the party? Belonging? All regimes last eternally, and each one eats its

117

servants – that's how they keep sleek and plump. Me?" he says. "I lived between the sun and sand. All I wanted was electricity. Current all day, to make a noise, my music, and keep those miserable women quiet, shrieking like peacocks, filling the house like armies of red ants."'

'He sounds terrible,' Susannah says, giggling, embarrassed.

'Oh, I love him so,' says Danièle. 'He's so different, from everything and everyone.'

'Really?' Susannah asks. 'He sounds just ordinary dissatisfied.'

'He says, "Without the family, what am I? I'm one of four legs, the table to eat on, or the corner of the carpet. Futile. Without me, everything's impossible. We wait, doing mechanical things until we die our dreadful deaths, knowing from the start we've not accomplished anything, there's nothing in the book or in the air we can." If only – he'd write his poetry. It would shock you, Susannah.'

'You must show me, Danièle,' Susannah says, thinking how brave Danièle must be, committed to a bore – a boor – like this.

*

'He went out in the evenings, saying he felt safe at last,' says Danièle. 'Lectures – on anything. A swarm of pictures – bronze Vishnus less than a metre tall; flat bellies, many arms; round breasts. Pallavas, Kanchipuram, the Kriveri River. Easy to get muddled and bemused. "The Chola lands": they thought in symbols. A tiger, a parasol, three fish strung on a frame. I said "wildlife, sunshine, river-fishing". A tourist ad. But he identified personally – he is the tiger, calm, shaded: he didn't eat the fish – the tiger does. So he's himself – the tiger too, it has its diet, a quiet animal, you don't know as much as her.... "They were lucky," he said. "Those peoples lived before the messengers. Those messages – they bring you trouble." He was so excited – and that night, he died.'

'A natural death?' Susannah asks.

'They all are,' says Danièle. 'He wanted it for himself so's to avoid the terrible one he thought was waiting.' She weeps. 'There was nothing like, he has no copy,' and she hugs, holds on to Susannah.

'Copies lifelike seldom happen,' says Susannah, at a loss.

'We buried him at once,' says Danièle. 'People from hot countries, they go off so quick. I have to face the family – without a box or bone.'

'You may be right,' Susannah says, 'that he found an origin, no message. I see him following the lord of Dance ... except ... I'm sure he's wrong. The past is never clean and simple, there's always been an empire, a poet, a foundry. Maybe there's a peaceful city, where the tigers lounge at midday, but usually they're flayed and on the wall or on the floor ... the symbols suppose the death of living things. Maybe he looked up all his suppositions – found there was no good primal place, there's always missionaries and hunts and trade...We all die of déjà vu. There was a revival, Danièle, religion. A luscious piety. We think we'll never manage, nor survive, without some help – invisible, that comes down from the clouds. Cholas made an empire, what Walid wanted came before, was finished by the time they made the statues. Never an innocence, never pleasure for itself. Always those rituals, bronzes carried round. Research a little, Danièle – and fantasy fleets away.'

'Oh yes,' says Danièle, 'there's always us, our schemes, or else we wouldn't know. You think he died of disappointment?'

'Tamil's a grown-up language,' says Susannah. 'Poets. Those always mean something has gone wrong. Walid started with a mistake – he thought the tip of India was primal, innocent. Instead, he came in in the middle. The war, the tigers – the killing, the warrior Buddhists, and the side that would be Walid's, only he got it wrong. Forgot. Chose to err, wanted it all to have been different. It couldn't be – even a new faith, a conversion, can't make it so. Everything starts as a mistake, an explosion – he's not alone.'

'You're kind, my dear, I suppose,' says Danièle. 'Walid is finished. Most things end so, mistakes carried through from the beginning. What can we do? A bit of justice here, spin the wheel, prime the furnace, jiggle the tiller – recognise this, forget that ... bury the dead and write something over them that might do you credit.'

'I don't mean to be kind,' says Susannah. 'It's a puzzle. The Cholas had those sexy statues made from the most unsexy stuff. Metal made to last, not to be cuddled.'

'You're not in tune,' says Danièle. 'You haven't understood. Those statues, the dancers, the couples divine and not – it's life, cast in bronze, not separate things, but nobility, connecting everything, exalting it. But Walid – he was unyielding. No luxury, no self-indulgence. That India – wasn't him. Maybe what he'd like to be, have been... He could have been a Zadig, ruler of wisdom, justice – but he didn't have the time or place. King of Babylon? That would be some place invented now, out of the map. He went looking, maybe he made mistakes.'

'You're making it all up. Next time you tell it, it'll be different; and Walid's never there,' Susannah says.

*

Something of past lovers you must keep. Something – there has to be, or be invented? If not – we don't please the gods, no more, our bodies might be led out in procession, but won't be fixed in bronze, with grace, with ecstasy.

Vishnu and Lakshmi – those bodies, perfect: the distant land Walid had sought, unlike himself. So thinks poor lonely Danièle.

*

'The first thing,' Victor tells Danièle, 'is disconnect the death from the life. Then, in the life, what was known, and what you think you know. If someone is too many things, your side loses you, it loses interest. I could set you right, Danièle, if you don't call it patronising. The tigers come before the Cholas. The statues were carried round to show what people loved the most – the beauty – was offered to the deities. The people gave back what the gods had given them – the love, the elegance....'

'I see,' says Danièle. 'There's no mistake. I'm sure that's what Walid thought – though cutting out the deities.'

'But, Danièle – that would be the contrary, the opposite of justice and of wisdom. Those gods are ideas, personifications – nothing wise. Justice is a principle, and a routine: it needs the real. Those statues are art, Danièle, where there's no equity, no real. Proportion – surprising how elastic that can be. Coherence too. The balance is in the eye, no more: if the gods fall, there's no impact, no splat. Splat is often what they are about. Justice can't be that.'

'Well,' says Danièle, confused, 'are we at a dead end? Is there a fork in the road?'

'Maybe Walid felt exalted. Nothing resolved – the heart can't take it. Not wise. An unjust end, that could be just – but in a minor way....' Victor says, stacking books on a table, putting on gloves. 'Alas, Danièle, no gods, no justice for us. You could have a body like Lakshmi if you went often to the gym,' and he imagines her naked, in jewels.... How well the sculptors managed extra arms....

'You've been taught to be unique,' Victor goes on, ushering her out. 'And yet you have to fit with hordes of equals, unique too and identical. So, your uniqueness is always shaky, it needs a propping, a cossetting. The past and you: fitting in to crowds, fans, believers, clans and tribes, corporations, city lives – quite alien and unimaginable. It can't be done.

'The life, the thinking and the wanting, is not concluded by the death. The death's irrelevant, but none the less defining. The grave is mute, Danièle, the road ends, the bus, the train, falls in the ravine, there's silence.Then the noise – it starts again, the condors and the owls.'

'You could trip to see the statues,' Danièle says, unconvinced. 'Or look them up. Buy a book, even.'

'I hope you will,' says Victor, locking his struggling bookshop, and holding one of Danièle's arms.

'He wanted something you could see and touch, something not infected and corruptible you had to keep on track, every day and in every way,' says Danièle. 'He wanted to be seen and touched – admired, even. He had nothing to be wise and just about, but you could work on that. It was the rest – everything he thought he didn't have … had lost … life, the breathing. People in the streets, enjoying their bodies, the peace, the beauty, easy beliefs, easily professed. All gotten wrong? It's beyond a verification, too precarious, a wisp. He folds, Victor. I love him, loved him – but he didn't have the cards....'

'And like us all, he never will,' says Victor, not wanting conversation of this kind, that ends in families, promiscuous groups and shades of feeling. 'It's a common misbelief,' he says. 'That slaving, empire, all the circling themes, are decisive, qualitative jumps. No – they're easy, like torture, easy to start and stop. Walid thought he could find the river where it flowed quick and clear. It's all flowing water, Danièle, red, grey, transparent.'

'Yes, Victor,' Danièle asks, 'but where's the sea? Is there one? Does the river ever end or start? Should we be looking for a source?'

'You mean – what do you do with him? What's left of him? He's gone,' says Victor. 'Do you make a life for him, what he might be, have been? A prophet? Destroyer? Your intimate? Or is it you who holds the torch, and runs with it? It's all turned quite different from how he lived, giving you little, probably nothing, not speaking out, without a voice, without a message....'

'Don't be a bore,' says Danièle, pulling away. 'It's all about you, you wanting to be chalked in, on someone else's wall.'

'Remember Madame Bovary,' says Victor, hammering home. 'Suicide? Insults from the computer – quite unanswerable. Murder – a revengeful spirit, under a metre tall, coming up the stairs – vengeance? Orthodoxy? The wrong address....?'

'No,' says Danièle. 'Time. It was up. You never know, there is no tick. Only a tock.'

*

It's a tragedy, no doubt – but: against the flow, against convention, there's a reason to rejoice.

That evening, before his death, under the influence of Chola statuary – and better many gods, or none, than the inscrutible and all-demanding One – Walid had had his eyes turned round, from inner desolation, his kingdom there would never be, of Babylon ... towards a joyful optimism.

*

'Of course, I'm not antique,' says Danièle. 'This religious stuff – is just a metaphor, for having goals, and rules, and doing it together, possibly witnessing in public.'

'You have to mourn,' Susannah says. 'And then we'll have to fit you up again – a lover, that you love, or who loves you.'

'Is that a metaphor as well?' asks Danièle.

'The war down there,' Susannah says. 'Didn't he notice...?'

'Oh,' says Danièle, 'that was now – he was interested in then. There's terrible wars where he is, or was. I didn't feel I could take another body back – the women shriek so.... Besides, a tent has no address. I sent a postcard – the sea, parasols and castles. It made me cry....'

'It's all around,' Susannah says. 'You can't feel responsible for conflict, danger – it's best not to feel at all, or, not responsibly, at least. Besides – we've had our trial, we've both been low, and taken wing....'

'I love it!' Danièle says, quite shrilly. 'As if we are all – no! Phoenix has no plural. We can't all be overcooked, dead and then – up we go – rising like leavened bread! Birds! Of malaugury...' and they laugh, then Susannah says, 'Danièle – your Walid. He convinces less and less. Are you sure he was alive? Here? That he's dead – that takes no effort to believe, but a life like that – a path going nowhere, but so full of signposts! Billboards ... prompt cards – a cut-out, cardboard for a silhouette, a stereoperson, a case, made for a show, an ideal type to jerk a tear or fire a rancour, or a fear.'

'Oh absolutely,' Danièle protests. 'He was authentic. How'd I prove what shouldn't be disclosed? He'd be indifferent, say there was nothing to expose, but the rest of us – we would be compromised. It's true he had no documents, but the life went on without, although it's true, he left no monument. Indeed, he told me not to make a record, leave no name....'

'How was he, really?' Susannah asks.

'He was my lover,' says Danièle. 'I can't speak for him, of course, if I was his. Nothing special. None of them is special, no one is special. It sounds superficial...'

'Oh no, Danièle,' Susannah says hurriedly.

'What's depth, Susannah, anyway?' asks Danièle. 'Do we all have depth? How deep is it? And do we know we have it, and how much and when it works? Do other people see it?'

Susannah ignores all this. 'And he was an Arab, that's for certain,' she says. It means nothing to her, nothing particular.

'I think everyone sailed everywhere, before the Europeans came and put their voyages on all the maps, and covered all the other tracks. Then there were the armies – into Persia, and beyond. They must have left a trace, before people were so interested in listing, labelling.The scientific turn, you'd say. They must have settled, procreated, melted into other landscapes. Before the Arabs called themselves such – what would he have called himself? What kind of answer can there be to that, why do I ask?' asks Danièle: 'It's interesting. Does it matter?'

'That's not the half,' says Susannah. 'Not even the beginning – there were all those Bosniacs and Chechens: – not everybody left. It all sorts out, then there's something strange – a discovery, a drought, the water recedes, the tide exposes the variety, pebbles, plants, the shingle, that was always there but invisible. Less visible. Look at the Turks here – how long will they stay? They weren't even running when they came.'

'Not like my lover, who arrived when I was at my lowest point. How I needed him,' Danièle continues. 'And now, it's good to be alone. Really good.'

*

'What a huge house, Susannah,' Danièle says. 'I'd no idea you were in the money! That's stucco – giants and antelopes! There's trees, and barley-sugar chimneys.... Staying with you – it's like the Little Trianon....'

'Yes,' says Susannah. 'But it's not mine. We're in the trailer, round the back. We have to feed the chickens too. Then they feed us, if luck's our way.'

'He may have felt the joy,' says Danièle, 'not shared it. Or seen that everything has always been – not identical, but similar. Or – he had no home, I wasn't it. Nowhere in any case you could return to...'

'Listen, Danièle,' Susannah says, quite brisk. 'There's apples here to pick. I spy a mango over there. Admit your tragedy, that you weren't up to it. Load on some guilt, and then forget. Eat this!' and she holds out a fruit – a pomegranate? caco? Something exotic, overrated, difficult to peel. 'It happens – death by tortoise falling on your head, there's no escape, no tale so odd you can foretell. It's logical, and yet there is no logic case by case, natural, but who knows why it's all set up like this.... Let's hear no more, Danièle.'

'It's perfect here,' says Danièle. 'There's something – a smell, beneath, a bourdon, like pigs....'

'No pigs here,' says Susannah, leaping, turning the phrase into song.

'That's catchy,' says Danièle. 'You can sing it, pigs or not.'

'We'll take off our clothes,' says Susannah, 'and frolic naked in the orchard.'

And that they do.

*

'You could help people,' Susannah says, 'if you feel there's something missing. People without homes, like we might be – though that is not the point. People who are left only with belief, something you don't have – or else nothing at all, which isn't either what you have. Somewhere between something and nothing. That's what you have to offer, Danièle.'

'Oh, I believe in you, Susannah,' Danièle says. 'And you in me?'

'Offering's not easy, Danièle,' Susannah says, not knowing where this leads: 'Anything beyond things – it could be a threat. An emphasising of what they've lost and won't have again. Sometimes you're a friend, but you don't need to be.'

'You don't have things, Susannah,' Danièle says. 'It's better so. We take what we can, and leave each other as they are. Nothing is changed. We eat the fruit, and the fruit grows again, it's a procession, going on for ever. It's all that we can know, we start to see what grows and then – our time is up.'

'You have to read the ticket,' says Susannah. 'It's written there before you start. I bet you didn't bother.'

'No difference if you do,' says Danièle. 'It's cold and dark. Where are my clothes?'

They put them on, nearly identical. Dew is falling. 'Friendship,' Susannah says, 'is not a side. Pacification – peace – is a general interest. Nothing is up to you. Mostly what's lost can't be found, or has become quite useless while you search. Don't promise yourself what can't be got, Danièle.'

*

'Money?' Susannah says, 'There's fieldwork – gets you tanned. But – you take a tough and temporary job. You won't get fired – you're leaving anyway. Then live on what you've got. Train hard and stick to it – nothing permanent, you'll age and die there.'

'Let's do the training then,' says Danièle. 'Fortify me, throw me around and put me in the churn. I'll go from milksop to the hardest cheese in seconds....' They laugh. 'Something always happens,' says Danièle. 'You can eat it all.'

How white they both look, under the moon.

Into the churn with them, delicious, both!

Danièle says, 'If Walid had listened to another talk, he could have ended differently: Kazimba, perhaps: Kuduro. Cultish: opportunist – naturally! Wanting the fullness: a completion, complete integration to make the whole. No more the division between the human life and some idea, a spirit, goal unattainable ... Lived thoroughly, nothing more to say. The dance! That's it.'

He casts a gloom, Walid, his death.

'That's what he got,' Susannah says. 'Whatever you just said. All he could ever have.'

*

'Goodbye, Danièle,' Susannah shouts: she's off –

'Oh no!' says Danièle. 'I thought we'd stay together.'

'Of course not,' Susannah says. 'Though it's farewell, not adieu. I'm cook on a Japanese whaling ship – it's not a gender type, we're all girls on board – could be an old movie from the States. And you're military, I hear – artillery or flying drones....You'll have checked "assisting peace", like I did: "working with animals".'

'Oh Susannah,' Danièle pleads. 'Let's forget the money. Stay with me!'

'Oh Danièle,' Susannah shouts – they're measuring her for aprons. 'This is the hottest planet, ever. Even the communists are singing capitalism – more for less, Danièle – that's economy. More production, less wages. I need my share of it!'

'It's true,' Danièle shouts back. 'But think, Susannah – those enormous fish! Up top they have the fun – harpoons, the chase, the symbol – desire unnamable. And you – a galley-slave, cutting them up below with buzz-saws, those denizens – just think! Snoek, Susannah. Blood and corset whalebones. Then making chips for all the girls – it's legendary – a life spent peeling, skinning ... all that oil! Oil is a curse, Susannah: the forests that went down – they are our last comeuppance – a second time they burn and stifle.... The dinosaurs – they fried: and now it's us. Get in your Maserati – your stiletto's on the pedal, pressing on the metal – but however fast you go, you choke. Whereas – I've the chance of being paid to kill bad guys. What could be nobler? Safer, too. If I'm a mercenary, I get paid per strike. But if they're cunning, enrol me as a proxy – I'm the next bad fall guy, the ally who's betrayed.... Those drones – their eggs – they migrate, and they come to roost, the same spot every year, above your head, your eaves....'

'Yes,' Susannah says. 'There is a snag. For both of us. It's not just cash that hangs above our head, no pomegranate nor a caco ... nor yet a drone. It's that black light – our bad star. It's for evermore the evil fruit, a promise dangled – full of serpents and their fertile eggs....'

'Revelation,' says Danièle. 'Conversion – from the small to the inflated, from a man-sized Buddha to a pantheon: the heavens overpopulated – deities major and minor, and demis, climbing down the stairs, hungry, aroused, tuneful and not, fat, lusting.... Well – is this our destiny – the species, risking the infarct, the blow-out, fear and trembling, prostration – Stendhal's syndrome – death from eating too much sweetened culture, laced with kirsch? Look at our poor friend Walid ... his organs overloaded, afflatus roaring up his pipes, a dreadful flowering of yellow teasels, nausea, pretty-maid faces turning to the sun, all gone to seed like onions – and pouf! All done....

'You're right, Susannah, I see you with your saw – the belly of the fish upturned and – oh no! Oh, save us, innocents and sinners all! A man, a prophet stepping out, his mantle stained with bile and krill – on to the galley table. "Help me, Susannah, hide me, clasp me to your breast, absorb me; shelter I implore.... There's thousands of us in those whales, each with a testimony, a dire forebode... Humanity deserves a moratorium – stop the harpooning! Let them regurgitate and let us out, and let us prophesy....'''

How to resist the plea?

'If you're a soldier, Danièle,' Susannah says. 'You must believe your fate lies more with one side than with the other. How do you tell? The armies aren't laid out like once they were: until the smoke came down, you did a count of probabilities.... Cannons, horses, men-at-arms. No! Now, it's all hidden: motives, friends and maybe fellow-travellers, materiel, the gas, the plague.... the end, the doomsday.... It's right you look for some deciding sign – a labarum, the corbies – do they fly from left to right? It's all a gamble, Danièle. No soldier's tale, no devil's pact! Forget the pay, forget the looting, don't write your memoir, don't sing your song, and don't put your adrenalin into poetry. We'll find a decent modest life: back to the chickens, Danièle...'

*

'Over here,' says Danièle, pointing, 'are the easy places. You'll be at ease, could make a fortune as a singer – but you'll accomplish nothing. Over there – they're difficult. You won't lose your head, but everything, perhaps. Which do you choose?'

'Oh,' says Susannah, 'that's not a choice. I'll take an easy one. And that leaves you....'

'I'll look out for you always – the place I'm going to,' says Danièle, 'is not for you – but you may come and seek me out....'

'I may, I may,' Susannah says, and weeps.

*

They say the future's coming here – well, it comes everywhere, and then it is the past, but no place is identical to anywhere, when it's been.

Whether the future comes or not – this is a difficult place. Susannah'd chosen – the easy one. You have to hustle, here: it's hard.

Danièle sees Blanchine, a tiny figure on some bales. She's desperate – you'd think the clothes worn here don't need a shape, they're just thrown on. It isn't so, for some are fat and some are thin. There's more besides – she needs someone who can measure, who can sew...

The people here are tall – the arms a lanky length, the joints like bowling balls.

'If you work for me,' Blanchine says, 'talk of the future if you must – yours will have come, and it will last, it's yours for ever. Forget the working day, forget justice. Truth and beauty, exact measurement – those alone, will be yours. But – don't patronise. Bodies come in different size – it is a rule of everywhere.'

'The colours, Blanchine – they're the colours of the world to come,' says Danièle.

'They'll be winning too,' Blanchine says. 'They're racing silks – Mister Crane, he has a compound here, and races fast and slow, organic steeds and not. These are to be his winning shades, and – the losing too.'

'Oh,' Danièle says. 'I'll sew anything, and wear those clothes, go in procession too.'

'I'll better that,' says Blanchine. 'You can make them all for everyone. But there's one special person: you. It's you they won't, they mustn't, fit. You're backstage, in the gloom.'

'I'm looking for my friend,' says Danièle. 'Your conditions – are conditional. I'll only leave if we can't stay. A place like this – it would attract. The sun – so near. A friend to love...'

'Of course,' says Blanchine: and she starts to cry ... such sentiment...

'I think of her so much....' says Danièle, tripping romantic – and there's a crash. Blanchine tumbles to the floor –

'No, no!' she shouts. 'No homosex! Not here.... We're clean. We're pure, we're as we're born.'

'Then you're a bigot,' Danièle says.

'That may be so,' says Blanchine. 'It isn't logical, of course; but how we're made and squeeze out of the maker's tube – is how we want to end.'

*

Nothing to be done.

*

There's a compound, with iron doors, and scuffling, mooing sounds.

'I hear you quarrelled with Blanchine,' says Crane, a baggy expat-looking guy. 'You're brave – refused a job for life. Here, all is chance. We run, and if we win or lose – we run again ... and then again. For my lifetime, everybody's, too. Each time it's unique. Repetition – always different, supposedly the same – so odd. And – I come from hereabouts. Colour, don't let it fool you – comes from the sun. Skin or cloth – the same.'

'Some work, dear Crane – even the shovelling,' begs Danièle.

'Oh, we take turns with that,' says Crane. 'A month, a year, and then it's turnabout. We're waiting for the future here, of course. Until it comes – we play, we game, we ride the beasts.'

There's karts and buggies, monsters too: there's camels, horses, donkeys – even a yak, back in the gloom.

'Besides what's here, for jobs,' says Crane. 'There's the police, unloading stuff, and sweeping up: there's mines that I don't recommend – there's offices, there's graft.... Your work here is desirable and blessed: straw to the camels, pumping up the tires – and don't confuse the two. You doss down with the little ones,' and there they are, he's hugging them, and tickling, lots at a time: indeed they're tiny, tiny as big toys, the jockeys.

There's many tiny people running round – you couldn't guess their age. Maybe some go to school, though Crane's against – knowledge comes so fast, it's obsolete, useless to run after. Best come in right at the end, or even when the school has closed, to get the latest angle, best intelligence. That's what he says.

The jockeys lie asplay in bed – their arms and legs don't straighten out. Up-facing, open to the sky, like beetles: and down, in crouch-frog posture, motionless all night.

They sleep embraced with Danièle, and there's pricking, maybe from the straw: they bond, the jockeys and Danièle. The tiny ones – they run, triskeles bowling through the legs and wheels.

'I'll not abandon you...' chants Crane, holding up an armful of them, trying to scoop up Danièle as well.

They want to win, and so does Crane: they go to lengths and lengths. How long, how fast – and how to beat the rest. A cut across the rival's face, a nail driven in a camel's hoof ... girls and boys, they're equal, fierce.

*

Crane's aware that like Blanchine, he has no class. They're artisans. It limits trade and prices too. He can't win elections here – there are politicos above, and at the top, perched on their heads, the drivers, from abroad, with capital. Then, there's employers of cheap guys, like Crane – how can we climb the scale, he wonders....

There's Chinese come – they don't bring animals of course.

'A race!' says Crane. 'We'll use my beast.'

So, they select a powerful one, camels are best, a horse may be as fast, but then they tire, where camels run for days, grow stronger still ... and Crane selects his champion too. There's drums; and compliments to hats, and corsetting: the silks blaze out, the trumpets blare....

It's over in a flash, and half the crowd is furious. They lost. The Chinese win! Crane's camel's first – and second too. 'I've won,' he shouts. 'Won twice.'

The jockeys come in winners too, first, second, and the field. 'We've won,' Crane says, they say. 'I won! though I was beat.'

Everybody's won. The Chinese laugh and laugh.

'If you're poor and win,' Crane says. 'You're rich; and if you're poor and lose – you're where you were before.'

*

If you don't care and don't compete – life's dull. Years pass, unmarked and swift. Danièle hears nothing of her friend, Susannah.

By night she climbs the compound wall, wanders beyond the houses and the trees – meets with the dogs, hybridises, runs in the desert to the ramparts, that divide the sand from sand...

It's clear she wants to leave. The little ones, they know.

'Take us, take us,' they cry.

'And how?' asks Danièle.

'Oh, three or four, in your case, we'll hold our breath,' they say.

'I have no case,' she says.

*

'I'm a hybrid dog,' she says. 'Between the house and nature... The flock, the wolf – in nature they cohabit, and it's right in custom too – although I hear the wolves are poisoned hereabouts. Someone, not the sheep, takes care of that: the shepherd, maybe – he eats the sheep, but he could share them with the wolf.'

'I'm not about to cut you in, Danièle,' says Crane. 'This talk! Am I the wolf? You're sheep, so be content! What you do, you do quite well, year after year – and when you die, you get your pay. It's how they do it here. Your family gets the lot, they dig your grave, they raise a stone....'

'It doesn't suit for me,' says Danièle. 'Who has no family – although it might be customary....'

'Don't patronise, says Crane. 'You get your food, so don't complain.'

'I'm finished here,' says Danièle. 'I've done it all, and it is all the same.'

'I'm not ready yet to let you go,' says Crane.

One night, the pricking wakes her up. The little ones tattoo her in the dark – they can't see – it's all a mesh, blue as on a Chinese vase. It's a new concept, fashion pays, there is some cash – she buys the ticket....

Out she flies, over the pig farms, cattle ranches, over the ramparts and the mines...the sand.... She doesn't see the future in the sky. and they go north, north into the dark.

*

Vikram says, 'Pour the vodka, then when the guys are full, dance on the bar... We're short of water – so, out the back, there's bottles – not water, if you think it's water, try drinking lots – it'll kill you. Vodka: – they bring it in in little boats – they make it from potatoes – those give a special kick.'

There's people come from everywhere, some shouldn't drink the vodka, but they do. They all work up and down the street, but all have origins from everywhere... 'I'm from Kanchipuram – right at the tip,' says Vikram. 'I've never been there, and I'll never go. That's my home.'

Roy, Vikram's cook, squints at Danièle. 'Left my eye in a keyhole, don't know where, it waits for me,' he says. 'Maybe I lost it – fell down the barrel, lining up my sights, like soldiers must. So, there's a paradox. You find a target and you aim, and when it's hit, you're Deadeye Dick.'

*

'There's so much disbelief,' says Vikram. 'You'd not believe what it is I don't believe. Those gods were real – but they were made of bronze. Were there originals? Better not to ask. Only the Americans thought – 'we'll split the heavens with a bomb. See what the gods are up to there' – see right up their knickers too! See their private parts – though they're not really private – they must be public, since there's demigods and bastards – everybody knows and tells the tale. They're birds too, and clouds – even golden rain can procreate. It's the heat, Danièle – the world's a kitchen, only the food is scarce. Pierce the dome to watch the gods – and the heat will dry you up. It's always warm up there, close to the sun, and most in beach clothes, some in none. They'll all come tumbling down, the gods, and look for water; since there's been no rain, they fall the distance – there's no clouds to hold to, float upon, no storm. And they're all dry, the gods – no sweat. We'll all be finished off by then, without a sky! There would be nowhere to be gods of – except, the last one of the faithful. Naturally, I, he, has a bar. I keep a bottle, the last water for a god – so they'll maybe carry me, up to the mountain, or the hall, the dome.... Except, there's nothing left up there....'

'We know belief is hard, the stuff it's all about's ephemeral,' says Danièle. 'The priests don't make it clear. That's why they cast the deities in bronze. Some certainty, a shape: those days, you couldn't snap, or paint....'

'Epochs is nothing,' Vikram says. 'Time's a net that scoops in everything. Nothing is separate, nothing defined. There's syncretism everywhere. The Kushans – took from the sky the sun and moon, the blacksmith from the Greeks – then there's Nana, Nanaia, all the rest, and Buddha too. The gods start off as other things, with other names. Things a cow might rub against, or that you could hang a hat upon. You try to fix them, your beliefs: the six systems of salvation – hard on the tongue, but try to practise them.... Tally the spiritual, and all becomes mathematical. Sixty-three of other things: that's tough! Then there's the poetry, goes for years, and not a line to be got wrong or blundered. To follow them, better objectify ... it's best to see them all, ducks in a booth, being carried round in solid form.... Ah, dear Danièle – faith is itself a suffering, before you start to look outside – the guys a-sleeping in the street, corpses that burn....'

'Even without the gods, there's suffering,' says Danièle. 'You could be king of Babylon, Vikram – but if you've rockets anyway, who'd build a tower up to the sky? That's the truth, but no one cares; you can have innumerable truths: it's justice that is never there. Would justice end the suffering? That's what they say, but if equality's a part of justice – when they invented gods, the people said farewell to their equality. As for the kings of kings, they mde a hill so high, you can't see to the top of it...'

'There's two ways out,' Vikram says. 'From suffering. There is the bomb, that splits the heavens, ends our life, and everything – the suffering too. Then, there is capital, the cash to end the pain. But if you read about the working day, you'll know the money's not enough, not ever; it's a serpent, swallowing its tail. You never end the suffering that way. The bomb is best.'

'Cash, though, is to be preferred,' says Roy.

They never closed, and every day sees customers prance in, recuperate – then wilt and fade – some can't return at all, and some rebel...

*

'I've never been in such a situation,' Danièle confides to Roy. 'No pay, no help; the drunks – I should be happy here, I'm not.'

'It's all subjective,' Roy explains: he winks his eye. In his pork-pie hat, his mustard weskit, and his salt and pepper pants – he is a cook become his condiments.

He tells Vikram all that Danièle's said, and they share a laugh.

*

The band's innocuous – marimba, *ondes,* lutes, and some trombones. The dancers glide or stamp, some cling, and others sway alone, there's incantation – and despair. There's no way out, you just go round and round. You think 'Vienna' and you wheel, you wave your arms, but no one comes.

Danièle says to Vikram, 'Roy's your friend, I know. He's always hanging on me – good for him, I'm sure. But he's sinister, and persecuted. What he says – it's beyond the limit.'

'I'm sure it's just tauromachy,' says Vikram. 'The bull fights, but it's not his show. He must be wounded – the more it hurts, the more he turns aggressive. And in the end, of course – it's steaks. They cool him down, or else the flesh, dead flesh, is tough. Then – it's the end – some of the applause is his.'

'He's master of his eye, his I,' says Danièle. 'It isn't lost – it's just the first of two. You lose your eye, you keep your I – even with no eyes, you never lose your I. But – what's the fight?'

'That's it!' says Vikram. 'He's a warrior. He has you in his sights, that's all. He cooks things – maybe me, and maybe

you – it fascinates.... He fights, it must be good – we don't
know why. He is a harbinger. Is he the bad we live with? No
need to eat his food. To me – he is a friend.'

'You're strange too, Vikram,' says Danièle. 'Though I
think you're quite a friend....'

*

One evening, there's a punch-up in the bar – men and
women, indiscriminate. For them there is no motive
necessary – everything's for fun.

'They'll close us down,' says Vikram, taking down the
breakables, the strobes, the glitter balls. Roy takes a tiny
trisul from behind the bar, and charges like a bull who has a
bandillero in his eye. He roars, 'The blind – they get
accompaniment – a dog, who is their eyes. With one eye
forked, you're half blind, best lose the two, so you can see
what your condition is. Blindness – is knowing already what
there is to see. Wall-eyed – you'd need to feel your way, but
when you reach the wall, you know it, however many eyes
you have, or may have lost.'

'I thought you lost your sight in keyholes, Roy,' says
Danièle. 'Oh no,' says Roy. 'A fork, a fork'.

He parries someone's knife. 'Yes,' he shouts, 'I was right
and royally forked. I had my eye on paradise, and ended with
the knives and forks.'

'Distract the crowd, Danièle,' shouts Vikram, and she
climbs up on the bar, undulates, she's left her breasts and
buttocks where the staff hang up their things – she's a long
blue cobra, wavering. She's calming, and a threat.

'It's just a ritual,' says Roy. 'It's like the keyhole – all
depends which side you're on. We're always hungry, we
Bengalis, because they made us so – the famines they

constructed for us. Being a soldier – it's no use. You're always hungry. And Empire, it's no help – all's rituals.'

'I hate rituals,' Vikram says. 'And Roy – you've never even been there, just like me. Be careful, don't fork the customers, and don't patronise: invent, exaggerate.' He sniffs the air, as tigers do. 'Burn resin, to drive out the energy the dancers left here.'

Danièle wonders, 'Is there another shore, another side? What would it mean for me to find it, and be on it? Swim towards it? How did those kids, who didn't move at night, put those tattoos on me, and I never woke? Maybe it was driving monsters, gave them the touch – and now I'm blue, I have the blues – a Berber, a Touareg – and yet I'm not. I am a vase, I'm hard, and if you break me, you'll have all the troubles of the world, at once, and on your head. Me – I want no luxury, no new machines.... And Roy – is trivial, and he's terrifying. He ends here, in the kitchen, no one eats his food, that's all *he* does....'

'Didn't you want posterity?' Vikram asks. 'All you have is ending, or soon will – you think it goes on forever – you slough your drab skin and hang it on a twig, and in a little while you grow another – a new drab skin.'

'Oh,' says Danièle. 'I don't mind the colour, not so long as there is something different. I've had training, I can ride a beast. You have only faith, Vikram, faith that you'll be honoured, that you're right, that you have origins however much you might deny them. It isn't so. You're cheap and superficial.'

There's peace, and everybody drinks.

'I saved the bar, pay me my hours, Vikram,' she says.

'Oh, hours are long and short,' he says. 'And some can last for days. Here – this is clean – goodwill,' and he empties out the mug for tips, into her purse.

'This is the end,' says Danièle. 'Though nothing finishes.'

*

'My friend, Susannah,' says Danièle. 'She must leave a trace....'

The guy, Ivan, looks at his tiny screen – there's smaller topless pics, with grins.

'Here she is,' he says. 'She's in Ukraine I feel a thing for her before we're there.'

Ivan is always truthful, so he swears; but – 'You're born with beauty and the truth,' says Danièle. 'You can't avoid. It's justice you must seek, and never find, along the way. To be optimistic, you can't hold people to account. You don't forgive, you just ignore.'

'I foretell, says Ivan. 'But I can go backwards too. In Ukraine – they're poor there, stuff's cheap, but it's not what you'd want to buy. They won't thank you either, just because you're rich.'

'When we arrive, we'll all be rich,' says Danièle.

'Going from north to south is best,' he says. 'Here it's the top – it's all downhill to everywhere. But you must concentrate. Nothing is easy, Danièle,' he frowns, as he's counting out her wad, his fee. 'Even drinks.'

*

'Oh, a train,' says Danièle, 'you get there quick, as quick as if you fly.'

'I hope not,' Ivan says. 'We work the train. Each compartment has its group, its speciality.'

'I never heard that,' says Danièle, 'and yet I've been on several.'

On the train, there's bound to be new, mature, public and private – capital.

'The guys here,' says Ivan, 'Berliners. They had poetry: "how long the journey is, how slow" – *wie schön ist noch die Welt...* They even caught us in a line Danièle; here's me – "a blind tiger, a converted warrior". A *"blinden Tiger ... ein bekehrter Krieger".'*

'No', says Danièle, 'the warrior was Roy, Vikram the tiger, possibly. I was converted, but it doesn't count. I exclude myself.'

'Well,' says Ivan, 'you see! Your past is everyman's. Here, they lost their souls. Ours were destroyed, with everybody bombing everyone. My friends, they slip a soul to me when I'm in need. It's grey, small as a button off your pants.'

Under the samovar, there is a tiny spirit lamp – he lights it: vodka.

He says, 'There's vodka and there's tea: if you take round the tea, you have to learn a word: it's *chai.*'

'I'm not a cretin, but a cretin could learn that,' she says.

'Forget the handicaps,' says Ivan. 'Take the tea. Compartment one – there's Chinese. They have capital, but don't give tips. I think they're mean, they think they're tough.'

'That's fine,' says Danièle. 'With tea you get goodwill, with vodka, there's largesse, but insults too.'

'Then there's the communists, they smoke cheap fags. No tips, on principle. Compartment three – New Age, and four, the movie moguls. Some have had their time – but if we stop, it could be days, or centuries for us. We'll all age the same, be moribund. When we reach the end, we'll come right back. The cops think that's just fine, it does their work... Mostly, they bring their own booze and pills, but they are generous...'

'Cops? I have no document' says Danièle, terrified.

'It's of no consequence,' says Ivan. 'Write on this manuscript – ten words, I'll know exactly what you are. I'll show the cops my topless pics, and they'll be satisfied. It's clear you're terrified and not a terrorist – nor warrior, proxy, undercover guy, nor shyster, hacker ... none of those.'

'The Chinese in compartment one,' says Danièle. 'Suppose those bags contain not capital, but hucksters' stuff they plan to sell....'

'There's worse,' says Ivan. 'In compartment five, there's soldiers – taking no vodka and no tea.'

'They may be on a side,' says Danièle. 'It could be yours. How'd you get rid of them? Besides, they may not know which is their side, nor tell....'

'I have a side, of course,' says Ivan, 'that I hope would win – and yet, the long term ... history, making a balance, creeping towards a justice, maybe ... religious patina and veneer ... it could be better if they lose.'

'That's crazy, Ivan,' Danièle says. 'No one wins a race, gives back the cash, and bets on all the losers afterwards. Even the truth can let you down, that's true, but when you bet, you hope your nag will win...'

Ivan pulls himself up, long as taffy, then bunches down like amber. You see – he isn't warrior, he's cook. 'I hedge,' he says. 'That's my belief. That's how I shall be here when you have quit the train, gone to the maelstrom.'

Trains stop in nowhere, and at stations too – but, they never terminate – when you get there, sit tight, don't leave, and then you're back, wherever, as if you'd never gone.

It's summer, but when the cops come on the train, there's guys who jump, and run across the snow.

'They paint the birch trees white,' says Ivan. 'In case the people think there's silver there. Maybe there was, and it's been melted down.'

Everything is white, but some is cold and some is paint –

'You think it's all coincidence,' says Ivan. 'You think your life is lucky chance, but no: you meet a person, becomes a

friend, they stroke your hair, they steal your purse, some die.
In all the world, you think it was for you it happened so.
What a coincidence – 'that I was there, and you were too....'
Not true. Things seem coincidence because there's limits to
the universe, things are duplicates, they resemble, but there's
no design. Nor is there chance. Chance supposes an infinity –
if it's out there in space, it isn't here for us, in our street, our
rabbit's foot, our worry beads. Think that way, you can be
optimistic – nothing is random, nothing repeats. Chance
doesn't win a race, your jockeys will have taught you that.'

*

The German poetry, she thinks, the tiger, warrior – herself:
nothing. It doesn't mean a thing. It isn't personal at all – it's
just a tale of what the earth is made of, what is in your head,
and how invisible force has some plan for going on for ever.
How and why? You get bored with all the false discoveries,
forget about it, leave it all to simmer somewhere...

*

The soldiers sit mostly quiet: sometimes they sing.
    'We must preserve them,' Ivan says, 'but impotent,
suspended in some sauce...'
    'Aspic, says Danièle. 'Plum cake. Or kipper them – the
commies' fags, the smoke...'
    It's useless. The train's stopped – it could start up, and go
off anywhere – they have no sight of where it points. It could
just stay here, waiting – deus ex machina, they say – the
spirit from the engine, picks up power, moves on.
    'This way, I shan't find her, Susannah, even if she's here,
the train,' says Danièle. 'Or there – Ukraine.'

She dumps the dented samovar, its handles amputated long ago, the spigot dribbling cold. The tea's been changed to vodka in compartment number one: no cash in number two, and three and four have mingled and they're signing things... Manifestoes ... contracts probably.

Ivan would like to send the soldiers on, to fight – for the flag, and for his mates – and yet, it would be better if they lost.

And yet again – they must be fed. What would appeal? 'Why, cabbage rolls,' says Ivan. 'Everyone loves those. And Polish sausage, the purple kind; a pasanda: chizhi-pizhi – that's my favourite. Then if we move on, the pinenuts ... clarify some butter, Danièle!'

'I'm hungry all the time,' she thinks. 'We're like those monsters, vegan lizards, who eat all the leaves they reach, then starve.'

'Black bread and caviar,' she thinks. 'Those scarlet mushrooms, my! how beautiful, but – better stick to lichens and to crawling things.'

Ivan is right, the train's not territory – it's rather gut, intestine. Stasis. This is no place, no thought of places a and b.

Danièle's as happy on the train as she has ever been. It could be the happiest she'll ever be, safe in a nowhere place. It's time to leave.

*

Danièle drops down, runs towards the trees.

In the wood – the soldiers don't see her: they are notching bark or doing exercises, staring at their screens. 'Where are we?' Danièle asks a soldier – he doesn't answer, he's a proxy; some guys in cotton pants are shivering uncontrolled. A boosted voice says 'The wood – is no longer there.' It's true, it's flattened, there is marsh and stumps, and Danièle wades to where its edge should be.

The house looks edible. 'Come in,' the lady says. 'The oven's on. I'm making cookies. Are you alone? No little friend, a brother, possibly?'

'I'm looking for my friend,' says Danièle.

'Most people come by here,' the lady, Lili says. 'Their journey never ends... I give everyone a face – but since the flood, there's some whose features blur.... Who knows where they end up, what's their journeys' length... They finish in the water, just a few metres, long and deep – don't go near it, it will do for you, my dear.'

'I know my journey ends in water, with a death,' says Danièle. 'That's how you start, and so arrival and departure are the same.'

'I see from your tattoos, you've been in jail. And did you join the gang? Susannah too? Being your friend is deadly, Danièle, it's dynamite,' says Lili. 'Come in – there's many guys a-chattering here. But first, go milk the cow...'

It's dark and empty in the shed: there is no cow.

'My lover must have taken it,' Lili says. 'Go try the neighbour's, he won't mind.'

'I'm so hungry,' Danièle thinks. 'I'll eat some cookies, have some milk....'

'I had the tattoos done when I slept,' she says. '– all superimposed, those little jockeys, so mischievous – a tangle, a mesh, though I got some cash for sporting a new fash....'

She looks into the house – although it's small, there's hundreds there, in uniforms and suits, with cases, folders you wouldn't want to read.

'I need my friend,' says Danièle. 'But I can't describe...'

'How did she look, and how does she look now?' asks Lili. 'It isn't memory you can rely on. Our time – is a design fault. In heaven, they've a better version, so that when you're made, a wrinkled mouseling, you coexist with what you become also as an ado, and what you are right now. The Maker makes a living sculpture, that's all ages, whatever is its date... Come in, we're here to sort things out... Borders and flows of people – we've the generals, people who draw maps. They were crafted in the same way too – you see them here as infants, youths and warriors, grey, some blind.... I'll bet the same *fabbro* crafted their briefcases too...'

There's a long table made of precious shiny wood.

The countries here are bumpsadaisy, all hugger-mugger. The house is on four boundaries, four nations. Here, they hope to sort it out, the flow, the rule, the settlement, the way things are and shouldn't be – although this time round there's only exercise and threat so far. The fight – is always possible, the way to sort things out.

Lili says, 'We're waiting for a captain Sykes who stopped the Syrian war....'

'Nothing will change,' says Danièle. 'And they're tired and hungry too, those generals ... and me...'

'You're right,' says Lili. 'Even the good guys here have atom bombs. But the people, Danièle – they must have their say: they're all inside, better informed than you, fired up, enthusiastic....'

'I am the people. The others don't always see it. I must get on, to Ukraine,' says Danièle. 'My friend....'

'Oh stiffen up, Danièle,' says Lili. 'Didn't you do boxing in your youth? You're soft as yogurt. And you're old, you droop all over, legs are bowed, the spine's a snake.... Will you be welcomed there, I wonder....'

She works, Danièle, she cries. Is hungry.

The cow is nearly empty.

'You're a good person, Lili,' Danièle lies. 'You could set the house on fire.'

'Nonsense,' says Lili. 'The house is in my name.'

We'll never know if she is good or bad.

*

There's smoke rising from the house, cooking goes on ... or arson. It could be.

Danièle decides – her friend is more important – anyway, with all those soldiers, she won't get to eat: she leaves, she wanders on.

*

At the station, you wait for your train as it comes back, if it's already passed ... but, what a surprise!

'Susannah!' shouts Danièle –

'My, what a coincidence!' Susannah says: 'I'm here to meet another person absolutely, who you have never known or heard about! I never thought I'd see you, Danièle – one makes the silly vows of friendship, then forgets....'

Susannah is much smaller than she was, her hair's gone blonde, if she's a singer by profession it makes no difference to her voice – it's rather shrill, and in Ukrainian, which Danièle can't understand....

'The train is late,' Susannah says. 'There's soldiers, and we hear there's been some shouting – or it might be shooting. My friend .... I fear for him...'

'It's never Ivan?' asks Danièle. 'Now, that would be coincidence. You, topless on the screen – we'd both recognised at once....'

'Oh no, Danièle,' Susannah interrupts. 'I'm not like that. And – it's not Ivan – he sounds a risky type...'

'He is, he was my friend,' Danièle says. 'The catering biz, you understand. It's quite hierarchical...'

'If there's deaths, there'll be a procession here,' Susannah says. 'It lifts you up, more grief, and then....'

'Oh,' Danièle says. 'I love the colours and the gold. Do they hold up those silver hands?'

Susannah cranes up to see the popes – she turns to Danièle. 'My! It's been fantastical, to meet you here. What a coincidence. I must find news about my friend....' And off she goes, following the cross, the other symbols carried round...

It's disappointing – but there's crisis. Where there are soldiers, there is always a confusion, they don't give news – they make it. Danièle expects no more. Poor Ivan – if it was him who suffered – a good friend, like the others she has had, their problem was a meanness with the cash, her cash earned, not paid and not acknowledged. But otherwise – all revealed their philosophies, their aspirations; if that's a mark of friendship, they were friends.... Ivan, Susannah – Walid long ago of course.

There's still a drama – Susannah, smaller, older than she was, joins the procession, goes chanting off the scene. If Ivan has been hurt – the train gone off the rails, the soldiers too – that would surely be coincidence! To lose two friends....

Everyone is up on tiptoe: beside her, there's a guy, a little sly, maybe, but alert, maybe a bad sign, worse, he shakes her hand, it's 'Yuri'.

Now, why wait in this shabby building? Does news come here fast, and nowhere else?

'I'm preoccupied,' she says – and Yuri tells her that she's safe. 'You're not in line for sex work,' Yuri says. 'You're old, and blue. But I must lock the door. Keep quiet – if the cops come, they'll think it's empty here....'

'I have no document,' says Danièle. 'But I am innocent. It's just that I'm a foreigner, that's not illegal yet....'

'Of course it is!' says Yuri. 'There's people quite abundant, we need capital...Our people leave, there's few like you who sneak in, no documents, no job... And then you went to Lili's house....'

'I milked the cow,' says Danièle.

'That's the most important thing there was,' says Yuri. 'Most culpable. Providing comfort....'

'Was it my friend,' asks Danièle. 'That Lili? She's told on me, and sold me, and you want the cash from selling on?'

Friends, she thinks – they are like water ... when you're thirsty, drink it down, as otherwise it goes to make the sea, undrinkable, and drowns you too.... Water – will take me: better not dissolving in the earth, but gone as if I never was.

She thinks – the only person asking nothing – was Roy, a mystery, a master of the paradox, himself a prime example: resister, patriot of somewhere, half-blind warrior: a spicy root, inscrutable, for soup.

Roy – a bad element? She didn't ask, he was a colleague, a boss; good and bad they don't come in but she's curious, takes it all in, peppers it up. Yuri for sure is bad ... something's wrong in him, in all of them, with how they see what is around.

'If only I'd Roy's fork,' thinks Danièle, 'I'd pick the lock, go from this place that's easier than some but difficult like all of them.... And Ivan – best if you're not sceptical like him, it doesn't help. Maybe a quiz from soldiers on the train, and then – his uncertainty's resolved: a bullet where you can't resist....'

In this room, empty but for knife and fork, you have to wait – she thinks they'll maybe come to feed her, or ... the fork's a trident, and she thinks, a cult implement, Siva, death, salvation, 'I am close to both of those.'

'Poseidon! – those Kushans never saw the sea, but Greeks in Bactria, how they must have missed it, cried, and worshipped rivers by default...' She pokes the fork – the keyhole's big enough to let it pass, and there's a yelp, the door is open – on the stoop there is no one, no I, no eye, but tears – 'A pool of tears,' she thinks – 'Mustn't fall in,' and yet the liquid spreads; it makes a slough, slough of despond, she thinks, it's like perfidious Lili's marsh... For certain, Yuri's not a friend, and if his eye is lost, he forfeits it by spying on his fortune, his captive ... income at least... 'Where there's eyes, there's spies,' she thinks, and maybe they're collected in a tray like – Einstein's brain was sliced and sliced, those memories of underwear and owls all scrutinised in case the universe was hidden there. 'My brain will go to mush,' she thinks, 'and better so, than end in that Soviet collection of them all, Lenin's like German sausage, white and veined, perhaps a better revolution lurking in the crease ... collectors know you must hoard everything because the passion's in the last, the missing, piece that gives a sense to everything... They'll have trays of them, brains,' Here, she remembers – she saw that white cube, 'Institute of Brain Studies', an immense six-storey cabinet. Trays and knives.

Still, she shed no blood, no sacrifice to be rejected or approved. An eye, an I despoiled. An act of self-defence, no more, the jailer, the surveillance – they do anything, and so can you. One thrust, you're on your own and out... She's free!

She is confined ... in an uncertainty....

There are processions, popes crossed up, their chasubles like in a game of battleships, but Susannah isn't visible – 'Quite probably it's good, – in God we say we trust, but the gods did for poor Walid, moving from the peace that equality is supposed to give to Muslims, no comparing of your body to the rest, now on to something more precarious, with bosses over you you must obey, and priests, like my friends have always been: – his was just an aesthetic choice, was it? –

those cunning bisex nipples, smooth bronze the skin, the vestments, and – were there flowers? – what women fear is torsoes, the upper body muscle-threat is always present, women being the inverse: – men's arms can pin you down, the bottom weight of women not much use except for carrying bags of lime, all fifty kilos of it ... sides of pig and cow.... There must be beauty somewhere,' thinks Danièle – 'but truth and wisdom, justice too – they're not it, not beautiful at all, not like Walid had wanted it.'

And she's out! Another country entered, indifferently, and she's free, with all the world around her, everywhere: and nowhere on her compass. So small now, her hunger fines her down, so she can creep beneath the wire.... There's vegetation, thick – it was easy leaving Mister Crane, the sand is smooth, you fly over it like on a camel running, but here you crawl, you sink. There's water, a foretell that you don't need, and shapes of ruined buildings, barracks, underneath your feet.

'I'd have died for Susannah,' Danièle thinks, then smiles as she remembers them – in the orchard, naked as mushrooms or as cods. 'You'd think Susannah'd have a memory of that, worth giggling for with me.'

*

Returning the way you came – there's the turf roofs of cowhouses, Lili's conference hall still smouldering. An old guy with a pitchfork – Lili's neighbour or her lover, could be both, a set of cowhorns on his head, he points his fork at Danièle. You don't know if he's good or bad.

'Exactly where you're from,' he says, 'is critical. Not your beliefs – the values you profess. Those, the right ones you must have. We, for example, we believe in courtly love, our scholars' wandering.... It's not much relevant, does not impinge. Yet – you're still unknown and unexplored: I see you rising from the marsh, like love-lights... Tell me your story, abbreviated, plausible....'

'Didn't you steal Lili's cow?' Danièle interrupts.

'She never had a cow – she took her neighbour's milk,' the lover says.

'I'm just a wandering waitress,' Danièle says. 'I don't mix with independents, owners – I serve cooks.'

'Let me explain,' says Lili's lover. 'Here, we used to have big plans, but they were to be realised through big wars, and those destroyed the plans.... So, now, there is no plan – there's peace. If you like – that is the plan. Vendetta is no more, everyone's tattooed, but not according to a clan ... and yet the people here won't pay for peace, there's hundreds coming in, like you, and dragging countries after them like skins they've shed.... And us, we feel the itch to fight again, do awful things and then repent.... And Danièle – no one's tattooed like you – all over, I would bet....'

'I know,' says Danièle. 'They say I am unique. But this here is a place I've always been in, even when I went away.... I was a child, here or hereabouts. Born without beliefs and values. Sometimes, though, you have to leave – your work, your room, vibrates, like there are tectonic plates all on the move, and you have to budge. Right now, the earth, it starts to shake again. You wake, and unadorned, you flee. There is a limit, though. I can't go to Babylon, to see if there the king is really just and wise. A flight to China, that is possible, but I hear it's hard there, very hard.'

'You may have seen the gatherings we have – like clan chiefs, or those mafiosi in the past,' the lover says. 'But I doubt that you'll be asked to intervene....' He peers down inside her blouse – 'You're blue, my dear. Sex work is difficult, no doubt....'

'I'm happy as I am,' says Danièle. 'I have my friends, my work – I'm always on a trek to find some more of both.... But, tell me: to stay here, what must I do, believe ... expound my values. Are values part of my belief?'

'It isn't that,' he says. 'What is required is what you do, the work, how much, and if you look like one of us. Belief's not interesting, it's inside, and you can lie. Let me guess: I bet your friend saw that the universe is quite indifferent. "Do the exercises, and believe," says the philosopher, the guru – then "If you can't believe, be good." I'll bet your unquiet friend settled for the beautiful. How long did that serve him, Danièle, your Walid?'

'An evening,' says Danièle. 'Not much, but I don't think more would make a difference. If you're an apostate – an hour is quite enough. Now, what work do you propose? We all start off with none. I used to keep the animals content and running smooth, the monsters too....'

'Oh, screw the animals,' the lover says. 'If they can't live, then let them die. We'll live on cabbage rolls – they give you everything you need. The animals are even more indifferent than deities, except – they need us: look, you've leeches on your neck...!'

It's true – Danièle is brusque with them.

'Beauty,' he says. 'A mistress terrible and cruel. Worse than bigotry and misbelief – and you see it everywhere if you are not alert. Sends you to jail, or hanging from a tree. Lili had it once and lost it – now it's politics for her. Who gives a snuff?' he laughs. 'Beauty – look! Don't touch. That's the rule – those little gods, for instance – just a metre high – could be kiddies: five or six, I'd say. Made to be fondled, cossetted.'

'It's an angle, I agree,' says Danièle, losing hope that he would give her work. 'Oh dear,' she thinks. 'Beauty and sex – I hadn't thought ... that link!'

'Don't stay here,' he says. 'It's desolation. You go in procession all the time, to stop you touching it, the beauty....'

Danièle trots round the hummock where Lili's house is built. Maybe the cookies are burnt. Maybe captain Sykes has not yet come. She hesitates – no work and no friends here.

'Gay Paree...' she hears the lover shout. 'There's a cult of beauty there... Go!'

She's not convinced, but – why not? Her plastic bag was left on Ivan's train – the water weighs her down, but that will dry – 'I'm like those ascetics in cartoons,' she thinks. 'Cut their rock house down into a sliver, then amputate themselves until there's just a tongue, wagging in the sand.'

It will pass – the blind tigers, the wounded warriors – they'll be put away somewhere ... they called the Russian soldiers samovars, when they lost their arms and legs – there's a destiny for everyone, their causes just or for the moment, undecided.

*

'Even something criminal,' says Danièle. 'Nothing hands on, but just to tide me over. Receptionist – for a boss, perhaps. Counting the cash, even – making his borshch, his carbonara or his egg and chips.'

No one is listening, besides, here in Paris you can't do a simple dish – though *rillettes* would be a treat.... One thing, thinks Danièle, that doesn't go away – forget who you were, and what we did together – it's hunger.

*

At last the station – if you've no bag, no ticket, on the train they put you off at every stop, you try again, it's very slow, but in the end, stop by stop ... it's free. You're there. Try it.

It doesn't always work, of course....

'Maybe it is you we're waiting for. A someone aged by moving round, waiting – for the future, probably. A mal d'Afrique? That, or some agèd lady from Vietnam. The tattoos are great – they cover all that's been. We can pay cash,' the tall guy, Alain says, pulling her into an eatery and ordering her *rillettes*....

'I worked for someone who owned and also trained the racers,' says Danièle, feeling much at home. 'He never lost.' She never tells what went on inside the compound – those rapid bodies, rapid lives, her own part, why Mister Crane was so attached to her – but then, she never talks of what went on across the land, the disappearances, the crowds with sticks, the cops, all that... It's past – and if there's curiosity, it's written down – she's not a messenger. She says, 'But – what's the job?'

'The job is doing what we tell you to,' says Alain. 'Now, about ourselves. We were New Age, Ryan and I – the new age never came, so now we're movie moguls – like the mongols off the step, attracted by the cooking smell – ah! the pasanda – and we left them all the architecture that hasn't crumbled down, the pillars – marble: pink and veined in white.... Now we make movies, India style: it explains why we've so much cash, make odd requests. We give a hand to wounded Tigers – they're our extras, if you understand. Not all are blind, of course, though it is true, there's many poets there. Takes centuries to write – those Tamil epics... Blindness accompanies that trade, of course: your memory is always better than the real,' he says, paying the bill – with a huge note, seldom seen, but irridescent ... 'because you wander aimless in the real and never see again what you remember.'

They enter through iron doors – a kind of compound: 'It's a converted *passage*,' Alain says. 'Paris had its day – as world of capital, they say – like the US, before it fell apart, retreated into enclaves – though that's the future of the world.... Enclaves. A club in there somewhere, a claviger, and old boys, old bonzes in armchairs...' Still foretelling, Alain stops to fondle a TransAm, battered and rusting, doorhandles off, wheels too: 'Ah,' he says. 'Once it was TransAm, racing coast to coast, and now it's Trans – the movie we've sketched out. An ending: overlooking China seas, crackle-glazed and blue and white. Move with the time, you've no alternative, the days are gone when motors could outrun the years... best movie ever made – you remember – fork in the throat. Then in the eye. The blood! The tears! And then the starlet quit he should have fucked – we were all waiting – and so they had to change the end. There was no end, of course. What genius! What luck!'

Ryan, instead, is almost mute. He stares at Danièle, and doesn't speak. Nothing's known of Alain, though he talks a sacred river without pause, but without a word, Ryan tells all. Alain kisses the top of Ryan's head and says: 'He was in the best movie ever made...'

*

'Cooks incline to anarchism,' Alain says. 'But, you're promoted, Danièle. You're a slave, but no more a servant: we can still pour our own drinks, we've still our arms and legs. We love Paris – Rome is so provincial – but here you must do everything yourself. That's why we call the outfit "The Mohican". The last – it shall be first. Everything is up to you. The prejudice all round – you find it helps. They leave you on your own.

'We do science, poetry, crime and cookery. It all pays well, but all you do, Danièle, is sit here at the desk and channel all requests to one of our directors...'

'But,' says Danièle, 'it looks like it's all you two. The blinded Tigers, all the others I see here – they can't be much use.'

'Aha,' says Alain. 'You see well – it means you'll have spare time, and so, I told you, the job is doing what we tell you to. Aside from being mostly blue, you're also white. Ryan – who got his colour straight from Africa, the sand, and me, who had to go to Philadelphia for mine – we are the generals, out of sight. You are our flag, white, that shows there's nothing here to hide.'

'People are curious – when they see you, they'll go away. It's ridiculous, but it's life: nothing to do with colour, but that can't be changed! As the song says, "Everybody's looking for something": that made a fortune, though it's rather trite. Or is it "for somebody"? – that's worse. What the people really stroll about, asking, peering, looking for, is the bit that makes the money. In the songs, it's always the arrangement that makes the hit, and it's what people never hear. You're employed, anyway, Danièle, to soothe their curiosity. You do the simple things, the planning, execution. If you hesitate, there's him –' and he points to a large Ganesh by the door. 'See, he has two tusks, no one has whittled one to use as pencil – he's all new, ready to be used. Any problem – ask Ganesh, don't bother us, especially if it's guys in uniform that call....' And Ryan cracks a smile at that.

All day, it seems, Ryan watches a screen, skimming tiny sums from accounts somewhere, like working at the checkout in a supermarket. When he has huge sums accumulated, he shifts them round and starts again, more tiny sums. They must be rich, and Alain talks continuously – how to use the money to cook, to drive, employ some Tigers, a trans; to use a fork, to film 'a sex scene held up till after the last – the final credits roll and then – there is the scene, with almost everybody watching exited. The ones who like the movie –

they walk backwards, watch the screen go blank, then see the sex. Those are the ones who'll star in our next hit,' Alain says, his face aglow with genius.

No one comes. Danièle is bored. 'Excellent,' says Alain.

Danièle thinks, 'These are days of Brahma. Brahma's hundredth birthday is tomorrow, bikers up the Champs ... then we wait more billions of years for another lookalike of Brahma to appear. A successor who does much the same. More tedium.'

'The days drag, Danièle?' asks Alain: 'Ryan's delighted with your work, your silence. It is quite inspirational. You're a quiet dog, watching what moves, better than the cameras we can't instal. Cameras attract the crowd. He wants this to be a frozen point, in a universe where every point is still, eternal – equal to every other point.'

'I understand,' says Danièle, thinking of the hectic days pushing the samovar in the corridor, before Ivan's death, his being taken hostage, or maybe giving orders – and to who? Bandits, terrorists, contractors – that's for sure, but who exactly? This fixity – could mean she's for ever in the first hour, not Senior's last – the first, which can't ever be computed by accountants, paid for by the boss. 'At least, you could give me cash,' she says. 'I could eat outside, once at least, a couscous, instead of cooking from your cans.'

'It's an awkward moment,' Alain says. 'Cash is a bit off these days – we're into other metals, alts, wooden tokens – titanium, some tin alloys, or river gold, even nacre: leaves....'

'Even that,' says Danièle.

'You have to find some other guys who'll play with you,' says Alain. 'To use your money. Not easy – these French, so snooty....'

'The movie,' says Danièle. 'At least, tell me what it should achieve.'

'Oh no!' says Alain, turning pale. 'You haven't understood at all. Philosophy? Aesthetics? That's all gone: the explanations, making a land with beautiful people, their docile animals – harmonious and all true and good.... all those disappeared when idealism died. Suicide and murder – fork in the throat and eye. You can't create a land, a happy one, they're all already there, all different. One has black lizards, another, flowering fly-traps – neither swims, and so they yearn, yearn for each other, or for any kind of food.... I know you're always hungry, Danièle. Idealism – that was the universal food – with a side-dish of metaphysics, or cruises on those great economic seas – the waves! the regularities, the logic – tides and swells: those Austro-Marxists! Then, when materialism tried to be the daughter of idealism – and died by its own hand, on cellar steps and in those camps – then, they tried again, to build some provinces of meaning. Maybe those would lead again to unity, communication – a universal language, even friendly to reality... New novel, new age, the auteurs' cinema.... Nothing, Danièle. Curiosities and peepshows. Philosophy was – it still is – dead, the messages simplistic. Fritz Lang and Fatty Arbuckle – much the same. Camp-fire stories, that is all.

'We do our Bollywood – a cheap and serious parody. Everything is teetering – into parody. The musical. Who's waiting now, anxious, for a revelation? My dear – we've given up. The driver now's invention, new machines – whatever may turn up.... Technology determines all. The genres, their publics – each runs, tires, finds a desert, dies of thirst, exhaustion... While you can see them still, down there, moribund and morituri – from your drone – they're enclaves! I told you. Guys piling in, each with their two cents: life, oppression, transit, migration, hope born of misery, some humane slant... Everyone's involved – .ready to fight and sure to die... Ephemeral! Hypocrisy! No unity, and no

autonomy. Is there a Veda underneath it all? A first account,
a primal understanding? Rude potent deities – the earth,
Danièle, the growing seasons and their death? The Ur-
condition? – sprouting philosophies, dealing in numbers
freshly named, touched for the first time.... Rajahs and
maharajas, mathematicians, pure guys wearing nothing, times
immense, all to affirm the attributes of potentates divine, or
semi-such. Gossip from the clouds: who snatches back a
trisul, who trebles up a role – guardian of warriors, keeper of
prisons, dweller in the rowan tree? There is an origin, you
say; we need to know about it, return, even inhabit it. When
the first embers cooled, the lava made a blob, a roughly-
round – a unity, and then the sons and daughters came,
roiling, stabbing, coupling. Some claimed to be divinities, but
mostly not: profane, now dead and irretrievable.... The earth
solidified, but they brought – chaos! Maybe we all hear one
unique music still, a throb, an echo of a voice, a melody, a
rumbling, played in every style and scale, on instruments of
bone and gut.... The species' first exposure, the first day and
night, the première, the gala. Much sought after, the tickets –
but so what? If it started simple – it's not simple now, no,
nothing is. Who cares, if there's some beginning, inaudible,
that mystics strain to hear? It's meaningless, Danièle; there's
no philosophy, no truth vital, original, forgot. Don't make
yourself look silly, seeking one. There is the real, that's all;
the new age comes and goes, all in a night, then there's
another, then some more, they live short lives, all
simultaneous and discreet.... It's good. That's what there is.
Be humble. Humility's the only hope: it's optimism. All
elaboration's a mistake: pretension. We all went wrong, we
started wrong, we keep on going wrong. Does it mean we
have to start again: taming of animals, figures drawn on
rocks, re-invention of the playing card, perhaps.... Do we get
it right this time? Or is it just the same....?'

Ryan turns back to his screen: he's listened, an exasperated smile ... he says, 'You're incoherent, Alain. Write the story, get the guys together, rent some stars – if really you're convinced it's worth another go ... remember what happened to the last.'

'Oh, yes,' says Danièle. 'I am so curious. Do show!'

'It was the painters,' Alain says. 'They got it wrong, made it unwatchable. Then, in those costumes, the ladies couldn't do high kicks. The philosophy was there, of course – eternal return, but after some hours, even that becomes a bore. This time, we'll do the casting from the pack – so long as they can kick their height... we'll stripe the music on another time.... Should you be in the movie, Danièle? I have my doubts – you're so morose, then there's the catering to do ... a credit hangs on that as well.'

'I am in doubt,' says Danièle. 'My sadness – I don't know if Ivan was my friend, and should be mourned....'

'The vodka man?' asks Alain. 'Trains do stop, they must, and have to start again. Dead or alive, it's more important you decide if he'll come here and trouble us....'

'That's exactly it,' says Danièle. 'What is he? Where? Just tell me, will the movie help?'

'A quest? A journey? Make it about him, Ivan – a bandit chief? Victim? Secessionist? My new age past lets me put all that in – but it won't help at all,' says Alain.

'You've no idea, what it's to be about?' asks Danièle, shocked.

'No,' Alain says. 'It will go on until it makes its point. Emotion and sacrifice, bad guys and big events.'

'Imagine – couscous for hundreds,' Ryan says. 'That's your task, Danièle, and your reward. We'll use the whole city, its people and its streets – that way it's free.'

Alain whispers, 'Ryan – was in the greatest movie of all time – alas, he was the bad guy, not redeemed. How'd you get over that?'

*

This might be the *passage* where the 'young, beautiful woman' called Labsolu worked – without philosophy. What she does, has done to her – it doesn't need philosophy – the point is cash. You can hear the music of the Opéra from here.... It's central, clients of the better sort. It's been looted, this *passage*, but it's recognisable, it's where they traded everything, wandered up and down in it, a refuge ... all luxury, the shops, the gloves, the strass, the novels, fans – and Labsolu.

'Talking of philosophy,' says Alain. 'Labsolu was in charge, the principal. She was the boss. The problem was – you couldn't call them happy. If that was the goal – they missed it. Happiness was what they called "a fantasmagory". Boredom assailed them – dense and clammy – with the rain, the fog, the traffic. The spectre prowling round was – eternal return. The everlasting subject. Instead of what seemed eternal novelty, they saw everything was "existence as it is", without a sense or aim. The production of quantities – making money, but being one of thousands, millions – of similars. Winning, losing, the same people. Millions – in the bank, and in the trenches. Millions. Of bodies.

'The trouble is, Danièle, you fit in here so well with us. You have no story. You could be selling gloves, instead of being cheated like you've always been.'

'Oh,' says Danièle. 'I'm used to it, don't bear a grudge. I'm lucky to have you, bossing me. If you're like me, you live in metaphor, if you've the luck. You can ignore the other people who surround you. Most are worse off, some are the shepherds who are fattening you, living off you, until one day they eat you. I'm not like that – all I want is friends, preferably friends who're good. It's not been easy – but it's useless to bear a grudge.'

'You haven't understood,' says Alain. 'I'm thinking of the movie. Bodies for sale, the rain: the resignation – people coming in, being cheated, being bored... Then the song, the dance. Mmmm – loving those long flicking legs.'

'You could pay me,' Danièle says. 'Instead of inventing tales, those new expedients, those coins.'

'Yes, we could,' he says. 'Of course we will. But: everything – it's in the script. The glass, the marble – that went long ago. There's dirty walls and motors, now, with graffiti. We'll get a high class star to play the prostitute. An aria in the front seat – a trans in the TransAm. Labsolu – more than a trans – the versatility that means, in sex and all the rest – everything and nothing. Everything not fixed – is nothing, but it can be – you understand, Danièle? – anything you want and everything you didn't know existed, that was waiting for you, inside you, but in the air, the trees, the smoke, the breakers. You're inside, outside too – your skin feels, is felt... She knew about the Absolute, but she wasn't it. She was an artisan – you only find her, her absoluteness, abstraction, in a movie. It's a length, you jig it, denying time and place, it's nothing, nowhere, and you pay to sit and watch what's more real than you. Abstraction, the over-arching presence – it's quite simple, but quite hard to flesh it out. Start and finish – but no bones and blood. It isn't a gadget, an item, gratification, what you want; it's what is there for you and everyone. For sure – you'll never recognise it....Forget it, Danièle. The actors – they're well-read, friendly guys. You could pal up.'

'It's feeding them, I guess,' says Danièle. 'That is my part. Dates, milk and couscous – it's in the Qur'an, you can survive on them. Remember, I want to find a friend who's good, remembers me, and doesn't die – at least, not the first day.'

'We have to clean our money,' Ryan says. 'Do two movies, Alain – one, the musical. The other – the refined one. The dull one, that grips. If you prefer, weave the two together, have the same crowd appearing in them both. That's new age – if anyone remembers what that was.'

*

Ryan says they need more warriors. They can rent an army, out East – put them on ponies, have them make their return, eternal, from the steppe. Singing. Palling up with the Khwarezmians – all those women, fearful for their jewels, eager to find a warlike friend....

'Leave the ideas to me, Ryan,' Alain says: 'But – if they're at peace, soldiers are adaptable: I guess you can dance on tanks, a sequence. Singing on horseback – like Siegfried?'

'I've told you, Alain,' Ryan says. 'Don't toss everything in. It shows you know less, not more. People are ignorant, but they're snobs – one reference they may recognise – more, they feel humiliated.'

'Something without beauty,' Alain says. 'Without beautiful people. I see it clear – beauty for the market: what's it worth? Labsolu? Where is she, when you're having your expensive screw? I think she's untouched, pure, the cleanest prostitute you could meet. Even if she's not – you still have the Absolute – that's pretty immaculate. Of course, there's a chance you're wrong. I love it, chance. That's what movies should be about. Mine are – the others – aren't. Your Ivan, Danièle,' he asks. 'Was there around him – a border, a trim, a foulard, shawl – of beauty?'

'Him? More a sallow rat-face,' says Danièle. 'A poor body, too.'

'Well, pass over it,' says Alain. 'I see him none the less a charismatic. The assault on the train, the Trans-Siberian, of course. The trip takes seventeen days. It could be a series. There's the divide – the branch that goes to Vladivostok, the other to Beijing. We need to bring both in, but – that way they're of equal weight. No drama. I see a process, followed by – explosion. Russia becomes a vassal state. Maybe Ivan has a thing going with the President. A touch of sentiment, of cuddling. China ascends – I'd put in a reminiscence of Kublai and the Yuan. We see the actual Chinese ruler and his squad: – they topple. Then, there's the Mongols' revenge. Ivan – I hear him say to someone... "I'm so sorry..." I wonder who he's talking to, what's that catastrophe: and what becomes of Ivan....? Who's the Genghiz...?'

'It's interesting,' Danièle says, reluctantly. 'There's lots there about eternity, the empire where the sun will rise, return, and rise again, as every day it does – maybe it's an opening for the sequel. The Americans, you have to put them in...'

'There! There's the nail,' says Alain. 'The twist, the prick. Finally they realise – their weapons are unusable – they would kill us all. And kill them – probably first off. Their strength is suicidal.... I realise it's a reiteration, but guys forget. The world goes on without America, they are muscle-bound, stuck in their armchairs....'

'If you could pretend, discover it, naively, for the first time, Alain,' Ryan says. 'It could be brilliant. But – as you tell it, it's a dish gone cold; it's bits of other movies.... Of course, you're right: we can go anywhere, do anything. We're giants, in your nutshells, germinated, starting off. Just wait, Alain, until I fix the cash. Your idea – in our minds still....'

'So it is,' says Alain, wistfully. 'And we never know if there is good or bad, or if anybody is....'

'The army doesn't come in much,' says Danièle. 'It's wasted. If it were me, I'd make a story of us here, in the *passage.*'

'We don't know why we're here, or what will happen,' Alain says, pouting, unconvinced.

'There'd be emotions, though,' says Danièle. 'A puzzle. But solvable. Time passing.'

'Our emotions?' Alain asks, laughing. 'We'd need to root those out. Dig for them.'

'Desires,' says Danièle. 'Those hats, gloves, and fans: things made of tortoiseshell, jet, nacre. Little bottles, tiny boxes for pills and powders. All beautiful, too expensive for me – obviously I don't make them, but I long for them. I sell them, they're under my hands all day... That's love, a love for life.'

If there's not nothing, there is something. Alain's setting is almost nothing: you grow to love it, depend on it, the powdery land. The animals – they forget their destiny, and they love you as you guide them to their food, the green. Even the dust storms – they're your movie screen ... the train, making steam, coming round the bends – of course, there are no bends... Even, you can love the big Chinese cities in East Siberia, the last symphony orchestras there, still playing Brahms. The secret – they have it: making commodities by means of commodities... What we once knew.

It's Alain's world – Ryan is staring, sitting, at the wall.

'Pay her, Alain,' Ryan says softly. Alain hugs him, kisses the top of his head again. He hands Danièle a bag – it's light for coins – unlocks the iron gates.

When she's outside, she looks inside the bag: they're leaves, poplars, it seems – quite apt. Normandy – red skies?

*

'No one cheated me,' she thinks. 'Even if they did – I'm clean. I left, I'm myself. Friends will come and will be found. No one depends on me – that's good, that's very good. Having enough to eat ... that's where you start....'

*

When there's not much that you can do, in Paris, they're keen that you improve yourself... There's lectures, videos – the French have a notable stock of stuff – they looted it for centuries – from Egypt, also Algeria, deeper into Africa, and India, China, Syria – they killed a lot of people getting it, every one, each cadaver, was worth it, and if you have an academic bent, or if you want an evening keeping warm, it's special.

There's cops, of course, looking for people who might be angry about things, but Danièle is only interested in the culture and holds in tight, anxious, even fearful, that she'd be swept away like Walid, that she gets sucked in and dies that night.

The cops aren't so concerned with talks and artefacts – they look for submissive types, militants, humanitarians, isolates and groupies. They look for activists, obsessives, people related to other people, people from afar and people from the street – it's absorbing work, and if you get it wrong, there's deep deep trouble for you. They don't see Danièle as a terrorist, or as anything at all. She teeters, naturally, not to the political, but crime, there's always openings – most everyone would profit from it, if they got it right, there's no course to take to show what you're most suited to.... She isn't interested, not at all, in making points. Besides, she's small and getting old.

'Ibn Rushd, Al-Mawardi and juridical thought'....
'Treasures of Pondicherry....'

Cops? Of course not! Then ... who? Who's listening?

*

'No, I'm not French,' says Danièle. 'Only the name has the accent.'

'You're here, then, waiting for a tuktuk,' says a tall guy, Leon, coming from the slide show, laughing.

'No,' says Danièle. 'I'm here, fully, no other place in me. All I want is to be free to leave.'

'If you've no card,' says Leon. 'You're nothing, or a slave. Climbing up the legs of someone, if you're lucky.'

'No,' says Danièle, moving away. 'No submission. I haven't found my equal yet.'

'Much beauty, in a conventional sense: some truth,' says Leon. 'In lectures. Don't look for justice, though.'

'It's about obeying good laws, the wise king. Knowing it will pass anyway, and that he or she has title,' Danièle says, fearing a trap. 'Anyway, if you protest and land in jail – it's way too late.'

'I may have some work for you,' says Leon, tiring of the justice question, and seeing Danièle is carrying only a light rustling bag, no document.

'I hear it! You come from Africa,' says Danièle.

'The future's coming there,' says Leon. 'I don't believe in all this identity nonsense – you come from somewhere, you go somewhere else. You sign up. Give a word. Need a document: "take a card, any card", so long as it's the ace of trumps: the less you, and they, know about where you go, the better....'

'I come from Africa too – in that way,' says Danièle. 'I had friends – they're lucky, they don't need to leave. They can't.'

'No tears,' Leon says. 'They're poor there – and you're poor here. It doesn't mean a thing. At least there's lectures here – if you're there, there's lectures too, about Paris, and its treasures.'

'I know,' says Danièle. 'Those poplar leaves won't take me far. I'm always hungry. But – it's the contact. My friends – they're artists, they know me, for always. They have worlds under their hands. They don't make them, but they sell them.'

'That's the point,' says Leon. 'I get hungry too. I help people – for money. Their worlds aren't interesting – there's an infinity of them, I'm not involved. And they've left all of them, the worlds.'

'They're here?' asks Danièle, feeling stupid.

'No,' says Leon. 'They're there, but they're free, they see the future's somewhere else – Kosova, Mali, Kurdistan....' he continues, a long list. It could be any time, and any place.... Guys who've left and haven't moved.

There's rows of neat books – nrf, Gallimard, Minuit, Pléiade, all cut, it seems, and in decay, the pages going cookie yellow, cookie brown, then flaking off – fragments like potato chips. She's hungry. She reads a fragment, '*le cerf broutait l'herbe d'enfer*'.

'"The stag was grazing on the grass of hell..." Where's the rest?' she asks.

'Oh, poor Max, Max Jacob. Conversion didn't help at all,' says Leon. 'All's vanity. Vanity. So it might seem.... I often think my work's a pebble dropped in the well, to see if there is water there. Of course, water might be poisoned. Or if it's just a hole, no bottom, no end, a well of silence....'

There's shelves of history, poetry, and architecture, the mathematics of each, jurists – some Assyrian – and folders – 'Personal Pandects'.

'What would my job be?' Danièle asks, though she would rather eat. 'People who leave find there's a legion of guys who help and take their cash.'

'Oh,' Leon says. 'The guys I mean – they don't know about documents and places. They know escape and refuge are illusions, that if you leave hell, there is another hell you stay in before you reach another place, and that could be the third hell, then a fourth.... If you slough your skin and leave your horns – maybe you graze. Otherwise....'

He sits, lies, in his tall chair. 'See,' he says. 'I don't spend the cash. It isn't current either – no matter,' and she sees the notes.... Sun Yat Sen, his face – Sun, Stalin, and swastikas, guys in suits and guys in caftans, guys with pens and guys with swords....

'You see,' says Leon, growing faint. 'They don't want another place. What they seek – is justice. That's what you must explain. If they come here, and speak to me.... I shall explain, and then they pay.'

'And get justice?' Danièle asks.

'Oh, you do rush on,' says Leon, laughing, coughing too. 'First, we deal with truth and beauty – easy, but they've maybe missed them for a while. Then, we must distinguish – my, our, justice – and life. What you might call chance, coincidence – is really life itself, which doesn't recognise those abstract things, or rules outside its own, even if we still do, a bit. Truth, beauty ... and justice. It sounds last century, I know.

'Life blunders on, Danièle, it doesn't give a fuck for what we do, or what may fall on us, erupt as buboes, eat us up within. It doesn't know the good – but there's a good in that, there is no devil either. Hah! you say – what's capitalism, then? Part of life, natural, indifferent; or entered in our special realm? Protagonists will say it's life, it's nature, so we cannot judge. Then, there's the others: "It's run by men, so it comes within the rule, like all the other ways of making cash, staying alive."

'Justice is hard: even if you say "What's just is not what's just for me, but specially what's just for you, and maybe everyone...." Well, Danièle.... Is it justice? What you say? And what I say? Is that what's so difficult to resolve, just by our saying?'

'It interests me,' Danièle says. 'Like the movies. But they cost so much. And with justice – I've never got further than your questionings.'

'Mostly, guys who ask,' says Leon, growing faint. 'Don't move away. They do other things – take arms, go to jail, or wait in patient suffering.'

'I select, then,' says Danièle. 'The guys who seek justice. Explain there may not be solutions, no happy place, no document. Or if there are –'

'Yes,' says Leon, turning even paler than before. 'The solutions may be in the Pandects here.'

He tries to move, but he's immobile, weak.

'They're so beautiful,' says Leon, faintly. 'The towers ... the places where all the people gather. Brick, terra cotta – structures immense, cracking, resisting, converted ... Wisdom, Danièle. That's why there's people there. They seek. Not Holy Wisdom – I don't find that adjective a help.'

Danièle forgets her hunger. She says, 'Then you – you, Leon; I recognise you! Your discourse, and your laws. You are the king of Babylon!'

'There is a line of us,' says Leon, turning grey. 'A line of infinite length. But, yes – we are the kings of Babylon. Wise....'

The word comes out – a whistle...

'And maybe just,' says Danièle, thinking to humour this old guy – but ... too late.

He dies.

*

'These goddam lectures,' Danièle says, looking for cookies. 'They fire up weak organisms, the guys croak. We are as we were.' She remembers Walid. 'Where does love go, without an object? Is it all remembrance, even as it goes along, tramps its road...?'

*

She said she's interested in that stuff. The king, Leon – he's passed his task to her ... she's nothing better she has left to do....

There's no kitchen here – he must send out for food.

The banknotes say, 'Promise to pay....' more notes...

Ah – here's a voucher. 'Two for one', it says.

'I'll have the second one,' she says.

The guy brings eats: the box says – 'City of Peace'. It's good, she finishes everything, and dumps the box.

She could shelter here – but there's the cadaver, quite a noble one. Best not be caught with that.

'Economics,' Danièle thinks. 'That was an interesting point, though what's to do when you decide: – is it nature? Or us?'

*

'You can sleep in the kitchen,' says Abbie, her new friend. 'But don't touch the food. And don't forget to take those folders when you leave.'

They're not mine, Danièle thinks, and yet – they're only mine – they're leaves blown to rest in my hair, then they'll journey on ... to ... What's that place called? Ur. The beginning, the original.

'You should go back to Africa, Danièle,' Abbie shouts, as she sets about the many things she's not doing well. 'It's your "elsewhere", the other place you look for. The other person in you.'

'I don't have origins,' says Danièle: 'My life is not the mirror of myself. I walk in and out of it, the frame – sometimes I'm there, and it shows nothing. When I'm not there – it holds my picture.'

Abbie hears none of this. She's noisy, and it's good, in her. She thinks of Danièle as someone who leaves Africa, comes to die in Europe, maybe doing business, selling dangerous things, explosives, salt – things people have killed to have, and things that kill you....

It's not like that. Danièle rejects nothing, transgresses because it suits, no place is poetry, there is no spirit that you must seek out by voyaging, making a fortune, risking, courting death because you've done the rest.

'Yes, Abbie,' Danièle says. 'If you mean the Touaregs. They're in a hard place, that they can't leave, they'd disappear. I have no place. I'm not ready to disappear....'

'Well,' Abbie says, 'I love you, but I can't have you living here.'

'That's how I feel myself,' says Danièle. 'You're right – a season in hell for both of us. A winter.'

'I've many friends,' says Abbie. 'So should you – keep your distance, and they'll help you out.'

'It seems I have missions,' says Danièle, laughing. 'They collapse, but on the way, I'll have picked up a friend.'

*

'Abbie will have told you,' says Salar. 'I'm close to her, an acquaintance – and you were a friend of Leon – poor, poor Leon... An omnivore. Come to nothing, with no one. No one to close those eager eyes.'

'He trusted me,' says Danièle. 'It was his choice, not mine. He died because he couldn't unravel justice... Frustration, obstacles, a fear of failing, then ... dead end.'

'Yes,' says Salar. 'He shouldn't have gone there – he was a jurist, every jurist tries, and can't find, justice. It's like those mathematical jousts. Everybody tries, there even is a prize, and when it's accomplished, everyone forgets. Everything's been said and written about justice – there's no solution. It isn't lost, and it has never been found. It's not a puzzle to be solved, it's quite discursive, quite political.... Leon set out laws. It's that which interests me, if he left ... some leaves...'

Jurists wear blue raincoats, long and ancient, you've not seen them since you were at school, and mothers chose the clothes, hand-me-downs, jurists' cast-offs. Danièle conceals the folders: 'Laws are easy, Salar,' she says. 'Every place needs two sets – one to go by, and another that is what you want.'

'That spare is what you need,' says Salar. 'Not for one place only, but for many, if not everywhere.'

'It's something I don't know about,' says Danièle. 'Law doesn't interest me, and it causes me great bothers.'

There's not much in the folders, no revelation.

She peeks inside – a page in each, 'lex dura', one says: 'do as you were done to...', 'Hammurabi? check? ....' 'be done by as they wish' ... just scribbled.

'After family,' Salar says, 'it must be friends. Family is necessary for the start, then – enough. They are a heavy weight, and interdictions hobble everyone. We have been wonderful, Danièle. The steppe, the desert: we sculpted memorable lives, made marvellous cities, crafted songs.... Then, it started winding down – the alien empires, they arrived, the wars, the oil, the potentates without remit.... It's time to break away. Already there is talk of where to go when all's been eaten up and mined – and here we stay, in stereotypes, with family rules, customary laws: it isn't viable, it's stuff for lectures, not to live.'

'They say you can find hosts of friends – they're all there on your screen, if you have time...' says Danièle, not much convinced.

'Oh,' Salar says, 'that's Proust. Real people jiggered into phantom dress ... words they've not said, sexes they've not been. Alas, poor Leon – he was a nostalgic type, but he saw we'd need new institutions, reality, fresh laws that served us all.... Unlock the women, Leon said: "Bury the stuff of lectures – all the sayings and the faiths that were not said and mostly not believed. Stick to 'treasures' – those stand, even if they wobble.

'"They led you on, the wise men, they pushed you out, into the dark. They said if you would trust them, open wide your eyes, you'd see the dark was light..... The idea was to celebrate 'as if'. As if there was the best and truest, if you believed.... tiny, but still a possibility, that smudge on the horizon not the campfire smoke, but – the tower of Babylon, with its king, kindly, wise and just... *Slava, slava, knyaz!* Shout it out – long live the kings and queens! If they're deposed – try the bearded ones, the wise men, wise monkeys.... Just journey on. And on."

'No, no, Danièle – if you've been taken in, forget all that. No friends by chance, but always by design. No cynicism, no commands off-handedly diffused, to obey until the death; no loyalties undeserved – no, Danièle. Nothing left to coincidence or chance. Reason and reflection.... Something for everyone – no more particularism, spotting a king here, queen there....'

He carries on – Danièle is amazed, shocked to hear the wise, just, king so summarily dethroned.

'You shake the structure of my optimism, Salar,' she says. 'Maybe you're right – it may be time for something fresh.... they'll call it heresy, a revolution.... But – I've a past. It's all I have. That, and a corpse slumped in his chair, a brain that maybe held our laws, and now – lost. Deleted. Damaged: error irreparable, one lecture enjoyed too much....'

'Are you sure,' asks Salar. 'You took all the folders? You didn't bin some when you'd ate and dumped the box?'

She doesn't know. 'This stuff about space colonies... People like you who want to live out in your own space the time that's made for earthly clocks – it's all a genre that I don't recognise...' she says.

'Oh, Leon went all over everywhere,' says Salar. 'Harar, where I first met him, and he'd given up on poetry. Bukhara – where his music finished, Damascus – where he just got out in time – his time, of course, and only saw the world we'd made in lectures, sitting in the cold....'

'It's relatively warm,' says Danièle. 'If you've nothing more. But all the sci-fi stuff – more colonies, more aliens to displace ... looting and shooting, Salar, who wants that?'

'I was there, in California,' says Salar. 'By day – the laboratory; and by night, in movie studios, painting monsters, raking sand.'

'They'll be making lists,' says Danièle. 'Of people who'll go. Or people they would like to send.... I wonder if I'm one of those....'

'You may be,' Salar says. 'I'm not. It's an honour, they say, to be shot up – with a touch of suicide and life imprisonment. 'Cast into the desert and beset by devils...' remember that? Except there'd be no temptation. First, up with the soldiers, in those suicide suits. Then the mining engineers. Then explorers – topees and bearers too.'

'I've heard all this,' says Danièle. 'It used to be in cheap *bd*'s, kids' comix – then it got taken up.... Would this mean that when we dock in second earth, we were a different species, selected special, wafted off the globe, set down in all difference from what there is – or there is not? Evolution starts again – a new environment to be graffito'ed on.... Or are we just colonials there?'

'I think we'd be the same as now,' says Salar. 'That's my point. It's a pain not worth the suffering. Be sure they'll take those videos: treasures of the earth.... Crying as they watch, filling those fishbowl helmets with their earthly tears....'

'Everybody knows,' says Danièle, 'the world will end, and we must make the best. That's where our optimism lies. But – we thought it would take years...'

'Oh no,' says Salar. 'They are hard at work. If the maths is right, it could be Tuesday next....'

They laugh. 'Then, those guys who want to go right back – to re-run all the feuds and heresies,' he says. 'They're right to see the end, but there is no return, eternal or just one-off. Of course, they have their history wrong: their time is out, a fiction, but, most of all – the earth won't be renewed, can't have second editions, or remakes.'

'I always laughed,' says Danièle, 'thinking of those martyrs in their caravelles, cruising on for ever in their void, all alone and shrivelled up, still going when the earth is dead – as if Columbus, sailing on, had fallen off the edge. On and on he goes, the buffaloes, the Cree – all disappears, he never sees *Blade Runner*, never goes to a drive-in, joins a gang, sees Buster Keaton, *Hellzapoppin*.....'

'The only place to go that's viable,' says Salar, ignoring her, 'is on the moon. But – that's already dead, worse than what we have to perch on here: it's much smaller – a barren annexe....'

Where'll he let me sleep, she wonders.

*

It's a van. In California, it's quite the thing for playful space explorers ... they have other possibilities, of course.

'I live here. Home?' asks Salar. 'I've never been there, though it's where I come from. In the movies, it is like the moon. The moon with camels. Dust, horizons. Unforgettable, moving, so beautiful.'

*

'We can't get anywhere,' says Danièle. There's no cooking. She's glad. They send out. 'Nobody knows us, we can only travel, move around.'

'That's good,' says Salar. 'We two are different anyway. I know a lot, and on top, I am unknowable. That's good. After booze and other stuff and sex – the unknown part is precious. What I do know – is not a comfort. We come after, Danièle; everything tried, emotions extinguishing. I know what was before: maybe it's different for you. What's next? Us? You and I? I hear hooves and half-tracks. Dust and smoke. Fight as heroes, or fiddle and strum? We'd look silly as a band, us two.'

'I wanted to wear torn clothes and swear,' says Danièle. 'Then it was "Great guns, unawares, shook all our coffins as we lay."' They laugh.

'When I found the working class had seen its moment pass,' says Salar, 'I thought it best to join the non-working class. It takes intelligence ... or you die. But – the van is mine. You'll find it really rocks – five times a day, I do my

exercises – my body ... it is worshipful. My line, those
forebears – is honest, but obscure. Unpretentious. You might
say, eternal Goths – the gothic bricklayers of Babel.
Cementing the infrastructure, while the justice and the
wisdom buzz overhead. Maybe you should find some work,
Danièle. My project....'

'No, Salar, wait!' says Danièle. 'Not your project. I might
cut you in on mine. It's clear – you've no idea where lies the
key to what we seek – in a vase, a cabin trunk, even a
commode ... instructions on surviving in the happiest
mode....'

There's no threat – the project that she doesn't have
involves going out to find the menace. That should be easy.
Salar though – he chatters, listens to old rock, and boasts.

He's empty, thinks Danièle: he doesn't want to open up his
box.... 'There's no solution, nothing is coherent, nothing you
try to do is fixed....'

'Yes,' Salar says, 'life is a tragedy. We look for folders
and – surprise! – they're skimpy. So – I prefer to sit here in
the van – if you want to see a fight, starvation, cholera, or
just have land stolen and be bullied – it's easy, Danièle. Just
take a flight and pay some guy to run you in to there.'

*

Sometimes Abbie comes; she and Salar quarrel, shout, then
go in his bunk.

'You want to live in Beirut style,' says Danièle. 'Me, the
old wife, Abbie the girlfriend. Me to tell stories ... she to
scream....'

'I've concluded,' Salar says, yawning, 'the road to justice
isn't through the law. Unless you hid the folder, Danièle....'

'We can't go anywhere,' says Danièle. 'We're up on blocks. You have the recipes, Salar, but won't throw the spices in the pan.'

'We could go shopping,' Abbie says. 'Like when we met. But – we'd quarrel: I like that, but you don't. Ordinary life, Danièle, it's passed you by. You prefer your tales: "fork in the eye"! Wonderful!'

'Of course, I'm an obsessive, Abbie,' says Danièle. 'But if you look for wisdom, you find friends, perhaps you're happy too....'

Abbie doesn't hear, or maybe she can't think how to react. She's not family, not to Salar, nor to Danièle, and even if she were.... 'It happens on TV, Danièle,' she says. 'All the action worth seeing and feeling for. And you don't have a set. So....'

*

'If you're leaving,' Salar says, 'take your spirits. Unless it's them that's calling you...'

'There's some I'll leave – the ones everybody knows and fears,' says Danièle. 'The crab, the horned goat, the archer. I'll feel free, at least, of them.'

'I'll work on those folders,' says Salar, 'though I think I'm free as well – the law won't find me here.'

'Living rough, with rough people – does it make you tough?' asks Danièle. 'To end up here, I must be soft. Best go to Georgia, live to a hundred and twenty years, then find another body, a young one, that can leap and walk: jump into it – and maybe walk to Babylon... I won't live in Tbilisi, though, and nowhere to do with manganese. No mines. Everybody's roamed through Georgia – amazing there's some Georgians left, or coming back. Abkhazia, perhaps, is more evocative....'

'Salar is lucky,' Abbie says. 'No one knows where he comes from, what he believes, why he's cast out. But – devils are made to be cast out, and they're always dangerous. So, maybe he's a devil, and he gets a space – not respect, just room, and fear. But you, Danièle, you move around and everywhere you're different, a foreigner, a miscreant, a woman of the streets, a woman – coloured, dirtied, yet you speak an unknown language like a toff... You're what they call an "object", like a stone cigar that's not a meteor, nor comet – but you leave a trail that frizzles out. Never quite employable, never quite indigent....'

'Oh yes, Abbie,' says Danièle. 'I do need cash! Now! You never know if this adventure is to be the last.'

'Then you don't need money, if it is,' says Abbie briskly. 'Be careful of the metaphors you live in, Danièle. Kings are exiting, Babylon's a Yankee parking lot. Everybody's punished – justice would be just too much on top of that. Just say you wander! – that's the truth, enough. Is there a purpose? There's your stories – you should learn to tell them better. You're soft, so you won't fossilise, no one will puzzle you out, Danièle, you'll leave no skeleton.'

*

No one believes I'd go to Georgia. But here I am, thinks Danièle, on the bus, with Georgians. I suppose I must eventually speak to them. I'm studying the language, when they were present, before they were scattered, and came back. Except. Except the book is heavy, and I understand Colchis and Iberia, but the words start to fall off my lap, the Asomtravuli script, which looks like coming from somewhere else, and here's a sentence in old Tamil, 'He brought distress and her body lost its beauty' – and well, how true, and how Walid would have laughed and learned the phrase, the bastard, and there's another lurching of the book, and 'I'm going to Georgia so's to live over a hundred years.' But I shan't stay...

'I'm learning many languages,' she says. 'Now, if I had a Mayan dog, I'd call it "Pek".'

'No!' says the guy beside her. 'If you had a Mayan dog, it would be called Pek already, or more likely tsul...'

'But you can't call "tsul!" even if that's your dog's name,' says Danièle. '"Pek", though, is easy.'

'We don't now speak and write in early Georgian,' the Georgian says. 'Nor believe in the second coming, or that a monarch can be persuaded by our prayers. Those are sentences, but we served our time ... now, it's all just – only – us.'

'I plan to move to Babylon,' says Danièle, feeling important and stupid. 'Like a word; slipping from person to person, till I get there....'

'Yes, yes,' says the Georgian, laughing. 'But we're on a bus – not a rebus! Only one place, one thing, at a time. I know you'll say "it's in the book" – and there it is, moving along, you too. Like everything, in its way – it's true. It moves, all moves. And, of course, you know the wise king's been long gone, his wisdom too, his tower knocked down, by rockets, and in any case – it's all sexist, what you say is true and what you're looking for is true and non.existent, and much is cultural appropriation too....'

'Of course,' says Danièle. 'I'm against all that, naturally. But – where do I go? Where do I look?'

The Georgian asks to read the book. At the next stop, he gets off, taking the book. Enters the lavatory ... you never know, some pages may come in handy. Danièle waits – he never returns, never takes his seat. 'He'll come back,' Danièle thinks. 'It's typical. Not long ago, Tbilisi was populated by Armenians....'

The bus moves on – 'Pek!' shouts Danièle – she sees an old-style dog, a chow, almost extinct, a cloud of orange fluff – it looks away, and she thinks – 'the wisdom of the king – that's extinct too, for sure.'

She scrambles off the bus – 'You're unwelcome here,' the driver says. 'And it's the same back there...' But back she goes, back to the city. Nothing accomplished. They say that only what exists is true – but what Danièle says – that's true too.... What's true, then – what is, what isn't? Both?

'I'm hungry,' Danièle says. 'And that's the truth.'

The Babylon she's going to – it's not the Babylon there is. She's right to get off the bus. There's no book, no lexicon, no morphology. The city Voltaire evoked – did not exist. A joke – everybody knew: no one expects to laugh. The original, that *did* exist: but it's been rocketed, don't bother seeking it.

*

'It's temporary,' Danièle thinks. 'These seem the people who've exploited me, but here they've all been punished, they're in the holes they've eaten, they are weevils, omnivores – we're all on mattresses like life-rafts, eyeing one another to see who we'll board and eat. All raw, you're not allowed to start a fire....'

It's tough – you make a group by sex, language, country and religion – and Danièle's been everywhere, and prayed, and spoken words quite promiscuous – Akkadian, some Urartian – for use, in Babylon, and all the way down, she thought, maybe she'd have found some commonality passing through Baku, a chat ... how comforting. 'What I requested, the gods gave me,' and I sat 'on the paternal throne of kingship'; you need to know that turn of phrase. Too bad the book the Georgian took – it had no map, 'what language, where.'

Maybe Hurrian would be more practical, she thinks, But when you travel, you don't hope you find what you had sought, but rather that what there is should be more interesting....

In a group, you are attacked. If you're a loner – you get hit. She knows too much to join a group – best feign some ignorance, be hugged and taken in.

The first night, someone pronged her in the eye – probably a fork, and probably there was no intent ... not especially to blind, just hurt: but there's a good side, you have another eye, that's what they say, and that one's full of wisdom that you get when someone puts the other out. She thinks – if it was a trisul, since it clearly doesn't mean I'm dead, with luck I am immortal ... I'll try out Akkadian, I'd barely mastered it.... 'When you have reached the waters of death, what will you do then?' An excellent question: – and there's a picture – 'after he cut his enemy's feet off, he kept him prisoner...' It sounds quite plausible, though mysterious....

'It's lucky I kept my feet,' says Danièle. 'An eye gives depth, but that can be deceptive. You don't need a field if you want to hit a guy, just using fists....'

She's with the Bosniaks – they don't fight so well, but they let her join: the Banglas and the Buddhists are quite fussy, although she'd go along with them.... 'All the languages I've learnt – at least a phrase, no one speaks them here, nor maybe anywhere, and....' she starts to cry, a fountain. It's possible with just one eye, 'I keep forgetting ... where I was headed does not exist. You study history, try to be thorough – then you find there's no place to stick it on... The people outside this tent, the city people, for sure, they are enlightened, revolutionary too – the king's decapitated, and they should be happy, having achieved everything...but coming all this way, this history, knowing no other language ... it hasn't made them wise or happy either...'

*

'Come with me,' the lady says. 'Danièle – I have a place for you.'

'I aways have a place,' says Danièle, weeping harder still. 'I'm in one, and seek another.'

'I have some birds, they need your care. And me – I have a levée – that needs two at least....' the lady says. 'I feel I have to volunteer, to help you guys with no destination and a past in ruins....'

'Tamara, I know you come to help,' says Danièle. 'But you are blind, your legs don't work....'

'I feel I must do what I can,' Tamara says, letting Danièle guide her, pull her up the steps – an old house: one bird is one-eyed, painted on the wall, the other is a greyish black, that squawks ... and Danièle sets Tamara in a chair.

'Now, Danièle,' Tamara says. 'Which is your bird? The one like you, or what you'd like to be?'

'Oh, Tamara,' Danèle says. 'Your wisdom overpowers. Of course, the one-eyed painted bird – that's me. I love myself, and it – it's always hungry, never satisfied. It's me....'

'Well, take care of the other one,' Tamara says. 'And, above all, take care of me.'

'I've worked, I've been promoted, been desired,' says Danièle. 'Fought for Yugoslavia, run, lost all my friends... I know the meaning of that dark one-eyed bird, painted on the wall, that's always hungry, can't be fed or stolen – I'll bet the thieves...'

'Oh yes,' Tamara interrupts, 'the thieves can drill through solid stone – this house is full of passageways, blind bulwarks, bastions of all kinds – the thieves have taken everything, at night you hear them mining, looking for a secret chamber, yet I lie, naked, in full view, under the moon, on the flat roof... You should hear the bulbuls....'

'You must fear the birds, then,' Danièle says. 'In the dark, the moonless nights.... You'll hear them gyring, maybe soft feathers on your face...'

'Of course,' Tamara says, 'we all hear, the fear is terrible: at least it is within you, so you can let the thieves take everything, if that is what they want, and what they find. Now, I suspect, that when they sell it on – the bar around the corner, where the appetites are great – it isn't worth their while ... the risk .... snap judgments made of what is valuable, what they can lift, maybe the murders they commit ... those involve expenses, and the moral suffering too....'

'And now, Tamara,' Danièle says. 'I'm left with you. I am your eye, your legs, your gut. I am your nakedness that every morning I must clothe, and dress your sores, and stir you into your despair and your complaints....'

'Yes, Danièle,' Tamara says. 'And you must thank me, say a prayer, respect my wisdom and my justice – for I have rescued you, saved you from the shelter where you'd have ended everything....'

'Maybe you see clear, Tamara,' Danièle says. 'Blindness permitting. I've lost my destination. Heavy with knowledge and desire – I cannot move, my legs weigh heavy, like they were painted on the wall....'

'I told you, Danièle,' Tamara says. 'It is incumbent on me, on us all, to volunteer, to help. First me – now you.'

'The dark bird, with the one eye you can see,' says Danièle. 'They're painted when they've had a story made, and then it's ended. I don't trust that it can protect.'

'Of course not,' says Tamara. 'Feed the squawking one, look after me, like I said. No new age crap about protection – you have none, Danièle, no one looks after you, no one ever will. Be satisfied with that.'

'Maybe you're right,' says Danièle. 'No one, no one at all sees what we do and why. I'm free: I'll feed you till you die and leave me this fine stone house that runs back for ever, where there's nothing left to steal except itself and you. I'll leave your body in a secret room, and every night go off to drink, carouse, around the corner in the bar....'

'Yes, yes!' Tamara shouts. 'Do that! Enjoy yourself – no one else will! It's our imperative. I was the greatest courtesan of all our times – I couldn't count the kings, and then the presidents, the kings of kings, commanders, fathers of the people – lying on me like a petticoat of sweat, grunting and farting, reaching their ruined Babylons and the drooping tower ... rocketing, discharging the last one.... Drink if you can't fuck, Danièle – that is the natural law. That's what powerful cheeses said to me....'

'Then?' asks Danièle.

'They paid,' Tamara says. 'Cash is the best, but jewels, though they deceive, are saleable ... ask in the bar....'

'No, no, Tamara. Nothing physical for me,' says Danièle. 'No potentates upon me like an eczema scurf....'

'No,' says Tamara. 'You are wise. Stay off the game – look how I am reduced....'

They laugh. What joy!

'You, Tamara,' says Danièle. 'You are – you could be – my friend!'

*

'You are my body now, Danièle,' Tamara says.

Danièle lets the grey-black bird fly out the window. 'You're too big and greedy to stay here,' she says. 'And too much trouble. The hawk, the falcon, on the wall – it's not a threat, it's life as well as death. It is succession – one thing, one king – after another. How they cling to life,' she says, as the big bird beats on the window to be let back in. In its despair, it takes a rhythm, like a human heart. Thump.

Thump thump thump. 'It's hungry, like me,' she says. 'When we leave, you see us holding on, as if our body's finished but it won't let something go – not spirit, that is non-existent, but something like air, not what you breathe but that you've been flying on, all your life, and suddenly it goes, and you are falling....'

Tamara shouts – 'Listen to this!' – turning up the music, drowning out the bird: and there's an indifferent group that sings, a catchy but indifferent song, 'By the waters of Babylon, Where we sat down....'

'They'd no idea what Babylon really was, and why we cried, for all this time,' Tamara says. 'How punishments go on, quite indiscriminate! No one knows why – there must be answers, Danièle – you should try exploring politics.'

'I remember the movie,' Danièle says. 'The song was a relief – though it didn't fit... I wish I'd been in that film, behind the camera: *Série noire*, by Alain somebody. It's a place, a city, where I'd like to be, and where for sure I'd stay. The great river – watching it sail by and I can sit, relax. Eat dates, eat centuries!

'Politics? I've always dealt with that – you have to follow me quite carefully. I don't always spell it out, but it's all there. Crimes. Punishments as well, and the psychology – they go together in the book, though in the life, I'm not so sure. If in doubt about the politics, just ask me.'

'You let that fucking bird out, Danièle,' says Tamara, angry. 'It was the only living thing here. It knew this house as if it was its life.'

'If it's hungry, it'll come back,' says Danièle, offhand.

'That's what they said about the slaves in Babylon,' says Tamara. 'They were well off in the city, the centre of the world. Maybe they did well to leave, hungry or not. It's all been rocketed.'

'It's not germane, Tamara,' Danièle says. 'Nothing you say is. It's dementia. Memory's gone to mush. You have to stay put now – remember, I'm your body, and this place is a fortress.'

'Then don't think of leaving,' says Tamara. 'It's not a prison.'

'No,' says Danièle. 'It's worse, with you complaining.'

They quarrel, like Salar and Abbie did, but they don't bunk down together.

They suppose they are still friends.

'At least you could get a drink there,' says Tamara. 'Water. Euphrates. The great river. Go get a drink in the bar round the corner – when you come back, I might be dead. I leave you nothing. The house – it isn't mine, but if you live here, no one will want to throw you out.'

'Work it out, Tamara,' says Danièle. 'There's been different kings – and queens. Not all just and wise. Not everybody was enslaved, I'm sure, besides, slavery – it's an interlude. Everybody was enslaved some time, and many did quite well – the caliphate was run by slaves....'

'You're unlearned, Danièle,' says Tamara, wearily. 'Go to the bar. Find your level, the glasses intercommunicate, all level off ... shake off your obsessions: rock and roll!'

*

The bar is perspex and neon – there's a sign. 'No mutts or lurchers', but the guys have every other kind of hound, their chains snapped round a row of rings on the far wall....

The guys are dealing in old, stolen stuff, and making books, and paying out and raking in. It's market, stock exchange, museum acquisitions – humming like a nest of flies ... old masters and old mistresses, drips and daubs and Mickey Mouse....prices inestimable, values higher still....

My! there's the big black bird – 'How much?' asks Danièle. 'It should cost nothing, they drift down from the skies.'

'A million roubles, or a thousand yuan,' says the guy – rat-faced like Ivan, a body folded like a pair of wings, a wind-tossed gamp. 'I take dollars, but there is a premium ... often it is negative...'

'If I buy it, it'll fly away,' says Danièle. 'That means it's worthless.'

'It costs because it steals. That means it's priceless. Potentially Golconda. You need lock it up. It's life ... the bird will bring it to you in its claws. It's how things change, and how you got the things you have, have lost, and want,' he says.

'There's nothing round here that's worth a million roubles, even if you slice it thin and cut and cut and come again,' says Danièle.

'If that is so,' says the guy, the fence. 'I'll let it into nature. Up and away! That solves the problem: "us or nature".... Experience has shown. It's deals and free exchange. Dialectics – everything will interact. We are nature, nature's us – the problem is resolved – if problem there was, ever.'

'It's not what I would call an answer,' says Danièle. 'My answers are a yes, or no. "Both" is what you find in superstitions. My trisul, Siva's trident – he's death and battle: darkness and purity. Time that bears all things away.... And, he is the life ascetic. That's the life I have now, though I'd sooner have had it stay an aspiration. Of course – that's all a story that my lover told. He went to lectures, made me laugh and cry, and everything had a sense....'

'The guys here say it was a plastic fork,' the fence says, tickling the bird. 'You'll say it's all a metaphor, like the story of the king, Babylon like it was once, before....'

'So, if it's metaphor,' says Danièle. 'What isn't? You can't stop living by it, it's snow, you can't stop it, it is useless, you hate it – people keep on saying it is beautiful, transforms the landscape. Certainly, it transforms your life. You feel it more when it's anomalous – I guess Finns live in it eternally, but here, where we are, the heat each year climbs up and up, the water disappears between the stones – then, when it snows, we see another life comes, touches us, buries us ... see the pratfalls!'

'I hope you're joking, Danièle,' says the fence.

'Give me the bird,' says Danièle. 'You found it, so you're good. It's raucous, stupid. I'll take it, so I'm good, better than you. Tamara will be happy... Everyone is just, and some are happy too: and wise.'

Danièle takes the bird – 'on approval' says the guy.

When she's opening Tamara's door, it flies away. Tamara's forgotten all about it.

It has friends all round, so – it can be happy, high up in its tree, and it's wise.

'That bird meant the world to Tamara,' says Grigor, the fence.

*

Every statement made by him contains two quesions...

'I'm her body,' says Danièle. 'That bird was her brain. You say it steals. She must have stolen much – the mausoleum house, the bricked-up rooms....'

'I can help you search,' Grigor says. 'Out the back, I have a squad who will do everything – everything I ask. Special forces, rebels, fiscal inspectors, guys who run the currencies.... And guys with crowbars too, tridents to prise open secret chambers....

'Your eye poke, Danièle, has finished off your quest. Philosophy? Enough! The wealth, the treasure – for sure it's

behind those peperino blocks ... we'll assist, and add it to
your bill ... you never settled for the bird....'

This house is not a home – it's treasure. They knock it
down, they blast it down, they melt it with acid ... they forget
Tamara's somewhere inside...there's many secret hidey-
holes.... Each one resists, has recipes on the walls. The guys
steal all they find...Tamara stole Danièle's quest, all that
philosophy – fitted in a handkerchief... The house is no one's,
especially now it's not a home, and not a house....

'If, like you, Danièle, you've nothing to give, and haven't
given – then you must take. Take like me,' Tamara says,
sitting in a peacock chair, Ethiopian, fragile and tall,
dismasted now, grimed by the winds, bought long ago to
seem a cosmopolitan: 'Take stories, and take votes, take
favours, take respect and money, everything you can and
don't let them take it back. Take people, take a following,
preach and pray – they'll flock around, so then you fleece
your flock. The world is yours, no one owns anything. It's
there to take – if they want to put their spigots into you, then
take their seed and make it cash: you've won the round! Your
error was to think: "they had their Babylon, they'd water and
an alphabet, so they gave their everything to us". Not so –
they had everything and didn't give, and those that couldn't
take, they had to give *their* everything to the guys who made
the laws that helped *them* take...

'Look out the back – the action's there, the guys don't
drink, the inside's just the place they leave the dogs.... The
garden out the back, that is the marketplace, inside is just for
writing contracts, not the bargaining.'

'Your house, Tamara!' Danièle says. 'It's been knocked
down....'

'There's always one last hidden room, no bigger than a
walnut's shell,' Tamara says. 'That's what you have, your
most important space. As for the rest – it's gone. Too bad.

Maybe then you'll starve – but in a block of stone they haven't cracked, there is a breathing crevice, room for a comma, fly's dirt, a snick, a mini-snot, a snug – too tiny for a mouse, a beetle cannot wave his legs, a flea can't jump.... It's yours! It doesn't sing or chirp, or whistle when no air blows through. It's yours. Inedible, and dark. Your hole.'

'I'm so sad, Tamara,' Danièle says.

'My little farm, Danièle,' says Tamara, turning her blind face toward her. 'My river, my water, a tree where my bird could sit. How it sang up on the branch – before, it only squawked! Singing, dancing – it's all sex. If you're alone, it's easier to squawk. It's usual to lose the rhythm, then you're a cook, a hooker, wandering like you... I'm in luck – I piled these stone blocks and made a bigger block, impregnable, lived in it, waiting for the resurrection, and I had slaves, a million, piling up and smoothing down, and every secret room they made I had the builders killed and stuffed inside like giblets....'

'Oh, Tamara,' Danièle says, 'I don't want that. I want just payment, that is all. These themes you mention – they don't fit with what I am and what I want. They make up a construct, a stone city where we all must live, a termite heap, where every spring the sacrifices go trudging up the steps and lose their skins to make the maize go green....'

Tamara laughs, 'Oh yes, so long ago. It all dried up, was drunk. Now there is no green – there's sand abundant to be put in clocks, and watch it trickle up and down....'

'Listen, Tamara,' Danièle says. 'Just wait here, since you can't move. I'll go out the back, and see if someone wants to buy me, the little that I have to sell. Then I'll come back, and help us both, like you did, helping in the shelter where I began to lose my sight....'

'Oh yes, my dear,' Tamara says. 'I bought you out – what a mistake, what disappointment. See how we're reduced....'

*

'Tamara,' Danièle tells Grigor, 'sees almost nothing now, can't show you secret rooms, or anything...'

'Her memory too has gone,' says Grigor. 'It will happen to us all, it's our salvation. It's how we disappear and leave our heap to someone else who takes it on, is blinded, has the past scrubbed out, erased completely, to leave conundra of a brand-new kind, resources to be stolen, new slaves to lift the blocks and make the mausoleum, full of hidey-holes, a gruyère that soon is crumbled up or melted down, and so we start again, and all the stock of things is passed on to new folk ... and so, and so....' he finishes with a grin – not too concerned, and not much interested.

'Let's see what we can make of your resources, Danièle,' says Grigor – and others gather round to watch.

'The house – not yours, but...' he starts –

'It's a ruin,' Danièle says.

'People love them,' Grigor says. 'They're no one's, so there's no one to be envied. Think of the Egyptian pyramids, rust-belt of noble spirits – people love them. They were a pathway to the stars – now, people are curious, want to try another way. Those were the prototypes. The sphinxes – like big dogs, waiting for their walk – up to the constellations. Immortality, Danièle!... Death sciences – always such a draw for youngsters... Instead of wallpaper, a recipe: – how to embalm your aunt....

'Then – there's the bird. People think all animals are just about extinct – maybe they are.... Folk come to look at one and think "maybe it's the last, and I, this morning, have seen part of creation's end. It's winding down...." Well, there's a thought – always about ourselves, of course. We slip and slide, earth trembles, and it signifies – each one of us becomes extinct! It's bathos, Danièle. The black bird – it's our life and death, our soul, our inexistence.... See us throng to watch it search out carrion....'

And the guys all laugh and nod.

'Then, there's the body in the chair ... our mother. When she spins round – she's the murderer, bewigged ... that movie with the knife.... It's all there, your fortune, Danièle. Exploited right, curated well....'

'Oh yes,' she says. 'I have it all. And most of it is what I do not want – the gods, the tales: – enough! Inventing new magicians, new transforming stories that don't work. A fork is just a fork.'

'Come down from your ambition, Danièle. See what there is around. Consider having all those dogs compete, not running; just walking up and down....' says Grigor. 'You could be the judge – take backhanders, sweeteners. Have your hand licked...'

'Yes!' Danièle says. 'A promenade. Dogs on the catwalk.To me, dogs all look the same. They all should win. They all will lose. It's better so – that is justice, and I love the derby days, the silks, the tiny jockeys, horses on grass, camels on sand ... hats of Africa.'

'You see, Danièle,' Grigor says. 'You're rich! – though nothing can belong to you. You don't need to skivvy – not even for the president of all the world, the universe. That's all run by machines, of course. Is the power model here the American one? The Chinese? Secret jails, or public executions....? At your leisure, with your life's friend, under the lime trees with your bock to hand – you can discuss all that: hegemony, the regime, the rights of man and woman....

'The vans go up and down the boulevard, there's guys inside ... you guess, but you can't see – I bet they're terrified! But you're not scared, Danièle. You're clean.'

'There is a thing, Grigor....' says Danièle.

'Stop!' shouts Grigor. 'We all know, life happens to you according to your clothes – you're born a human, but you come in frock or pants, even jeans: shades or hijab. Like it, or probably not much – you've been a woman in your life. Gender's a determinant of course, Danièle, though I have a friend who could, with trowel and scissors, change your life....'

'I know all that,' says Danièle. 'But I'm not into it. Wisdom and justice – nothing gendered. That's my goal. If it can't be grasped, I'm trapped. Sex wars – an infinity! And so – I'm in another castle or a trench, another Armageddon, Vimy Ridge, Mosul ... there's no way out, I'd never see the river and the palms, the king, his breasts, his beardless face – not in-between, not transiting – he is above! Remember, Grigor, "with the International, the human race arises...."'

'It's catchy,' Grigor says, 'but without the contacts, writing songs can be another flop. If you don't want remodelling, accept: either you're a visionary, or you've failed. Just now – you judge dogs.'

'Bring on the dogs, then,' says Danièle. 'They're quite like us – incontinent, scabrous, multi-coloured and obsessed.'

There's guys with hammers breaking stones – 'Tamara's in one of those,' says Grigor. 'The basalt will resist, but we shall shell her, break her out.'

'She's tiny, Grigor, but as strong as air – you can't break the breeze with sledges,' Danièle says.

'Here come the dogs,' says Grigor. 'Tamara'd be a sweetmeat for the winner.'

There's yellow dogs and black dogs, dogs by the day and by the hour, running dogs and dirty dogs, hang dogs and gay dogs, groomed and fawning, back-combed, polled, cropped and docked, huskies and russkies, samoyeds and afghans, Bourbons and Hohenzollerns, ridgebacks and Maremmanoes, Germans, Switzers, Belgians, pekes and dash-hounds, hairless and hirsute, to eat or be eaten by – "I'd like to see an original," says Danièle, 'before they were all customised.'

'Oh, they all belong,' says Grigor. 'And each has the wolf entombed, safe sealed inside – a bad, a single, cell.'

'Gender doesn't count,' says Danièle, 'but I don't want to see their tongues. No lolling. No hounds' tongue. Anyway, what is the prize?'

'It's stupid, giving dogs a prize,' says Grigor. 'They don't compete, unless they're greyhounds. The prize is you, Danièle You are the judge, and that's the law – I hope you believe in laws?'

'I obey,' says Danièle. 'Unless I'm breaking them. Philosophers are much taken with that stuff – obeying bad laws: maybe they sold drugs or had a still... It's tempting to write in something that gets you off – probation at the most. But – you mean I'd be a slave?'

'Call ownership as you will,' says Grigor. 'These dogs are owned, they're equal, each one has respect – they're coaxed until they sit or stand. It's not so terrible – as you say, gender doesn't count. My comrades here will bid for you – the more they pay, the more they value you. Read about the working day – these dogs, mostly, they don't work. You will. It's their condition of being owned that says it all. They have to go for walks – pee on the cinemas, the opera house, the rock arena. You stand and watch – it's culture, Danièle. The crap – you take it home....'

They all laugh. Each guy wonders if he'll win Danièle. Each dog will try its best, of course.

'It's not at all what I had hoped and wanted,' Danièle says. 'A friend I longed for. Maybe work – guarding the ruins. These are stone – don't send me where they're only thatch and clay, Grigor.'

Her prospect's all jigged back to Africa, and Mister Crane – the races and the shows, the colours of the world to come.

A waft of putrefaction ... maybe it's Tamara's zephyr; they've cracked her strong box – the dogs catch the scent ... and off they go! A bone! A bum! The guys run after, naturally.

Your dog is your best friend. Your brother, your *semblable.*They teach you that – maybe a dog thought that one up.

'I'm free!' thinks Danièle – the last tail wags away, in the long grass....

The guys are calling, 'Here boy! Hey girl!' further and further – the dogs scamper into liberty, still longing for the leash, for sure.

'Judging's not for me.' she thinks. 'Nor's to be a servant of the law, of the guys who lay them down.

'"Through law – no justice" – it's been written down.... Those folders; Salar with his exercises, lifting his weights until he finds one so heavy that he can't.... Gravity, *gravitas.* He'd like to weigh heavy, but can't escape the weight that holds him down.

'Nothing changes me,' she thinks. 'I am a fortress, made of rain and fog.'

*

Brave talk. Grigor – an innocent: the traders – perpetuating; round and round stuff goes – there's swells and crashes, in the end, the old things dull and break, the new ones – their price for ever lower – into the stream they go.

It makes reality. It is all we have and know.

Realism – the mirror of the senses....

Everything must change and yet stay recognisable. It's *montage;* you need an editor, not a demijohn of holy spirits. Without exchange, trade, and speculation, everything would be unreal. It might seem that from the start, nothing need change. There'd be no purpose – except the living things would die, not be replaced, and so reality would have no public, no spectators. No actors. So – Exchange. Time's clockwork. The queen bee. The buildings tumble, ruins are bought. The old's the new, the new's the old. It's nature too. Grigor and his mates – renew the world and make it seem the same, all connected, all trotting in the process, total continuity. We all age. We, the dead, we are replaced.

'They're sharp,' thinks Danièle. 'Those guys – they do no harm. And how they love their dogs... People race, they're small and light so's they can win, be carried in processions, they all compete – there's pictures on the barroom wall of four dogs playing poker ... although, they run, escape, those dogs! It's not conclusive – they run, and then run back. They love the leash, the guided walks, the chase – a ball, a fox, an escapee – it's all the same – the bounce, the double-back, a slaver...

'And I want none of that. I want my friends.'

*

The barman says, 'The traders – they all left. They do that. Find a new place. You just see the dog-rail, the art upon the walls, the rings where the fetters hang, broken and rusty, the chains, the thongs, the leads. They move on, find a new bar, new drinks, but we two, Danièle – we could play a game.'

It's that or getting drunk alone. 'What game?' asks Danièle.

You throw a ring that's on a chain over a horn set in the wall. The barman does it twenty times straight off. It's very difficult. You need space too. Danièle is hopeless. One-eyed. And there's the off-putting crow outside.

'Now we can be friends,' the barman says, pouring a big drink for Danièle. He puts on some raw music and it fills the walls.

'No,' says Danièle. 'I want a friend who can do great harm – and doesn't. You're just an expert at your game.'

'This must be the Last Chance Saloon', they say, two flames lit by the same thought – and laugh.

*

You have to take a side. Or the sides take you. There's wars, quite complicated – so you take many sides. Maybe you're elected – priests, or family, choose you, maybe it's the rich guys eyeing you....

The first morning, in the temple, you lose your innocence. They tell you what it's all about, the sides, what the fight's really for, show you your weapons, say who's your enemies. Spill all the secrets, swear you to silence. You're broken, ready for the ride.

'Power,' says the guy, sitting by Danièle on a broken rock, fist on chin, elbow on knee, a Hercules without a club. 'The hero dies, his power is buried.... The new hero – finds the power anew. Where did it go, where is it stored? – a mystery.... It's the magic sword...'

'The murder weapon,' Danièle says, and laughs. 'War – the secret armament of the poor.'

'Don't be deceived,' says the guy. 'For them, it makes a bang, doesn't explode.'

They are silent for a while. History spools through their heads – different speeds, maybe different scenarios too.

'Values,' says Danièle. 'It's what you do, not what you see afar. Besides, if you're at the helm, why complicate your life? Being a boss, a despot – has its own appetite. They do what there's to do – that's wisdom. Justice is – not falling off, not sinking, keeping a balance... I've become a sceptic. Why be wise and just when you've already all the power: the ace in the hole? Add to that the judicious whipping of your horse, the rap upon your camel's nose – much resented, but ... it keeps you out ahead. The others – far behind or at your back – it really doesn't matter how near or far they are....'

'I'll explain,' the would-be hero says. 'Just follow me...'

'No cooking, though,' says Danièle, taking his hand. 'No babysitting jockeys. No more tattoos. And tell me: why do guys struggle so to be heroic?'

'Oh,' says the guy. 'The best Masters have been Slaves. They understand, they have a memory. They escaped, and don't want to go back there.'

'It's not an explanation,' says Danièle. 'But I'll go along with it for now. I prefer the story of the monkeys, or the wolves. It's winning contests, being old and sly...'

'This "just and wise",' says the guy. 'What person would ever say they weren't? Who doesn't want an outlet to the sea, kick out those foreigners, bring in the craftsmen, sign the new bands, reward your friends, have more flat land, settle disputes without a brouhaha, know everything, write new laws? The trouble is, Danièle, your position at the start is wrong: you think justice, wisdom, are so hard to find. No! They're in abundance – everybody knows exactly what they are. We're all experts, we're all kings of Babylon.'

'It's having power to do the application right,' says Danièle, cowed, impressed. 'Winning consensus: no cutting off of feet.'

'Your quest is done,' the hero says. 'We're all just and wise. So, seek no more.'

His mother called him Balthazar – a fine name, for the king of Babylon. His father didn't want a son – they take things over when you've gone...

'There's freedom, equality as well: long ago they hadn't been invented,' says Danièle.

'Come, see how I live,' says Balthazar. 'I'm just and wise, so all the other abstracts you slip in, you can be sure they have a place.'

It sounds simple, but it isn't clear.

He pulls Danièle along, turning often to smile and wink at her.

*

The gate says 'Carefree', and Balthazar says to Danièle, 'You're sure you're wise? Prepared to be just? If not, you're in danger here.'

It's all said with a smile. She says, 'Those are my two lodestars, the two "o"s in Orion's belt. They're constant – not a twinkle.'

The gatehouse is large, martial: through a dusty window you can see a big dog asleep, it's like one of the poker-playing mutts on the bar wall. 'Of course,' says Balthazar, 'Potsdam penetrated far to the East. To Harbin and beyond, even Hong Kong. Always a wee bit alien. Yunnan's too far, saved for us, I'm glad to say. The military cant, spreading nearly everywhere, "service before everything" – means there's those Cossacks riding everywhere – that's a real downer. One's supposed to say it's a saving grace, but... It doesn't save a thing. It's a beachhead, maybe. Following orders no one needs to give. Metaphor, Danièle: hold to that. Metaphor's a style; life lived, not a prescription. You need the dacha – a hideout. It always needs painting, even when your hands are claws and they have to tie the brushes on.'

'You have to go to school to learn architecture,' Danièle says. 'And I was so bored I was caught nicking stuff I didn't want from supermarkets.'

'Well,' says Balthazar, 'you won't nick this.' He spreads his arms –

The main building's made of logs and fronds – it's more a long house than a palace. It's on stilts. 'I thought so hard about it,' Balthazar says. 'How it should be, a castle? permanent, a populated hermitage? – that meantime, we'd made this and lived in it, and so we and it stayed as it is. I keep four-square and stucco in my mind, though. Siberia's my bedroom. That's what I love... The white, the silver trees....'

'Maybe you're not wise and just,' says Danièle. 'But it's still an honest vision, this long house. Out comes the sketch you make when you've just a charcoal stick, an empty wall... when the wind blows, the whole thing flies away ... the rain dissolves graffiti...there's stick people too ... their singing's like sugar dropped into the pond ... those cheap oil paints blear down like butter-icing....'

'I know the styles,' says Balthazar. 'If I'd the money, I'd have built something else. But if you build something else, it's money-spend. You can't knock it down without you all being put out in the street – in the workhouse, my grannie used to say. We'd never seen a workhouse, yet we lived in one,' and he laughs. 'Everybody worked.... What you can do, Danièle,' he says. 'Stops you from doing what you can't.'

'Yes,' says Danièle, quite overawed. She's never even built a sandcastle. It doesn't matter – Balthazar seems to pay no attention to her. She says, 'I've lived all over, but the work's been much the same – the disappointments too. They're still discussing somewhere how to stop the war....'

'Or how the next will start,' says Balthazar, listening for once. 'Your life has been coincidence, Danièle. That doesn't mean a thing.'

In the wall of the long house, there are little plaques, some in Greek, some Albanian, some creole and pidgin.... 'That's where the workers left their bones,' says Balthazar. 'I guess you have to leave them somewhere, unless it's in the grinder, then you fertilise.'

'Were they killed in the constructions?' Danièle asks, fascinated. 'Pine-needles in the lungs? Woodpeckers?'

'Some just fell down,' says Balthazar, not reacting to the facetiousness. 'It's not a memorial, just a "where", you'd say a "where-house", Danièle,' just to show he sees a joke.

There's nothing else special here to see.

'This could be one of those companies that's bigger than a country, existing everywhere, supplying air and water, magma, swamps...' says Danièle.

'Could be, could be,' says Balthazar. 'Or it could be scrub. It's not there's nothing here – the scene is always full, a unity – like a book in a strange language, music written to no scheme; a picture of nothing in no colours you're familiar with....'

'There must have been a family here – bosses, slaves, managers....' says Danièle. 'Even a something that you do. You can't just sit, be powerful ... or be nothing.'

'Like they used to do,' says Balthazar. 'Not wise, just – just old and venerable. Yes, it could be, could be – you can't see things like that, not with your eyes. Now, Danièle – up the ladder...'

'I always wanted this,' says Danièle, looking everywhere in the raised long house. 'An attic, with no house below, no people you don't like beneath. Ladder without snake...'

'Don't jump,' says Balthazar. 'To that conclusion.'

'There's no people,' Danièle says. 'So – there's no need for tolerance, rights, all that. I guess they've gone somewhere, or be coming back – another bunch, perhaps. And we sleep up here, Balthazar? It's welcoming, in a cool way, the mattresses, equal, just like it was, when we lived as a rackety company in the trees.'

He doesn't answer.

Then, he reasons – 'They must all be out,' he says.

'Do they all do the same work?' she asks. 'All work for different things?'

'I don't know what you mean,' he says.

'Are they all blood relations, then? Your family, your tribe? And if they're out, they must all be well,' she says.

'I don't know what you mean,' he says. 'It's hard to give a yes or no. Each question's easier to answer at some specific time, one that it fits.'

'Now it's me who doesn't understand,' says Danièle, not caring much, since there is no one here. 'Tell me – are we against those – those intercontinetal corporations, who do everything for us, the TV, messages, deliveries, water and food, all that?'

'Well,' says Balthazar. 'If we're against it – what happens next? Do we win? What happens if we lose? If we lose, what happens after? Do you know, have you looked? Do you trust your *semblables* if they're on the mattress next to you?'

'I guess that's so,' says Danièle. 'Run a circus, run a prison – it is much the same... Train a nurse or train a soldier...'

Balthazar laughs, a sonorous laugh. 'You pick examples with such skill, Danièle – it all connects...makes a picture. I imagine being in a jail, with legs so fragile – like a flamingo bird – I could overleap the wall, the others pull me down. In confinement, with one of those legs broken – where'd you end up?'

'That's awful, Balthazar,' says Danièle. 'Not taking off....'

'Only flying when you can run far on,' he says. They reflect on that.

'You may not have read,' says Balthazar. 'There's still kings that call the shots.'

'I imagine – someone has to call,' says Danièle.

'And you,' says Balthazar. 'Remember – you've only got one left. The eye. I bet you've lost the depth – it's like a panorama painted on a canvas reel.'

'Thank you for asking,' Danièle says, lightly. 'Elected, appointed – there's lots to call those shots – there's thousands voting for those guys. The important thing is to be small enough to be carried in procession – don't get too heavy, Balthazar.'

*

There's people – not many – sleep briefly in the dorm. Some go into danger, or into odd-hour jobs – driving a coach, a truck, to somewhere difficult. Mercenaries ... in new clothes. Some – possibly they hadn't much, and now that's lost too: they've run lots, think of running more. They sleep deep, disturbed, then leave in silence.

Balthazar sleeps somewhere else:

'It's cold,' he says. 'I don't close the door at night. There's movement – even the stars... I found a pistol – don't know what to do with it.... You wouldn't need it here – nothing to rob, nothing to defend....' He's worried. His four-square beard has lost its edge: unwaxed, a hedge....

'There's a guard-dog in the guard-house,' says Danièle. 'Give him the gun. That's what guards have – there is no hazard, he can't use it, but it's right it should be his...'

'That's true,' says Balthazar. 'You are a joker, Danièle, I'm not sure you fit the norm. We set much store here by normality, or else the kilter's lost... But you are right. He would need it, if he could use it. He can't, so there's no danger. Well thought, my friend!'

This place is rich – if it were poor, there'd be families living here and doing trade, living lives and losing them, all hugger-mugger.

'That's true,' thinks Danièle. 'But the ones who flit through here – they're unhappy, apprehensive, whatever side they're on.'

She doesn't mention this to Balthazar, it's not a thing you can discuss or reason over, and besides – she's the one who sees them come and go.

It's normal, prudent, always being fearful.

'What shall I do?' asks Danièle.

'Do?' asks Balthazar. 'You know, I'm "be" rather than "do". If it's work – you could cut the weeds. Paint. Count the snipe and grebes, if they visit here. You want to volunteer? "Will" is significant. We must be all the same, and want it so, or there's no game. Some guys say – to be wise, you need to go to school; to be just, you need to sit in court. I don't agree. School's dull, derivative. Staying out of court is wiser than to study it. Forget that though: what you mean, Danièle, is "why am I here?" Just to be normal? To be afraid? Forget paradise, but maybe you'll get there all the same? Bet on wealth and immortality, but hope your last crust will be uneaten when you die?'

'Oh yes,' says Danièle, 'all of those. You know, the people who've lost everything, even if it wasn't much – what hurts them most is abandoning the animals. We suppose the beasts don't know about their death: – it's nonsense, but it's convenient to pretend that they don't comprehend....'

'That's beautiful, Danièle,' says Balthazar, preparing to shed some tears. 'That's a wonderful insight, a marvellous observation. The unity, yes! Nature, all the species – not a biology, but the mental matrix, the grid – the sentiments and their logics ... the ways to live, fear, conquest, when to sing, when to parade. Forget mechanics, the brain as driver up there in the skull, waving the arms and waggling the legs. Reason isn't that, Danièle – you know, you've been through almost everything.... If it were truly everything, then clearly, you'd be dead. You've lost an eye, but nothing more that you could see.... Reason: it gets you through. Survival – that's its prize, its goal. Losing cash and friends – and going on, to lose more cash, more friends, amassing enemies and threats.... That is your value, Danièle.... that you remain, integral, hopeful, firm... That's mistress reason for you!'

'But, Balthazar,' says Danièle. 'I'm beaten down, unhappy and confused. I'm optimistic because it can't get worse....'

'Exactly so,' says Balthazar. 'We possess nothing, no one belongs to us, nor cares. And we are wise and just, Danièle.'

'What is this place, and who are you, Balthazar?' asks Danièle. 'You're not the king, and not the gardener. You don't legislate, nor do you scythe the reeds....'

'I told you, no one owns anything, though we may nail things to our wall. Yet there's a paradox – I know almost everything. In that sense, I own it: knowledge. It's hard to take away and inventory. Everything, from where the Yue Zhi came from, and where Betty Davis went. Power – invisible – so there's no suprise if I tell you I have vast amounts of it. I attract, I lead, I dominate: you, Danièle, are one tiny proof of that...'

'This place....' asks Danièle unconvinced.

'I cleared it,' says Balthazar. 'It's ready. Catastrophes are happening – this enormous waste is for the bigger one. Hosts, Danièle. Hordes; nations, peoples. All will end up here. They'll swarm on this emptiness.'

'And here we are, waiting,' Danièle says. 'Two persons and a dog. It's typical. But why...?'

'Interests over-pumped, or ignored, popular suffrage without foresight, one man rule with spies and massacres, little world wars, uncontrollable weapons, rich and poor, vanity and ignorance, intelligence and revelation, dearth of everything – a disaster,' says Balthazar, thinking to expand further, then clamming up. 'You, Danièle, you shall write the laws. You've seen them, laws, and chancers too, at closest quarters. You knew the best of jurists there has ever been....'

'I'm a sceptic, Balthazar,' says Danièle.

'There's a secret,' says Balthazar. 'With the laws. You can change them as you go along.'

'And if the people don't obey?' she asks.

'No punishments. They don't get food, that's all,' says Balthazar. 'I have a store of it: to tell you where would be a bore...'

'They'll steal. Or plant,' says Danièle. 'Whittle and daub – poor things, to sell and trade.'

'Exactly,' says Balthazar. 'That is how it starts. Civilisation. Culture. Lawbreakers – indispensable. It's just and wise that it should happen so.'

'They'll paint,' says Danièle, enthralled. 'The long house – after Gauguin. The lines for flour and oil – a touch of Repin. Make their movies – Los Olvidados, over and over, many times.'

'The sculptures, if they find the stones, can stand against my lean-to,' Balthazar reflects. 'They'll need invent – chisel wings on ordinary things, there's not much here. And no religion, blood or ghosts. If they can't do without, something totemic. Nothing high up, in the sky: just spirits in the canebrakes and the palms.'

*

They feel the world – a wobble, like a top that's running out of spin. 'Start now,' says Balthazar. 'Here – these books may help.'

The Invention of Truth, The Invention of Difference, How They Invented Heterosexuality, Language Without Content, After Reality – there's a big pile.

'Everything will have fallen down,' says Balthazar. 'We'll see how they'll build new pictures up. Will it seem catastrophe? Or will everything be denied? Shall we speak one language? Or none? Think these things through, Danièle. what's happened, and what will – these aren't situations you can see. Two years to go? Two hundred? Did it all already happen, there is nothing left – except the scrub here, the few birds that flutter down – what's happened in the sky? You have to take it into your account. They'll say it's speculation, about a future that there'll never be, and then they say the opposite....'

'These "they"...?' says Danièle.

'Oh, normal people; look like us,' says Balthazar. 'We look like them. That's not the way to go, Danièle. Those cities smashed, the ruins sprouting murderers, the murderers who order it – all normal people, no less reasonable than us.'

'I wanted to stay out of this,' says Danièle. 'Mostly, I was in the kitchen, tasting the best bits.'

'I'll leave you with the quiet books,' says Balthazar. 'There's awful facho writings everywhere – don't let that bother you. That crowd already got all that they need. Work from your experience, Danièle.'

'Oh, I'll use my intuition, you can bet,' says Danièle. 'I never trusted science – all hypothetical, and yet the stores are full of it. As for fiction – I have never seen the need. There's processions, carnival.... There's no better stories...'

What if no one arrives? Suppose Danièle has made some rules, and no one's interested? She doesn't read the books – you can guess what's in them anyway.

'They'll come, for sure,' she thinks. 'The other people. Not yet.'

She draws some monkeys climbing up some trees. It's trite. But – they're done rather well. 'Perhaps that's where my talent lies ... they're rather good,' she thinks.

The drawing – she slips it in a folder.

'What we need,' she thinks: ' – those date palms take an age to grow – trees! Magnolias. Jasmine – and monkey puzzles too.'

*

It's hot. There's frogs in the pond. The good life for a frog is making more frogs. There's lilies too – they don't seem to have ambitions.

She hasn't seen Balthazar for days. He must feed the dog in the gatehouse, though she hasn't seen the dog for days.

He must have made preparations for what's to come.

'Balthazar is the best friend I've had,' she says aloud. 'He knows the past like a book he wrote, and we're ready for the future, whenever it comes.'

Maybe he's gone up the road to see if anyone is coming.

*

There'll be an immense crowd, mostly silent, enough to raise the dust you'd see from far away.

About the author

John Fraser has lived in Rome since 1980. Previously, he worked in England and Canada.

www.ingramcontent.com/pod-product-compliance
Lightning Source LLC
Chambersburg PA
CBHW031329170626
46807CB00002B/619

9 781910 301586